Tony Montana Jr.

I0573595

Qualo Lowery

Cadmus Publishing
www.cadmuspublishing.com

Acknowledgements

First, I would like to thank God. Without him, there would be no me. Secondly, I want to thank my parents, Brenda Blackmon, and James Silas. You two have been my everything, over the last five years. (Life is Good.) I like to thank my grandmother, Betty Brown, AkA Big Momma. I love you with all my heart. I know it's been awhile since we have spent some time together, but that day is coming soon! I like to thank both of my sisters: Tanika Moore who is also an Author of

Vanilla Setbacks Part 1 and Part 2 and Isha Moore AKA poo. Thirdly I would like to shout out all my kids: Shaquala Givens, Jaquala Givens, Qualo Jr, and ZZ Givens. I love all of y'all and this is why I do this writing stuff.

Thirdly, I like to shout all my aunts, uncles, friends, cousins, nephews, nieces and anyone that help make this project a dream come true! I like to send a special shout out to Tanya Thomas, Rhonda Norris, Andrell Givens, Lacresha Woodard, Ladricka Perry, Ieisha Brown, Mr. Ridges at Bennettsville Prison Mrs. Mack at Leavenworth Prison. You all were blessings from God. Thank y'all for helping me during this process. Last but not least, I have to shout out all my Old Dalton Village people: Travis D, Big Jasper Lowery, Big Tiff, Nikki Mavay Smith, Lorin, and everyone who was at Dalton Village Day who showed me love in 2022 on May 7th. Much love. Shout out to all the guys in C2 Unit at Bennettsville, and (The Cell0Phone Crew.lol) It was real when I was there. Shout out to, (21 from Pelham GA) South Ward, Mookie, Ghost, Kendell Martin AKA DA Sauce, Ra-low from Hickory, AKA Cattown. North Carolina, Wok from Atlanta, S-Dot, Curt, Big D, Fig, Buck, Berto from St Louis, I still don't like Kansas City Chiefs, Sam aka the cash appt man, and everyone I forgot. Oh, Kevin Moss from Charlotte, I can't forget about you. You saw the vision. Mc, I love you man. I told y'all, I was going to do it. Please enjoy this story! West Blvd for life.

Shout to my editor: June Bug. Love you man. (I almost forgot. My three Mexicans: Mummy, Chuck, and M-30. Y'all are some real guys. Much love.)

An extra Last but not least, I would like to Thank Frank at Cadmus Publishing and his crew for their help. Ya'll are truly some God-sent people. Thank you for your help on this project

TABLE OF CONTENTS

PROLOGUE

Year: 1984.

Place: Miami, FL early summer.

Following Tony Montana Sr.'s death…

Heart broken by strife, Ms. Clara Montana stood motionless in her small living room crying after she saw her son's face on the local evening news! The news cast reporter who covered the story went into great details on how Ms. Montana's son was Miami's biggest Kingpin drug lord and concluded the story on how, Tony had been gunned down along with several of his men at his Montenegro Beach mansion. The reason is unclear at this time. Possibly waring Cartel factions.

It had been two years since Ms. Montana spoke to Tony. Her last encounter with him didn't go well. She could remember it like only yesterday.

"What are you doing at my door step Tony?" She greeted him.

"I'm here to see Gina!" Tony responded excitedly.

"Come Gina! Tony is at the door for you!" she announced loudly.

Gina came walking swiftly into the living room and while Ms. Montana looked on, Gina rushed into Tony's arms and after their greetings, she observed the conversation between the two.

Gina asked, "How long have you been in Miami Tony?"

"Not long." Tony replied.

"You look good Tony." Gina commented.

"I'm successful little sister. Your brother has made it to the big times, and I have something for you." Tony had said, and then presented a diamond encrusted woman's necklace for her.

"It's beautiful Tony!!" Gina had said while she let Tony assist her with putting it around her neck. After she got the necklace secured on, Tony handed her some money.

"Thank you Tony!" Gina had said, then looked at her mother. The conversation took a quick turn after they entered the kitchen and took seats at the table.

"I'm in hair school Tony!" Gina had said.

"That's good Gina." Tony had said.

"I want you out my house Tony! You aren't welcome here!" Ms. Montana said, in her quick demanding tone.

"Why mama?" Gina had asked.

"Because he's a bum! I'm ashamed to say he's my son." Ms. Montana said.

"Please mama! Don't talk to Tony like that. He's your son!" Gina had said.

"You come around here dressed in your fancy clothes, jewelry and throwing money around like you some type of big shot! You may impress Gina, but you're nothing but filth, and I want you out my house. Right!! Now!!" She yelled at Tony.

"Stop mama!" Gina shouted.

"What do you know Gina? You're just a girl," Ms. Montana had said, waving her old wrinkled hand at Gina dismissively.

"Get out Tony! Get out my house now! Go!" she had said, pointing at the door.

"I have to go Gina. I'll see you around." Tony had said as he headed towards the door.

"Don't ever come back here, Tony. You aren't welcome here anymore. And take your blood money with you." She had said, as she snatched the wad of money out of Gina's hand and pushed it into Tony's hand.

"Now get out!" She demanded as she held the door open.

The sound of the car engine humming brought Ms. Montana back to reality. She walked over to the window, and pulled the curtain back, and noticed the blue Buick with the white man in it in her driveway.

"He looks like a policeman." She said as she hesitated to go to the front door.

Standing at five-foot three with dark hair, razor sharp eyes and a slim body that made her look younger than her seventy years, Ms. Montana had a low tolerance when it came to dealing with law enforcement officials. She had been abused physically by police in Cuba and her dislike and distain for them did not change, but increased invariably.

A tall, slim built, white man with big hands stepped out the vehicle exposing his pale skin to the Miami sun. Everything from his black suit, brown loafers and gun on his hip said he was a cop.

"Please God have mercy on me." Ms. Montana said as she grabbed a napkin off the living room table and wiped her eyes. She started towards the door as she continued to look out the window at the man who was now reaching on to the back seat for a brown box. His demeanor told her that the material inside the box was important. Her assumption was confirmed after he pushed the door closed with his butt and cradled the box like it was a baby.

When Ms. Montana arrived at the door, she put her ear up to the door, and listened as the man made his way on to the porch. The man's knuckles pounding against the door came next!

She was startled form the sound, but it didn't stop her from wanting to know what the man wanted.

"Please God don't let this be about Tony!" Ms. Montana whispered to herself as she turned the lock on the door, and then she opened the door. As she swung the door open, the man had his hand in the air like he was about to knock again.

"Who are you? And what do you want?" she said. Her demeanor was serious.

"First things first, my name is Agent Terry Tadeo. I'm with the Special Drug Task Force Department." Ms. Montana interrupted, "Get lost! I don't want to talk to you."

Then she made an attempt to shut the door. Agent Tadeo blocked the effort by sticking his foot in the doorway.

"Ouch!" he shouted as the pain shot up his leg.

"I don't like police. I don't like police. Get away. Tony isn't here." Ms. Montana shouted as she kept the pressure of the door on Agent Tadeo's foot.

"I'm not here about Tony. My visit is about your daughter, Gina!" He shouted as he continued to struggle to free his foot.

"What about Gina?"

"Gina is dead Ms. Montana!"

The statement was like a sledgehammer. It sucked all the air out her chest. She let the door go and stepped away from it.

"Are you okay Ms. Montana?" Agent Tadeo said as he slipped his foot from the doorway.

"Is Gina really, dead?" She asked as she looked directly into Agent Tadeo's blue eyes.

"Yes. She was murdered at Tony's place."

"How? Why?" She asked in a whisper.

"Can I come inside the house?"

"No!" she yelled.

"I really need to talk to you about your daughter. I want to help find her killer."

"Where is Gina's body?"

"I really think you should let me come in so we can discuss this. Your life may be in danger!"

Ms. Montana couldn't control her emotions. Tears formed in her eyes right before she yelled, "Just leave me alone… Get away from here."

"Okay! Okay! Calm down. I'm leaving." Agent Tadeo said.

The neighbors were watching now. Agent Tadeo placed the box on the door step, turned to leave, turned back around and said, "I'm sorry for your loss Ms. Montana. But Tony is dead too."

Ms. Montana slammed the door in Agent Tadeo's face. "Well that went well. All part of the job." He said and then stepped around the box. Then he headed to the Buick.

Ms. Montana watched from the living room window as Agent Tadeo got back inside the driver seat of the Buick. She let go of the curtain when he looked in her direction. She took a moment to gather her thoughts as the sound of the Buick took over the atmosphere. While backing out the driveway she could hear Agent Tadeo shouting, "I'm leaving now Ms. Montana. Sorry, again!"

Seven months later…

Agent Tadeo had been sitting in his vehicle outside the Drug Task Force headquarters, when he heard the high pitch voice of the dispatcher come over the airwaves of the police scanner and said, a woman had overdosed at a downtown hotel. The hotel was two blocks over. Agent Tadeo put his vehicle in drive and drove over to the hotel. As he arrived on the chaotic scene in front of the hotel, a medical van was exiting the parking lot with a woman in the back of it.

He hopped out the Buick and walked over to the policeman that was in charge who was an old friend of his.

"Is the victim going to be okay, Jack?"

"I'm not for sure Terry." Jack said while writing out his report on his clipboard.

"Can you give me a run down on what happened here?" Agent Tadeo said.

"Can't you see that I'm busy writing the report?" Jack said while looking up from the clipboard.

"I think this case could be linked to Tony's case."

"You still trying to find out who murdered Tony Montana?"

"Yes…"

"Well, this is going to knock your socks off! The victim is Tony's wife."

"What?"

Agent Tadeo was familiar with Tony's wife, because his investigation against Tony. She had helped him identify some of the players in Tony's world. This was why he thought that one of the players could be behind the overdose.

"Why are you so shocked? Everyone knows she's a coke head." Jack said.

"I'm not shocked. I'm just worried." Agent Tadeo said as he lit up a cigarette and took a pull from it.

"You shouldn't be worrying about her, Terry. It's our job to solve crime not to worry. Leave the worrying to the public." Jack said as he went back to writing his report.

"I have to get over to the hospital!" Agent Tadeo said.

"What, you got a thing for her?"

"No!"

"Well, why don't you leave this alone and Tony's case too?"

"I can't. Now, I have to be going."

"Where can I find you if anything comes up?"

"Over at the hospital. If you find anything that you think could help me, give me a call."

"I have something you might not know about."

"What is that?"

"The Source is out on Bond."

"How do you know?"

"I have connections."

"That's messed up."

"That's the America way."

Thirty minutes later, Agent Tadeo pulled up in front of the hospital. The sliding doors to the emergency room opened as he walked in front of them and as he made his way over to the nurse behind the counter in the lobby, he took in the chaotic scene. There was a couple with bandages on their heads and there were people that looked like they had been in a car accident with blood on their clothes. A mother with a sick baby in her arms was waiting for service too.

After flashing his badge and asking what room Ms. Montana was in, Agent Tadeo made his way to the third floor where the operating room was located. He stopped at the rim of the door and put his ear on it.

"We are going to need more blood for the patient and the baby. Get an IV ready for the baby. Hurry everyone because time isn't on our side. The baby head is wrapped around the umbilical cord, and the blood isn't circulating properly. The baby is under weight and has a very slim chance of surviving." Agent Tadeo heard the deep southern voice in the room say.

Agent Tadeo wanted to know the outcome of the operation but was interrupted by a nurse as she pulled the door open from the inside of the operating room.

"What are you doing?"

"I was listening."

"Who are you?"

"I'm Agent Tadeo."

"Are you family?"

"No…"

"Well, you need to go to the lobby."

"I'm investigating the case."

"What case?"

"The lady in there overdosed right?"

"Yes. But right now she can't talk because she's fighting for her life."

A loud beeping sound took over the atmosphere. "I have to go." The nurse shouted and then rushed back into the room. Agent Tadeo knew the sound. He had heard it on many occasions while doing other investigations at this same hospital. He knew from the sound that something was wrong. Very wrong!

The evidence became transparent when more nurses came running down the hallway with breathing machines in their hands and two heart devices.

Agent Tadeo was very familiar with death. He had seen hundreds of people gunned down in the streets of Miami for drugs. Death was normal now. This was why he didn't inquire about Ms. Montana when the nurses rolled her out on a gurney 30 minutes later. As he stood up, the nurse that he spoke with earlier said, "The mother didn't make it. They tried their best to get her to breathe, and she lost a lot of blood during the C-section."

"May I ask? Is the baby okay?" Agent Tadeo asked.

"Yes. He's okay!"

"What is his name?" Agent Tadeo asked.

"Tony Montana Junior. The mother wanted him to be named after his father."

CHAPTER 1

21 years later… Early summer.

Place: Miami

Year: 2005

As Tony was walking down the South Beach strip towards his job, he could smell the scents of hot dogs, onion rings, and other delicious foods that were permeating in the air. He could also hear the sweet sounds of Cuban, Mexican and American music. He had been enjoying these different cultures ever since he had left the grasp of Social Services, and every time he walked the Strip, it reminded him of how far he had come in life. The Strip was also a place he could come to, to envision what life would have been like with his father in it.

When he arrived at his job on the east end of the Strip, he noticed a group of young slim built women dressed in bikinis. They were all wearing sexy heels too. He observed them as they strolled past the front entrance of Mr. Castro's store. Then he turned his attention towards the five elderly Cubans who were sitting in front of the store. He watched them as they shouted at the women.

"Hello lovely ladies!" Fred said. He was the fat Pillsbury dough boy looking one, out of the five men.

"You ladies are too sexy to be walking. Can I offer you all a ride on my back?" Guru said. He was the alpha male out of the bunch.

"My name is Cowboy. Do you ladies know how to ride a horse? If you do, I've got a big one you call can ride," Cowboy said as he took off his silver brim Western hat and placed it on the corner of the table. Tony interrupted, "Excuse me, boys! You boys need to stay in your lanes."

"You need to stay in your lane, Tony. This here is our turf," Cowboy said while displaying a disapproving facial expression.

"Yeah Tony, this here area is our playground. We have been working this area since Mr. Castro opened the doors. You need to chill out little puppy," Guru said.

The store bell interrupted the men as the door swung open. Mr. Castro stepped out and said, "Now guys, go easy on Tony. You know he's still got milk on his tongue."

All the men let out thunderous laughs.

"I may be young, but I've got more energy than all of you Cubans put together." Tony said and then looked in Mr. Castro's direction.

Mr. Castro said, "Okay Mr. Energizer Bunny, you've got work to do! There are customers inside that are waiting on you to take their orders."

The five Cubans busted out laughing again. After their little laugh, Tony and Mr. Castro walked inside the store and served two Mexican girls. After the girls walked out of the store, Mr. Castro asked, "How is everything going today, Tony?"

Tony turned in Mr. Castro's direction after putting a box of cigars on the shelf. Then he said, "I'm fine."

"I can see that you are early today! May, I ask why?" Mr. Castro inquired.

"I have some questions for you," Tony responded.

"What's on your mind?" Mr. Castro asked.

"I want to know the full story about my father's life," Tony said.

Mr. Castro made an unhappy facial expression where he had tightened his eyes and poked out his lips. Then he said, "Not that again Tony."

"I need to know what happened to my father, and why." Tony responded.

"I promised your grandmother that I wouldn't say anything about your father to you when she asked me to give you this job," Mr. Castro said.

"I'm a man now," Tony said.

Tony had been working for Mr. Castro for three years.

"That's the past Tony…." Mr. Castro responded with conviction in his voice.

"The past brings forth the future. This is what you taught me," Tony retorted.

"It's complicated Tony." Mr. Castro said as he stepped from behind the counter with the help of his wooden cane that he grabbed from the cane holder. He headed straight towards the box-shaped back room as he favored his prosthetic leg. Standing at six feet even, he was three inches taller than Tony. His black hair was the same color as Tony's, but longer and his eyes resembled some old American money.

Tony was used to Mr. Castro's evasiveness, because every time he brought up the subject about his own father to Mr. Castro, Mr. Castro would do exactly what he did today, disappear to the storage room. But, Tony was okay with it now. There was no need for him to get upset or go on about the subject, because he knew he wouldn't get an answer.

Tony put his right index finger on his chin. Usually, he took on this gesture whenever he went into deep thinking, in which he was in deep thought at the moment. He was now reflecting back on the day when he had first met Mr. Castro. He remembered how calmly he had walked inside Mr. Castro's store with his grandmother. They were there to purchase a book bag, because he was starting junior high school. While he was walking around the store, his grandmother and Mr. Castro were engaging in conversation. Even though the conversation was in Cuban dialect, Tony had understood every word of the conversation, and when his father's name was mentioned by Mr. Castro, this made him want to know more about Mr. Castro, because he figured that Mr. Castro could be the bridge to his father's past.

After that day, Tony returned every day to the store in search of the truth about his father in which he didn't get the answers that he was looking for from Mr. Castro. Instead, he ended up building a bond with him. He even got to know the Five Cubans on a personal level.

Ms. Montana had found out about Tony's friendships with Mr. Castro and the five Cubans. She went to great lengths to get Tony to end the friendships with the men, because she had looked into their eyes, which she considered the eyes are the windows to the soul, and saw that these men were thieves and snakes at heart. In her eyes, they were no earthly good, but Tony couldn't digest her findings. He had returned to the men in search of finding some type of closure about his father's death. But every time he brought up his father's name to the men, they wouldn't say anything that would lead him to what had happened to his father.

As the store bell rang, a white man dressed in a Miami Dolphins T-shirt, brown shorts and a straw hat walked inside. The breeze from the man's body interrupted Tony's train of thought. Tony watched as the man grabbed a case of beer from the cooler as he was making his way to the counter, as Mr. Castro reappeared.

After Mr. Castro took a seat behind the counter, Tony noticed a beat up Nike shoe box in his hand. Was this the box that held the truth about his father? Tony thought. Mr. Castro boss was dressed in red shorts, Miami Heat T-shirt and black tennis shoes now. His boss's fake leg was now in plain view.

After Tony took the white man's order and bagged up the beer, he turned to Mr. Castro and asked, "What's in the box?"

"I promised your grandmother that I wouldn't pollute your mind with your father's transgressions," Mr. Castro said.

He looked deep into Mr. Castro's eyes and said, "I'm my father's son. I deserve to know the truth about my father."

"The truth is complicated Tony," Mr. Castro responded in a firm tone.

Tony asked, "What do you mean?"

"Times were hard and Miami was the Wild, Wild West back in the 80's."

Tony looked closely at Mr. Castro while hanging onto Mr. Castro's every word.

"Cubans were exiled out of Cuba before you were born. Most of us were criminals. I don't know if you are familiar with President Fidel Castro of Cuba," Mr. Castro stated.

Tony nodded his head, this was an indication that he knew of Fidel Castro. Mr. Castro continued, "Well, he was the reason that we were exiled out of Cuba."

Tony asked, "Why did he put you all out of the country?"

"He was afraid of mass incarceration. The jails and the prisons were getting over crowded, and he was afraid that there was going to be an uprising," Mr. Castro stated.

"I have a question," Tony said.

"Shoot!" Mr. Castro responded.

"Are you related to President Castro?" Tony asked.

"No. I just took on his name when I got here. My real name is Gallant Santo," Mr. Castro responded.

"Why his name?" Tony asked.

"He was powerful back then Tony," Mr. Castro responded.

Tony hesitated and asked, "What does all of this have to do with my father?"

"Well, your father and I were in jail in Havana when Castro decided to put the prison and jail population out of the country. We were put on boats and told that if we didn't go, we would be shot to death. Since the United States was only 90 miles away, we got on the boat," Mr. Castro replied. Tony interrupted, "Is President Castro as mean as the Media and the News has put him out to be?"

"Yes. He hated the United States because of the United States' beliefs. He didn't believe in free welfare and the way the American Government operated," Mr. Castro said.

"I'm still lost. I don't understand why you are telling me about President Castro," Tony said.

"You have to understand Fidel Castro to understand your father's life," Mr. Castro responded.

"What did my father's life have to do with President Castro's life?" Tony asked.

"Your father got here because of President Castro. Without Mr. Castro becoming an Ouster when he force Fulgencio Batista out of position, we wouldn't have been sent here. It may sound like I'm repeating myself, but you must understand that you wouldn't be here if Castro never cast us out of the country along with the Refugees. That's how your grandmother got here too," Mr. Castro said.

Tony watched as Mr. Castro pulled out a picture of Tony Sr. and placed it on the counter. His father had on a black tuxedo and was standing in a ballroom of a five star hotel with a group of men.

"You were cloned Tony!" Mr. Castro said with a smile.

Tony looked at the picture closely. He could see that he looked exactly like his father. From the black smooth hair to the slim built body.

Tony grabbed the picture and asked, "What year was this?"

"That was early 80's. Those were your father's glory years," Mr. Castro said.

"I'm not here to judge anyone, but was my father a common thief or worse?" He asked.

Mr. Castro stood up and shuffled his fake leg to get a better balance on the tile floor. Then he grabbed the picture from Tony, put it back in the box, closed the lid on the box, stuffed it under his arm like it was a newspaper and caned his way back towards the back storage room.

Tony spoke, "You didn't answer my question."

Mr. Castro turned around and faced him and said, "Your father did what most of us did to make a life for ourselves here in America."

"And what was that?" Tony inquired.

Tony could see that Mr. Castro's whole demeanor had changed. He could see this as he looked inside of Mr. Castro's windows.

He knew a little bit about Mr. Castro's past from the stories of the five Cubans. They had told him stories about Mr. Castro. They wouldn't tell him the name of the man that shot Mr. Castro's leg off, but they all told him it was over an old drug debt and that Mr. Castro carried around hate towards the man who had did it.

"You don't get it Tony. But one day you will figure it out." Mr. Castro said and then he turned, walked inside the storage room and closed the door behind himself.

Tony knew his boss had beaten the odds of death and managed to get the convenience store with the money from the man that shot his leg off. The five Cubans had told him this too. The money had been a payoff, because the man didn't want Mr. Castro to assist the state DA office in trying to solve the crime against him.

Tony understood Mr. Castro's pain. He had lost his parents before he had ever gotten to know them. He struggled every day with his emotions, and his emotions had him wanting to get revenge on the people that killed his parents, because he never got to experience life with them.

Mr. Castro walked out of the storage room five minutes later with a brown bag in his hand. "Are there any more questions, before I leave?" Mr. Castro said.

Tony asked, "What about Geno's father?"

Geno was Tony's best friend. Tony and him had met when Tony started working at Mr. Castro's store. Geno's father had been one of Tony's father's foot soldiers. This made Tony and Geno's friendship special.

"Geno's father knew what he was getting into when he joined your father's side. He was killed right outside your father's office door at your father's mansion, the same day your father was murdered. But I've got to say, they were two of a kind," Mr. Castro responded.

"Geno has a different version. His mother told him that his father was murdered by the Police," Tony said.

"That's not right. It was a war Tony! Tony, your father went to war with a powerful man and lost," Mr. Castro shouted. He was upset now.

"What is the man's name? And why did they go to war?" Tony asked.

"I'm not a snitch, Tony. There are rules to war," Mr. Castro said.

"But you are my father's friend, right?" he asked.

"There are principles. A man must find his meaning to the World," Mr. Castro stated.

"Why are you talking in riddles?" Tony asked.

"I'm not talking in riddles, Tony. You are a man. You have to figure it out," Mr. Castro said.

"What about the lesson you taught me about loyalty?" Tony asked.

"That lesson still stands. Remember, men are loyal to money in this day and time," Mr. Castro said.

"So, whose side are you on?" Tony asked.

"I'm no saint, Tony. Everyone has a price. Even me," Mr. Castro said.

Tony knew that Mr. Castro had been into doing crime too. But he didn't know exactly how deep. He also knew that Mr. Castro had given his life to God and was now trying to live a life without doing crime.

"What's your price? Or what was your price?" Tony said.

"Good questions, Tony. Good questions." Mr. Castro responded while displaying a smirk. Then he sat back down in the wooden chair and said, "It's time you know the truth."

"It's about time you stopped playing around," Tony said.

"Your father was deep in the drug business, Tony. He was major. He controlled the East Coast at one time. His main head quarters were here in Miami." Mr. Castro said.

Tony watched as Mr. Castro became animated. His boss stressed his words and used his hands to speak. There was a hate inside Mr. Castro's voice that Tony detected as the conversation went along.

"What are you talking about? You never said that he sold drugs. I thought he was a street hustler," Tony said.

"Your father was a bully, Tony. He bullied his way into the drug business here back in the 80's."

"Did you and my father really get along?"

"It was a love and hate relationship."

"Did you work for my father?"

"Yes…Yes Tony."

"So, you know exactly who murdered him?"

"Politics murdered your father."

"What do you mean?"

"Everyone wanted to be your father. He was bigger than life. He was God to some people. He had the clothes, women, wealth and I can't forget about the power."

Tony watched as Mr. Castro flung his hands in the air to express himself. Mr. Castro's windows were telling Tony that Mr. Castro wasn't telling the truth.

"Cut out all the bullshit! What happened to my father?" Tony said.

Mr. Castro pulled out a rag from his pocket, and then he wiped his brow. It was well over 90 degrees in the Store.

"It's time you get serious and spit out the truth!" Tony shouted.

"Okay! Your father made a deal with the devil!" Mr. Castro said. The sound of the shop bell interrupted them. It was Cuban

Sam. Sam was a friend of Tony's father too. Sam spoke, "Hello, comrades."

Tony was still staring at Mr. Castro. "If looks could kill, someone would be dead," Sam said trying to lighten the mood.

Mr. Castro spoke, "It's time for me to go! Lock up, Sam."

Tony watched as Mr. Castro grabbed a couple items from the store, and then Mr. Castro made his way out the front door.

Sam asked, "What was that all about?"

"Nothing." Tony responded.

"Don't lie to me. I know you two like the back of my hand, and I have never seen you two look at each other like that." Same implied.

"We were just talking about my father."

"What was said?"

"Not much."

"Sit down Tony! I think it's time we talk."

Tony took a seat in Mr. Castro's special chair. He looked at Sam after Sam pulled out a lawn chair from under the counter and sat in it. He liked the way Sam was dressed. Sam's slacks and cotton shirts were always neatly pressed like he had just retrieved them from the cleaners. His style reminded Tony of a Mafia Wise Guy look.

Sam spoke, "I know you want answers Tony, but sometimes you have to be careful who you seek them from."

"What are you trying to tell me?" Tony said.

"Everyone didn't approve of your father's behavior." Sam said.

"I've heard this more than once. Why are you telling me this now?" Tony said.

"Life can be cold Tony."

"Why does everyone have to talk in riddles today? I'm a man. I'm not a boy anymore."

"I understand that you are hurting son. I understand that you want to know the truth about your father's death."

Tony interrupted, "Tell me then."

Sam ran his hands through his salt and pepper hair. Then he stood up and walked over to the heart shaped mirror that was on the wall in the corner of the room. He looked at himself and then he turned back towards Tony and said, "There was this guy that your father got involved with. The guy was from South America. I don't know if he's still alive, but your father made a deal with him."

"What was the deal?" Tony said.

"One thing at a time Tony. First, I have to tell you why your father took the deal."

"Mr. Castro said something about politics."

"You can say there were politics with the deal."

"Why did my father take the deal, and why did he have to pay with his life?" Tony said.

"Your father was caught in a money laundering scam. He was cleaning drug money, and the Feds busted him."

"What does this have to do with the man in South America? Did he set my father up?" Tony said.

Sam pulled out a fresh Cuban cigar from his shirt pocket, lit it up and took a few pulls, then he said, "No the guy didn't set up your father. He actually tried to help your father out his jam."

"How?"

"Part of the deal was if your father could get rid of someone for him, he would get rid of your father's tax case," Sam said.

"Who was this person that my father had to get rid of?"

"He was a politician that had power with the United Nations. Your father was supposed to stop him from delivering a speech by blowing him up."

Tony asked, "What happened?"

"Your father didn't kill the guy."

"Why?"

"The guy in South America sent a Terminator to do the job along with your father, but your father had second thoughts about the job when he saw that the politician's kids and wife were in the car with him. Your father didn't want to kill the kids." Sam said, and then he took a pull from the cigar. He held the smoke in while he was waiting for Tony to respond.

Tony felt relieved to know that his father had morals and values when it came to life. He now knew that his father had chosen to put his own life on the line for those kids.

"What happened after my father and the guy didn't blow the car up?" Tony said.

"Let me finish telling you what happened that day. Your father shot the hitman in the head, right before the hitman could push the button to blow up the car."

"That's enough I don't want to hear anymore right now." Tony said, and then he turned in the opposite direction of Sam and folded his arms across his chest.

Sam spoke, "You need to hear this Tony! I think it's time that you heard the whole story."

"No! I've heard enough," Tony shouted as he turned around quickly back in Sam's direction.

Sam could see that Tony was serious. He took one last look into Tony's eyes, before he walked out of the store where the five Cubans were still playing a game of cards. Tony watched from the counter as Sam joined in on the five Cubans' conversation. After watching for a minute, he fell deep into thought. He put his index finger on his chin like he always did when he went deep into thought. He couldn't believe he had let his emotions get the best of him during his conversation with Sam. Even though he didn't know the guy that had murdered his father, he was upset with the guy. He wanted revenge against the guy, because the guy had taken his father from him. He never got to enjoy a game of basketball or baseball at the park with his father. These there the things that Tony had always wanted to experience with his father, and he craved these things as a kid. Every time he saw a father and son at the park playing ball, he felt like revenge had to be taken!

Chapter 2

After Tony's shift ended, he walked home by himself. During his walk, he got lost in his thoughts. He had always wanted to know the truth about his father's death but every time he asked his grandmother about it, she would always change the subject. On the other hand, his mother's death was always talked about. Especially, when he got into some trouble.

His grandmother had always brought up his mother's death any time that she saw someone doing drugs or selling drugs in the neighborhood. She would always say, "Drugs are why your mother is dead. Take a good look at what they are doing, because that's the road to death."

Tony didn't like the fact that his grandmother looked at his mother as a junkie, and as if his father had never existed. Growing up, Tony had always craved for both of his parent's love. Especially, before he got adopted by his grandmother. He would daydream about a life with parents. This had been an everyday occurrence until now.

Tony's life had been a mystery to him for years. Every time he looked in the mirror as a kid, he didn't see himself. He saw missing pieces. Yes, his father's features were there, and he knew this from all the pictures that he had seen of his father. But, something was still missing.

Tony stood six foot even, one hundred and eighty pounds, semi-built with black hair and hazel colored eyes that he got all from his father. He was eye candy, but he didn't feel like it. People didn't see what he saw when he looked at himself. They didn't feel the pain or see the person behind the beautiful and expressive smile. People only knew the conservative Tony that worked at Mr. Castro's store for ten dollars an hour. They didn't know that Tony was a risk taker like his father. He had never shown this side to anyone but Geno.

Tony's mind switched back to Sam. He didn't understand Sam's motives. Sam had taught him that everyone had a motive for something. Tony had always kept this in mind whenever he dealt with people. But this time, he couldn't put a motive on Sam. Sam told him about why Tony Sr. was murdered, but still Sam hadn't given up the man's name who murdered Tony Sr.

Tony had gotten what he wanted from Mr. Castro and Sam. He now had a person that was from South America. In due time, he would get the guy that ordered the murder of his father, Tony thought to himself. For the moment, he was still upset about Mr. Castro's demeanor. He had never seen Mr. Castro act the way that he had acted when they talked about Tony Sr. This confused Tony. This made him think that Mr. Castro wasn't truly a trusted Godly man.

CHAPTER 3

Mr. Castro called Mr. Stein on the store phone after he looked out the front entrance to make sure Tony was gone. He knew it was too late to be calling Mr. Stein's home, but Mr. Stein had instructed him to call him if trouble arose. There was trouble according to Mr. Castro's standards. For the last three years, Tony had worked for him, Mr. Castro had never seen Tony so upset or had never been disrespected by Tony. The tone of Tony's voice had sent a chill down his spine. This was why he thought that it was time to abandon the deal that he had made with Mr. Stein. He had gone against his morals and values when he had accepted the deal from Mr. Stein, but the deal was too good to resist at the time, because he had needed the money.

Mr. Stein came over the line after looking over at his alarm clock. "Hello?"

"It's me, Mr. Stein." Mr. Castro said.

"What is it Gallant? Do you know what time it is?" Mr. Stein said in his sleepy tone.

"It's a little bit after 11:00PM."

Mr. Stein inquired while stepping into his house shoes, "Why are you calling me so late?"

Mr. Castro could hear Mr. Stein struggling to gain his breath.

"It's about Tony Jr."

"What about him?"

"He's asking questions about his father."

"Give me a minute. I have to go into my home office on the other side of the house because my wife is asleep." Mr. Stein said.

Mr. Castro could hear Mr. Stein closing a door. Then Mr. Stein said, "What did Tony ask you this time?"

"He wanted to know everything about his father. He wouldn't stop asking until I told him what he wanted to know."

"What was that?"

"He wanted to know who murdered his father."

"What did you tell him?"

"I told him that a man in South America did it."

"Why did you do that?"

"Because he has his father's stare. He was looking right through my soul. He knows that I knew who murdered his father." Mr. Castro said.

"Did you tell him about me?"

"No."

"Good! We still have another six months, before he turns 21 years old. I have talked with his grandmother, and she said she will sign the money over if he doesn't want it when he turns twenty-one."

"I don't think it's a good idea to continue this. This kid is smart. He's been schooled by a street wise guy that I'm close with."

"Let me worry about that." Mr. Stein said.

"I really don't think the kid will just sign over the money."

"He's not a drug dealer, Gallant. He's not a killer. His grandmother has taught him the right way of life."

"She has taught him the right way of life, but he's cut from the same cloth as his father. You must remember that."

"Look Gallant, I found the little brat fourteen years ago in the hands of the Social Services. He doesn't know what to do with the type of money that his father left him."

"I can't do it anymore. No more pretending."

Mr. Stein interrupted, "When I hired you three years ago, you told me you wanted revenge Gallant. What's the difference now?"

"This time I saw something in Tony Jr's eyes. I saw Tony Sr. There is going to be trouble with this kid. I can feel it." Mr. Castro responded.

"He's just a kid, Gallant."

"Yeah, he's a kid but not just any kid. He's Tony Montana's kid." Mr. Castro hung up the phone in Mr. Stein's ear. He didn't know how he was going to continue this game of chess with Tony for the next six months. Things were at a head like a bump when it was about to bust.

Tony was close to the truth, Mr. Castro thought to himself as he walked over to the counter where Miss Valentina had left her card lying beside a New York Times magazine. Mr. Castro knew he could sell the place and disappear to another state. And, then there was the option of telling Tony the truth about the deal that he accepted form Mr. Stein. Mr. Castro had dismissed these thoughts, and then thought about the day that he met Mr. Stein. This was three years earlier.

Mr. Castro still remembered how the fat, bald headed, pale faced man walked inside his store that day. One of the reasons, Mr. Stein was at the store was to see where Tony was working after Ms. Montana had told him about Tony's job. This was told to Mr. Castro after Mr. Castro was offered the deal from Mr. Stein. Mr. Castro told Mr. Stein about his money problems which Mr. Stein had done his own research on him and knew that the building was being foreclosed on. As Mr. Stein wrote out the check to Mr. Castro, he reminded him that he had been the man at the Hospital the day after Mr. Castro was shot by Tony Sr.

The reason, Mr. Castro didn't remember that Mr. Stein was the man that brokered the deal between him and Tony Sr. was because of the medication he had been on that day, but he remembered what Mr. Stein had said to him after he received the money, "Trust me Gallant, this is the best thing to do by taking the money."

Mr. Castro had said, "The last man I trusted betrayed me and cost me my leg."

Mr. Stein said, "Get out of town Gallant if you want to live." Mr. Castro had done just that, but he returned when he heard Tony Sr. had been murdered.

Mr. Castro snapped out of his deep thought as the sound of a fire truck horn caught his attention. He turned his focus to Valentina's card that was now in his hand. He was now thinking about calling her. He could sell his business and leave town, he thought as he picked up the store phone. He tried the number and got her voice mail. He didn't leave a number.

CHAPTER 4

Tony walked inside the living room of his home after he closed the front door. His grandmother was sitting in her favorite chair sewing a blanket together as he walked over to her, kissed her on the right cheek and said, "Hello, Mama. How was your day?"

She said, "It was okay, Tony. How was your day?"

"It was okay." He responded.

"You don't look okay, Tony. Something inside of me is telling me that something is wrong with you." She replied.

"No Mama. Nothing is wrong. Really!! I'm okay." He said.

He watched as she began to cough. She grabbed a rag from the arm of the chair and covered her mouth with it.

He said, "You don't sound good Mama. Are you okay?"

"I have a little cold Tony. I'll be okay." She responded.

"Do you want me to make you some soup?" He asked.

"That won't be necessary Tony. I just need some rest." She responded.

He helped her to her bedroom and made sure she was asleep before he left her side. He liked the fact that she waited up for him every night, but he knew this was taking a toll on her. She had been doing it for three years. There hadn't been a time that she wasn't up waiting when he arrived home. The loyalty and the dedication that she displayed to him was what he wanted in a woman.

Tony made his way to his bedroom after closing her bedroom door. Once inside his bedroom, he took a seat on his bed and fell into deep thought. His mother came to his mind. He had always kept a picture of her and his father on his nightstand. The picture had been a present from his grandmother.

He picked up the old picture and stared at it while he as thinking about all of the people that told him that he had been a miracle baby. He had been three pounds when he was born, and the doctors didn't think he was going to make it after his mother died. This was told to him by the first Social Service worker who had put him in a home with a white couple that ended up giving him back after they had their own baby. This same Social Worker had tried to find someone from his mother's side to take him in, but never did.

He spent the next six years in and out of different foster homes, because there were always problems in these environments. After his sixth home, he went into a household where a couple had a child molester living in the establishment with them and after just two months in the estate, someone reported the couple. After another year in several different homes, Mr. Stein came to Tony's rescue. This was when Tony Jr. was told that his grandmother was alive and wanted him.

He had been so excited about the news of moving in with his grandmother, that he talked to Mr. Stein the whole drive to her house. He had asked Mr. Stein questions about her and he even asked if he had uncles and aunts. Mr. Stein kept it simple and didn't offer up too much information. He just said, "All of your questions will be answered when you get to your grandmother's house, Tony. Just relax."

After Tony heard his cell phone vibrating, he snapped back to reality. He looked at the clock on his nightstand, and it said

11:30PM. Then he looked at his caller ID. It was his friend Geno. He hit the Send button.

"Hello!"

"Que'Paso?" Geno shouted.

Tony could hear Spanish music in the background. He knew instantly Geno was at his new job Downtown.

He spoke, "Que'Paso to you Geno!"

"Something wrong Tony?" Geno asked.

"No! Why you ask?"

"I can hear it in your voice. Something is bothering you. What is it?"

"Nothing Geno. Drop it. Now what is it you want?"

"Hold on a minute, Tony. I have a woman here that needs some service." Geno responded.

He could hear the Spanish woman in the background who was trying to get Geno's attention, because she was talking in Spanish. She was asking Geno in Spanish, if he wanted to dance. He listened while Geno informed the woman that dancing wasn't his thing. When Geno put the phone back to his ear, Tony said, "You don't dance, Papi? Come on. Give the senorita a dance."

"Why are you talking in Spanish so much tonight Tony? Is there something on your mind that you need to tell me?" Geno said.

"I told you already, I'm fine Geno." He responded.

"Well, if there isn't anything wrong with you, I would like for you to join me at the club tonight! There are these two hot chicks that I want you to meet."

He said, "I'll pass."

"Are you still waiting on Miss Right to come your way, Tony?" Geno said.

"No Geno, I'm not waiting on Miss Right. I have to stay in tonight because Mama has a cold. Plus, I can't get my father off of my mind.

"Tony! It's a Friday night… you don't need to be thinking about your father. He's dead, Tony. It's time you let him rest."

"I think, I'm on the right path Geno."

"What do you mean Tony?"

"Mr. Castro told me a little bit about how my father was murdered."

"You don't need to be opening up old wounds. I think you should let it go. Whatever happened it the past, you should let it stay there."

"Okay Geno. How about next week? You get the girls, I'll go."

"Cool. It's a deal." Geno said.

"Be safe Geno. I've got to go now."

"I will Tony."

Tony hung up the phone. Then he turned his attention back to the conversation he had earlier with Mr. Castro. He couldn't stop thinking about all of the information that he had received from Mr. Castro. There were still some large pieces missing from the picture. Like, for instance, the name of the man that ordered the murder of his father. Tony wanted to know more about the man, because he needed closure about his father's death.

Chapter 5

South America heat was like being close to the sun. It could reach temperatures in the hundreds. This could cause dehydration, and the body could shut down completely after hours of being dehydrated. Resulting in death.

Federal Agent Terry Tadeo knew this, before he even decided to take on his new mission. His boss had given him the new assignment, after he turned in his weekly notes about a certain Mafia case. This case was totally different, and it had Agent Tadeo losing sleep, because the main man in the case had killed Agent Tadeo's family.

Agent Tadeo wasn't the type to take cases personal, but he took this case personal because he needed closure. It had been ten years since he had a lead on the man that killed his family. When his boss told him that the world renowned dangerous drug lord had resurfaced, Agent Tadeo was eager to go anywhere to capture him. He didn't care where he had to go in the world to do what he needed to have done.

Agent Tadeo picked up the bean off the ground that had been dropped by the Informant. This time, the bean hadn't been crushed like the last three beans. He continued up the path towards an area in the jungle where there was a waterfall. There was a familiar pungent odor of death looming in the air, and this scent gave him the warning sign that he needed to know that death was close. He made his way on up the path as his six-foot two inch frame ached with pain. He had been walking for over two hours with gear on his back. After being in South America for two weeks, eating all dry foods like he had been doing when he was on a mission in the Army, his black hair needed to be washed, and he needed a bath.

As he was listening to the waterfall, he could hear men laughing off in the distance. He was now sure that he was on the right track. As he was cutting his way through the thick brush with his machete, he could hear several male voices clearly. He wasn't familiar with the voices, but he knew the accent from being in town for the last few weeks.

He slowly walked towards the voices as he sluggishly pulled out his Remington 9 millimeter from his hip holster and put his machete in his backpack. Then he put the gun directly in front of him and used it to push the brush out of his way. In his path was a black snake and as he moved closer to the voices, he cautiously stepped over it. The snake didn't move. "Looks like a cobra." He whispered to himself as he continued on his path. "Damn… I'm getting too old for this." He said as the scent of gas hit his nose. He tiptoed over a branch that had been broken during the latest storm.

The storm was the main factor as to why he had lost the Informant's trail, the first time. The beans that he had given to the Informant to drop on the path had rolled off the dirt path because of the rain. But, he was still able to find a couple of beans. These beans had helped him navigate back on the trail of the Informant.

He reached the neck of the secluded area where a large pile of trees were burning. There had been a large patch of trees cut out of this area, which had been made into a perfect circle. There were stacks of trees lying around the circle. Agent Tadeo noticed the Informant was tired up to a tree with a rag stuffed in his mouth. This made him do a recon of the area. While doing his recon, he noticed two large men that looked like they were natives of Brazil, molesting a little girl. Another large man was guarding the area with an AK-47.

This was surely a challenge for Agent Tadeo; being that he wasn't used to this type of terrain. It would take a miracle and the luck of the Gun-God for him to kill all three men, save the little girl and free the Informant, he thought to himself.

He put his index finger up to his lip to let the Informant know to be quiet. Even though the little girl was screaming loudly this didn't break his concentration. He made his move. He came out the neck of the brush firing the Remington. This first victim was the man with the AK-47. As the man was hit in the chest, he let off a full round of shots before hitting the ground face first. This gave Agent Tadeo enough time to aim at the man that was having his way with the little girl. The man reached for a revolver lying on the ground after coming out of the little girl. He was too slow. The first shot hit him in the head, and the second shot was to the chest. This made the last man put his hands up. Agent Tadeo was too mad to let this man live. He shot the man in the head, and then he untied the little girl.

Agent Tadeo had decided that he would rather be judged by a jury than to let these men live. This is why he shot to kill. There were brain fragments all over the place, and some had hit the little girl who looked to be no older than 12 years old. Agent Tadeo took out a cloth and wiped the fragments off of the little girl's face after he took off his shirt and wrapped it around her naked body.

He said, "Wait here." Then, he turned his focus to the Informant who was known as Komo. As he walked over to Komo, he could see that Komo had been hit in the head by a bullet. His brains were laying all over the place. As he stared back at Komo, he thought back on the day that he had met Komo, and the little girl in the Village that was two hundred miles away. He didn't think that Komo would be killed. The screaming from the little girl brought him back to reality.

"Papa… Papa. No…" She screamed.

Agent Tadeo rushed back over to the little girl who he knew as Lace.

"I'm sorry Lace!" She continued to scream, "Papa… Papa."

After taking the little girl back to the Village, Agent Tadeo returned to his tent where his crew was waiting. The tent was their headquarters. There were all kinds of surveillance, search and detection CIA equipment that he had ordered to track down this drug lord, inside the tent. But the material wasn't helping. It was time for a new plan, he thought to himself.

CHAPTER 6

Ms. Montana was dressed in her housecoat, slippers and she was watching TV. It was close to 4:00PM. Tony had already left for work. She didn't know that Mr. Stein had been calling her all afternoon, until after she listened to her messages on her phone. The tone of his voice told her that he was upset about something. When he said he needed to see her, and he wanted her to call him, this really made her cautious of him. But, before she could do so, he showed up on her porch. She decided to tape their conversation, so she placed a recording device behind the picture frame on the living room table. Then, she turned it on. She walked over to the front door and let Mr. Stein in.

Mr. Stein was dressed in a blue suit and a red tie. His shoes were black and his bald head was freshly shaved. His fancy clothes and shoes gave her the impression that he was from a breed of people that were up to no good. The first time she had met him, they were in his office. At the office, Mr. Stein had told Mr. Montana about Tony Jr. He even told her that the doctor was told by her son's wife to name the boy after his father.

She asked, "What is your business here today?"

"You know why I'm here?" He responded.

Ms. Montana said, "I told you, I don't want the money."

Mr. Stein unzipped his briefcase and pulled out some papers that he wanted her to sign. This wasn't the first time he had done this.

Ms. Montana said, "I'm not signing them. I told you when Tony turns twenty-one if he doesn't want the money, then you can do whatever you want with it."

"I can't wait that long Ms. Montana." He said.

Ms. Montana said, "That's only six months away."

"Something came up. Some people at my job have found out about the money and they want to know what I've been doing with it."

"Like I said, it's up to Tony."

"After all I've done for you, you aren't going to help me?"

"No!"

Mr. Stein ran his hand over his head, then he stared at her.

She said, "Tony doesn't know anything about the money. Like I told you years ago, he probably won't even accept the money."

"Just sign his name."

"I can't do that."

He closed his briefcase. Then he said, "You are making a big mistake." Then he rushed out the door, because he was too upset to continue the meeting. He didn't want to seem too eager to get the money, but he had let his selfishness get in the way. His father had told him that his selfishness was going to get him killed or cause him to lose everything he owned. This was told to him after his father had signed over the family firm to his best friend. This hurt Mr. Stein because he thought his father was going to sign the firm over to him after his father fell ill from cancer. This had been over fourteen years ago. Now, his father's words were ringing in his ear as he watched Ms. Montana close her front door. The money was his mission, and he was going to get it. Even if he had to kill for it.

Tony walked into Mr. Castro's store after waving to the five Cubans in front of the store. He was an hour late for work, because he had gone to visit his parent's graves. This was his first time late for work in three years. He had always come early to work, but all the talk about his father made him want to visit his father's grave. And since his mother's grave was next to his father's, he changed the flowers on her grave too. Usually, Tony went to his father's grave on his father's birthday and on Father's Day, and these would be the times that he would talk to his father and tell him how, he wished he was in his life.

Once in the store, Tony recognized that Mr. Castro wasn't behind the counter. He was surprised to see Sam taking orders. After Sam finished up with the last person that was in the small line, Tony said, "Hello Sam."

"What's up Tony? Good to see you." Usually, Sam helped at the store when Mr. Castro had to make a run. This was usually around the first of the month and the middle of the month.

Tony said, "I'll take over."

Sam walked from behind the counter, went straight to the beer cooler and grabbed a beer. He popped the can, downed the beer, and then he said, "I needed that."

It was in the high 90's, the sun was shining bright into the store and the fans were on high. Tony took notice of Sam talking to himself after he grabbed another beer out of the cooler. Tony asked, "What's on your mind?"

"Nothing." Sam responded.

Tony knew something was wrong with Sam. He knew this because Sam never took in beer like he was doing now. Tony spoke, "You know you can talk to me?" Tony watched as Sam turned on the small TV that was on the counter top.

Sam spoke, "I need the Yankees to win today." Tony knew that Sam was placing bets on baseball but he didn't know that Sam was in debt, because he had a gambling addiction.

He asked, "How much did you bet?"

"A couple grand, Tony. I'm in debt with the local mob. I need this game."

"Are you crazy? How are you going to pay these guys back if the Yankees don't win?"

"I don't know Tony. I will figure something out."

"I think it's time you stop."

"I can't stop now Tony! I'm in too deep."

"Do you have another way you can get the money?"

"Rob a bank. But I'm too old for that."

A young white girl with thick long blonde hair walked in and interrupted them. Tony took her order and watched as she walked out of the store.

He spoke, "I'm worried about you, Sam."

"Don't worry, Tony. The Yankee's are going to win." The sound of the Yankees taking the field could be heard throughout the store. Tony watched the small TV screen as the first batter came up to the plate from the other team. Then came the crack of the ball from the bat.

Sam shouted, "No…"

CHAPTER 7

Mr. Stein had scheduled a meeting with Mr. Castro for 2:00PM. It was now 1:45PM according to his clock on his office wall. It had been three days since he had talked with Mr. Castro. After Mr. Castro had hung up the phone on him, after telling him that Tony had been asking questions, he called Mr. Castro back and left a message on Mr. Castro's answering machine to come to the Office on Monday evening. That was on Friday night!

Mr. Stein didn't know if Mr. Castro was going to show up, but he did know if Mr. Castro didn't, that he would have to arrange to go out to Mr. Castro's store and talk with him. He didn't want to go out to the store, because he didn't want Tony to put the puzzle together. This is why he decided to sit in his office and wait.

And hour later, Mr. Castro showed up. Mr. Stein spoke, "I thought you weren't coming!"

"It's no big thing, I just got tied up in traffic. Miami traffic can be a bitch sometimes."

"Well, I'm glad you could make it."

"I'm here because I want out."

Mr. Stein smiled, and then he opened his desk drawer. Then he pulled out a fat white envelope and dropped it on the counter. Then he said, "We have only six months left. This is enough cash to change your mind."

Mr. Castro pushed the cash back to Mr. Stein. Then he said, "No. it's too much risk." Mr. Stein went back in the drawer and pulled out another envelope. This envelope had twenty thousand dollars in it. He spoke, "Here is twenty grand. This is four time the payment for the month." Mr. Castro hesitated before he grabbed the envelope and said, "You have a way with money. You are a good businessman, Stein."

"I knew you would see it my way." Mr. Stein stated.

"When do I get my final payment?" Mr. Castro asked.

"Things are complicated. Ms. Montana will not sign the papers, and she now insists I get Tony to sign them."

"Is that so?"

"Yes. That's why you are going to find a way to convince her to sign the papers."

"How am I supposed to do that?"

"You are the criminal. You need to figure that part out."

"I thought you didn't want to hurt her or Tony?"

"Things have changed, Gallant."

José walked out of his bedroom bathroom after stepping out of the bath tub. The sun had gone down and the Compound always became much cooler after a hot day. The temperature had reached a hundred and ten degrees. The fans weren't helping much. The only thing that seemed to be helping José to stay cool was water. José was dressed in snake skin sandals and a linen suit. Then, he walked out on the balcony. Then he looked over his Compound and enjoyed the view. There was over growth all over the jungle area. This place was impossible to reach by automobile, because the terrain was so rough that when it rained most of the ground turned to mud.

After the War on Drugs had started in the United States, José had disappeared to Central Brazil. This was after he found out that there was a warrant for his arrest in the United States. His name was showing up on the International News too, and this alone was the main reason he returned home.

José walked back inside the main complex and grabbed his granddaughter's picture off of the night stand. He was proud to be a grandfather. After his son was murdered by some bandits, he took his granddaughter in and raised her. He sent her to the best school in the United States, and he had taught her about his cocaine business. He even made sure that she was given a spot in his empire after she had finished college. José snapped out of his daze as one of his female servants entered the room with a bucket of water in her hand. He put his granddaughter's picture down and waved the servant away. Then he grabbed his military phone that he purchased from a long time military associate off of the bed. He dialed his granddaughter's cell phone number. Once she came over the line, he spoke, "I hope you are in Miami."

She responded, "And how are you Papi?"

"All business, Valentina."

"Papi. I have taken care of the business you asked me to take care of, but I have one more building to buy."

"Make sure you get the deal done soon! Because I have more work for you."

José was always hard on his granddaughter. The reason being was that he was planning to leave her his businesses when he retired. Now that he was in his late 70's, he thought it was best that he put her in charge. This was why he sent her to the best schools and had taught her about the drug business.

"Okay Papi! I will get the deal done by the end of the week."

"Make them an offer that they can't resist," José responded.

Valentina Rivera stepped out of the new white Maserati and slowly walked to the front door of Mr. Castro's store. This was her last stop of the day. She had just finished closing several deals with other store owners on the block. She made them offers they couldn't refuse and now it was time to do the same with Mr. Castro.

Her grandfather had taught her at an early age about the value of money. She had soaked it in like a sponge, and the education that she had received from her grandfather had helped her finish first in her college class. She took International Business for her major and learned all of the in's and out's about cleaning up dirty money. Valentina greeted the five Cubans that were sitting out in front of the store. Then she asked, "Where is the owner?"

Sam responded, "He's gone out on a run."

"Well, my name is Valentina Rivera. I talked with Mr. Castro two days ago about selling me this place."

"He didn't say anything to me about that," Sam responded.

"Are you his partner?"

"No!"

"Well it shouldn't be a problem about the sell."

"Like I said, I have not heard anything about him wanting to sell the place."

Valentina had gone online and had done some research about the place. She had even come by the place after hours and left her card on the door.

"Well, I'm going to need you to tell Mr. Castro that I came by."

Sam responded, "I can do that if you can come inside so, I can get your number."

Valentina could feel Sam's eyes roaming over her body. She was dressed in a pair of Giuseppe Zanotti sandals that cost around two thousand dollars, Dolce and Gabbana earrings with a matching bag and outfit. Her whole appearance gave off superstar status. Her black, thick long hair was wrapped in a bun with gold pins that cost five hundred dollars apiece, her hair set off her lovely olive face and green eyes. These significant attributes charted her in a class of her own.

Sam escorted Valentina in the store to get her number for Mr. Castro.

After fishing out a couple cases of beer from the storage room, Tony interrupted Sam and Valentina when he walked back into the front area of the store. He sat the beer down. Then he looked up and met Valentina's eyes. He asked, "Did I interrupt something?"

"No Tony. Ms. Rivera was just leaving." Sam responded.

Instantly, Valentina felt a connection with Tony. The electricity between her and him was in plain view, and Sam could see it.

Valentina spoke, "Please tell Mr. Castro I came by." Then, she pulled a card out of her briefcase and placed it on the counter. Sam picked it up and said, "Ms. Rivera, I will tell Mr. Castro you came by."

"Thank you." She responded.

Valentina turned and headed towards the door, Sam interrupted, "Is that Mrs. Rivera as in married woman or Ms. as in single?"

She said, "I'm not married and I'm not looking. Been there, done that."

Tony asked, "Are you the woman that's been buying up all the properties around here?"

"That might be me. Why do you ask?" She responded.

"I want to know why? And why this place?" Tony replied.

"I have a client privilege agreement that I have to go by. I cannot discuss their business with you." Valentina lied.

"Mr. Castro didn't tell me that he was selling the place." Tony said.

"Like I say, there is a client privilege agreement that I have to uphold." Valentina had learned about business contracts from her time at Yale and how to lie while doing business.

"Well, can I take you out on a dinner date?" Tony said.

"Thanks for the invitation, but I don't think you can afford the places I dine at." Valentina responded.

"How do you know?" Tony asked.

"I know, because you are a nine to five guy. You are not my type." She said.

"So that means no?" Tony asked.

"Whenever you hit the lottery, look me up. Maybe I'll consider then."

"That might happen. Please don't count me out." Tony said.

Valentina winked at Tony and walked out of the store. Tony rushed over to the door and watched as the five Cubans that were sitting in front of the store whistled at Valentina as she made her way back to her fancy luxury vehicle. He smiled at her as she took one last look back at him before she drove off.

Mr. Castro strolled inside his store using his cane. He was surprised to see Tony behind the counter, because he gave Tony the day off. He asked, "What are you doing here today Tony?"

"I came here to talk to you, but Sam told me that you weren't here."

"Where is Sam?" Mr. Castro asked.

"He went to place a bet on the Yankees." Tony said.

"He's going to get enough of that gambling." Mr. Castro responded.

"How are you?" Tony asked.

"I'm fine, Tony. What do you want to talk about?"

"I was thinking about buying in on the store. I know you are in debt."

"How do you know?" Mr. Castro asked.

"The streets are talking." Tony said.

"Who? The five Cubans?" Mr. Castro asked.

"It doesn't matter who told me. I just want to help." Tony said.

"I don't want your money, Tony. This place is all I have and I want to keep it that way."

"Well, why are you selling it?" Tony asked.

"I haven't decided yet to sell. I'm still thinking about it." Mr. Castro responded.

"Why are you even thinking about it?" Tony asked.

"I'm just testing the market for now. Just in case I have to sell." Mr. Castro answered.

Tony pulled out the card that Valentina left behind. He spoke, "Well this is a card from Ms. Valentina. She came by yesterday."

Mr. Castro took the card out of Tony's hand. Then he said, "I think I spoke to her on the phone."

"She's a beauty." Tony replied.

"Forget her Tony. She costs too much for you." Mr. Castro said.

"She already let me know that. You didn't have to remind me." Tony retorted.

"Well, I did and I want you to know that she's all business so don't go getting any ideas." Mr. Castro said.

"How did you meet her?" Tony inquired.

"The Internet. I put an ad up on my Business page." Mr. Castro responded.

"She really wants this building." Tony said.

"How do you know?" Mr. Castro questioned.

"Her demeanor. She was all business like you said. But, she did tell me if I hit the Lottery to look her up." Tony said.

"Forget her Tony. You will never get her and you will never hit the Lottery." Mr. Castro retorted.

"How do you know?" Tony shot back.

"Do you know your chances of hitting the Lottery? Boy, you'd better start playing every day if you want to have any chance," Mr. Castro said then started laughing.

"Laugh if you like, but what makes you laugh can make you cry." Tony retorted.

"Dream on Tony. Hell, I had dreams at one time," Mr. Castro said.

Tony watched as Mr. Castro walked to the back storage room. He put his finger on his chin and fell into deep thought. His mind went straight to Valentina. She was the most beautiful woman he had ever laid eyes on. Her beauty wasn't the only thing that Tony liked about her. He noticed that she was witty and had charm and this was what was driving him crazy. He had to have her.

Tony had felt a physical phenomenon arising inside of him when he laid eyes on Valentina. He liked the fondness that she displayed even though, she put a road block in front of him when she spoke of money. Her lips had twitched for a second after they made their connection. Tony had seen it. It was breathtaking for him.

A customer walked in the store and set off the bell. This broke Tony's trance. He looked up at the tall African American male who had a T-shirt wrapped around his face. As soon as he made eye contact with the man, the man pulled out a silver and black 50 caliber pistol. Then the man shouted, "This is a robbery. Nobody move, nobody get hurt. Just give up the money. Right now!" Tony slowly opened the register and pulled out the cash. There wasn't much because Mr. Castro had taken most of the money to the bank. Tony handed the man the money. Then, he watched as the man looked at the small wad of tens and a couple of ones. The man shouted, "What the hell is this?"

"That's all the cash here." Tony responded.

"You've got to be kidding me right. Where is the safe?" The man asked.

Tony responded, "There is no safe." Tony was trying his best not to panic.

The man shouted, "All stores have a safe."

"Well this one doesn't. Sorry man." Tony responded.

Tony noticed Mr. Castro coming from the storage room with a bottle of cheap beer in his hand. The guy didn't see it coming. Mr. Castro swung the bottle and it connected.

"Bam…" The gooseneck broke in half. Tony watched as small pieces of glass from the bottle hit the floor. The guy fell to the floor on top of the glass pieces. He was out cold. Tony picked up the guy's weapon. Mr. Castro asked, "Are you alright Tony?"

He responded, "Yes."

Mr. Castro decided not to call the police after he took the T-shirt off the man's face. The man was from the neighborhood, and his name was Joe Black. (A known robber.) They knew him from taking his orders inside the store on many occasions. When

Sam returned from his errands, he was told by Tony and Mr. Castro that Joe tried to rob the place. And he didn't protest when they decided it was best to let Joe go.

CHAPTER 8

Tony arrived at home after pulling a late shift. Geno was sitting on the porch in Tony's grandmother's rocking chair, waiting. He was dressed in a linen suit and Polo shoes. His jet black hair was cut short in a new style. He spoke, "I've been waiting on you. What took you so long?" He asked.

"Waiting on me for what?" Tony responded.

"I've got us dates." Geno said.

"Tonight?" Tony questioned.

"Isn't today Friday?" Geno asked.

Tony had forgotten that he promised Geno that he would go out for a night of fun with him.

"I forgot all about that promise I made to you Geno." Tony said.

"Well, you need to hurry inside and get dressed." Geno replied.

"I really don't feel like going out tonight." Tony responded.

"You made a promise! Your word is all you have." Geno said.

"Give me a raincheck." Tony retorted.

"No can do. I can't stand up two hot chicks. You have to go with me tonight!" Geno replied.

"My word is my word, but you are going to own me." Tony said.

"After you see these girls, you're going to owe me," Geno responded.

Tony wanted to tell Geno about Valentina, but he didn't want his friend to think that he was in love with someone that he could never have. So instead of telling Geno about Valentina, he walked into the house and greeted his grandmother who was sitting in her favorite wooden chair relaxing. He kissed her on the cheek and said, "I'm going out tonight, Mama. I need to hurry and get dressed." Tony said.

"Don't pay me any attention Tony. I'll be here when you get back." She responded.

After Tony left the room, he took a shower, dressed in slacks, cotton shirt and hard bottom shoes that Sam had given him for his eighteenth birthday. Then he returned to the living room where Geno was entertaining his grandmother. She spoke, "Such a beautiful young man." Tony responded, "Thanks Mama."

A vehicle horn interrupted the family moment. Geno spoke, "That's the girls." Tony kissed his grandmother on the cheek and then he and Geno walked out the front door. When they arrived at the Wrangler Jeep, Geno introduced Tony to Sandy and Lisa. The girls said, "Hello," at the same time. Then Geno asked, "Where is your guitar, Tony?"

Tony said, "You didn't tell me to bring it."

Geno responded, "I think we are going to need it for our night cap at the Beach."

"That sounds like a good idea." Tony responded.

Sandy asked, "Can you play a song for me, Tony?"

Tony liked her Spanish accent. It reminded him of Valentina's voice. It had been a while since he had been with a woman. Geno and him just didn't have the time, because they were always working.

Tony said, "Maybe later…"

Sandy responded, "I'm looking forward to hearing you play. My father used to play."

Tony looked into Sandy's green eyes and could see the seriousness in them. Her teeth were perfect, and her breasts looked like two large juicy apples. She had the most beautiful slim fit body that Tony had ever seen. But she wasn't Valentina. Tony excused himself and went to get the guitar. When he returned, he got in the back seat with Sandy. Then, they were on their way. He played while they were on their way to the beach.

Valentina arrived at her eight bedroom mansion on Indian Creek Island. It was Dade County's most prestigious private island. After getting out of her car, she was met by her butler, Ms. Rick Long who she called Ms. Ricky. He had been working for Valentina for the last two years. They had become close friends after he told her that he was a homosexual. This opened the door for her to tell him about her addiction to sex and her openness about being bisexual. Valentina had been bisexual ever since her boyfriend Brad was killed. His death caused her to explore new territories in her sex world, because every man that she tried to have sex with after his death didn't satisfy her sexually. His death also lead to her closing her heart. She made a vow to never open her heart to another man. She had done great until she saw Tony.

The only thing Valentina could think about now was Tony. It was something about him that touched her soul, the moment they made eye contact. It was the same feeling she had gotten when she met Brad while she was in college. She could also tell that the feelings that she was experiencing for Tony were mutual. As Valentina reached Ms. Long her car keys and Prada pocketbook, she said, "It's been a long day. I need to take a hot bath."

"Your bath will be ready in ten minutes. I have prepared you a meal and there is a bottle of red wine on ice. Is there anything else you need?" He replied.

"No…" She said.

"You look like you have something on your mind. I can see it." He said.

Mr. Long knew that Valentina was an extroverted person. It was hard for her to hold her thoughts and interests inward. "What can you see Mr. Long? Or would you like for me to call you Ms. Ricky tonight?" She said.

"I see that someone has found love." He responded.

"You are reading me wrong." She responded.

"My girl side is reading you right. Ms. Ricky is never wrong about love, girlfriend. I've been around you long enough to know when you are in love." He said.

"I'm not in love Ms. Ricky!" She said.

"You can tell me. Is there someone?" He inquired.

"Not really," she responded.

Valentina took off walking towards the front door. Mr. Long said, "You only call me Ms. Ricky when you want to talk. I guess this guy is worth talking about?"

Valentina stopped in her tracks. Then she turned and said, "He works at one of the stores I'm trying to buy."

"How does he look? How old is he? You have to give me the dirt on this guy." He said.

"He's younger than me and cute as hell." She responded.

"Does he have a friend or a brother?" He said.

"I don't know. I didn't get that far with him." She said.

"Are you planning to get with him or what?" He asked.

"I don't know." She replied.

"I've heard that before." He said.

"He's not in my class. No offense to him, but my grandfather wouldn't approve of him." She said.

"You don't have to marry the guy. You can go out and have fun with him." He said.

"Let's get inside. We can talk later. Right now, I need to think." She said.

Valentina took off her shoes and handed them to Mr. Long. Once they entered the mansion foyer she said, "I might fuck him."

Mr. Long said, "Now you're talking my talk." They entered the house and Mr. Long disappeared up the stairs. Valentina's thoughts went to Tony. There were houses, cars, kids and money in the equation. She couldn't see herself taking on a pro bono case in the past but she was getting older. She didn't want to be alone when she reached old age. She wanted to love again, and she wanted to be loved.

Valentina had been taught by her grandfather that Love fades and wisdom is forever. She had always remembered this saying whenever she thought about making a commitment to a man. This was what made her into the strongminded woman that she had become. Even though she had a sex addiction, this didn't stop her from wanting love.

Valentina had attended Yale, one of the most prestigious universities in the world. Some of the ex-presidents of the United States had attended this same highly regarded institution too. This is what made her take pride in getting her business degree at Yale. While in college, she received the evil eye from her peers, because there was no background for them to look into when it came to her money, prestige or allotment ties. Her grandfather had made sure that there was no link from him to her.

While in college, her social popularity escalated quickly, because her major was International Business. She met people in high places before she received her degree. When she graduated, this made it easy for her to get business deals all over the world. This was how her grandfather had planned it for her.

While in college, she had met Brad Miller. He was a semi-Party Boy/businessman. He stole Valentina's heart the first day, they had met. His charm, wit and spontaneity was what she had loved about him. The day they had met on campus, it was raining, and he offered his umbrella to her. She had accepted the umbrella after he had gotten her to agree to a date in which they went to a movie of her choosing, South Pacific. A classic favorite. This lead to more dates and long nights of love making. And fulfilling memories… And connecting ever closer their souls.

When her grades began to drop, he grandfather told her to drop Brad out of her life so that she could finish her studies. She didn't listen. Brad turned up dead. Valentina believed that her grandfather had something to do with it. And cared not to prove otherwise. Her heart was crushed. She didn't get time to grieve Brad's death, because her grandfather wouldn't let her. He willfully instructed her to finish her studies, because it was the family business. She understood, and did what her grandfather told her to do.

Valentina had a feeling that her grandfather had something to do with Brad's death, but she never spoke of it. This was the very reason, she was cautious about dealing with Tony. She didn't think her grandfather would approve of Tony, because he didn't have anything to offer but looks. This was a big no-no in her grandfather's book. This was why she was always having one-night stands. She had been through her share of men and women. She never remembered their names. This was how she liked it. She did this so no one would get hurt.

She was like a vampire. She was always looking for a victim to stick her teeth into. This habit had come about after Brad's death. This was how she handled the pain. Most of the time it would be random people who she didn't even know that she had sex with. They wouldn't have any idea that they were going to be raped. Most of her victims she had had tied up were men, but women also suffered at her hands too. She had made sure that they were drunk, or she put the date rape drug in their glasses. Then after her fun with them, she would leave a thousand dollars to show her appreciation. This was business. Not pleasure. The unrelenting life of the rich.

Valentina felt like she could do Tony. But she knew she couldn't, because she didn't want to blow the deal with Mr. Castro. She didn't know if Tony was related to Mr. Castro. She dismissed her thoughts about Tony. Then she took a bath and dressed in the two piece sapphire Prada dress that Mr. Long laid out for her. She slipped on her matching boots and grabbed her diamond earrings and twenty-four karat gold wrist watch. She looked at herself in the mirror after she finished up her make-up. She didn't need make-up. Her beauty was natural.

Valentina ordered a suite downtown with her cellphone. She did this in a fake name on a fake card with real money. Then she went down to the kitchen and joined Mr. Long. She didn't want to talk about Tony anymore, so when Mr. Long brought up Tony's name she said, "He's an afterthought. I'm on a mission tonight!"

"You are so cold. That's why I love you," Mr. Long said. After dinner, Valentina left her mansion in a good mood. She was out to find her a random. Her craving for sex had started right after she left Mr. Castro's store. It was long overdue for her to release the stress. It had been three months since she had had physical sex with another person. During that period, she had been working for her grandfather to find a building for his retirement plan. It had taken a toll on her. She needed some sex.

She pulled up at Club Gambino's. The club was packed and there were two lines. After she gave the valet man her keys, she made her way over to the VIP line. This was her second time at the club. The first time she had attended was three months ago, when she found a random within twenty minutes. Then she was off to her suite that she had pre-ordered that night. Tonight was about to be no different.

CHAPTER 9

Tony couldn't believe his eyes. He had to blink to make sure he wasn't hallucinating. The marijuana that Geno and him had smoked while they were on the way to the beach had him high. This is why he had to make sure this wasn't the woman that he had seen at his job earlier. When the female gave the valet her keys, she turned in Tony's direction. He was now sure that it was Valentina. He shouted, "Stop the Jeep."

"We are not stopping here Tony," Geno responded.

He was in the passenger side. There were on the opposite side of the front entrance of the club. Traffic was heavy, and the club strip was live. There were people everywhere.

Tony shouted again, "Stop the Jeep!"

This time, Lisa pulled the Jeep into a gas station parking lot across the street from the club. Tony hopped out of the Jeep.

Geno asked, "Where are you going Tony?"

"I'll be back. I need to speak to someone inside the club," Tony responded.

Tony walked briskly towards the club and he waved at a couple of women as he made his way through traffic to reach the club entrance. He reached the VIP line as Valentina walked inside the building. There were two huge security guards dressed in T-shirts and jeans standing at the door. They both were white with short cut hair. The bold black letters on their shirts read: Security.

Tony spoke, "I'm looking for a friend. She just went inside."

The security with the black hair watched as his blonde haired co-worker asked, "Are you on the VIP list?"

Tony responded, "No."

"Well, we can't let you in." The second guard replied.

"She just went in. She was the lady that got out of the white sports car." Tony said.

"If you want to join her you need to pay the fee. And that fee is a hundred for you. Usually, we charge two hundred if you aren't on the guest list." The blonde haired security guard responded.

Tony knew he didn't have a hundred dollars to pay. So he responded, "Give me a break guys."

The other security guard responded, "No breaks here. This here is for ballers. Now move on if you can't pay the fee. Move on!"

Tony stared at the guy and said, "Give me a minute. I'll be back."

As soon as Tony turned towards Main Street, a Crown Vic pulled up in front of the club. Tony watched as three wise guys got out of the car, dressed in black suits. When one of the men opened the back passenger door, Sam stepped out of the car. Tony knew Sam was in trouble. Two of the men walked in behind Sam, while one lead the way into the VIP. They passed right by Tony, and Sam didn't say a word to him. Tony reached in his pocket and took out all the money he was carrying. Then he spoke, "This is all I have, I have to get inside." The blonde haired security guard took the money and counted.

Then he said, "Have a good time and don't make any trouble."

Tony rushed in behind Sam and the men. They were like ten feet in front of him as they made their way to the upstairs area. Sam looked back at Tony. This confirmed Tony's assumption that Sam was in trouble. It was time for him to call Geno, Tony thought as he stopped at the VIP stairway.

Tony took his phone from his shirt pocket and dialed Geno's cell phone. Then he looked around the club while waiting on Geno to pick up his phone. He could see that the second level was the VIP. A mix of soul and Hip Hop was playing. The speakers on the main level blasting Jay Z's 99 Problems. Tony knew the song because he had heard it while walking to work on several occasions.

Tony took notice that there were no cameras. When Geno answered his cell after three rings, Tony said, "Bring the guitar. Sam is in trouble."

Valentina was sitting in the VIP in the upstairs area when she noticed Tony. She couldn't believe her eyes. She had to blink twice to make sure the moment was real. What is he doing here? Valentina asked herself as she took a sip of her champagne. The reason she was shocked by Tony being inside the club was, because she wasn't expecting to see him in a place like this. She knew that his wages at the store where he worked couldn't pay for a night out inside this club, unless he saved up to do so.

Valentina called the waitress over and said, "Give me something strong to drink." The waiter brought her a bottle of vodka. Valentina grabbed the bottle out of her hand, and then she drank out of the bottle like she was a Bronc Buster Cowboy. This was after she reached the waitress a hundred dollar bill.

She put her bottle down after swallowing twenty-five percent of the liquor inside it. She was trying to build up the nerves to get her a victim. This was her ritual every time she came out on one of her sex-excursions. She decided to stick with her guy. Tony couldn't be her victim, because business came before pleasure. But teasing him wouldn't hurt, Valentina thought as she accepted another bottle of hard liquor form the waitress. Tony was still in her view.

Tony noticed Geno walking through the front entrance of the club five minutes later. The guitar was in plain view inside the snake skin black case. Tony had made a special compartment for the case to hide his Tommy-gun inside it. There was also a space for a small handgun. When Geno reached Tony, he said, "You know you're going to have to pay me back. It cost me a hundred dollars to get in here."

"Don't worry about the money. Sam is in trouble. I think some mob guys have him upstairs." Tony responded.

"What do you think it's about Tony?" Geno asked.

"You know Sam likes to gamble, Geno." Tony said.

"Well, I'm in. What do you want me to do?" Geno inquired.

"I want you to go up to the office with the guitar case and let the guys in the room know you're the live entertainment. If they try to push you away, keep talking until they let you in." Tony said.

"What do I do once I get in there Tony?" Geno asked.

"Play a couple songs until I come knocking." Tony said.

"Then what?" Geno asked.

"I'm going to come in and get their attention so you can draw down on them with the Tommy gun." Tony said.

"What if this plan doesn't work?" Geno asked.

"Then we all might be dead." Tony replied.

Tony watched as Geno made his way through the crowd and up the stairs. Tony slowly walked towards the stairs, as Geno reached the top. The lights from the disco ball flashed directly in Tony's face as he turned towards the upstairs VIP window. He made eye contact with Valentina.

Valentina noticed Tony staring at her. She had been watching his every move, and she even had seen when he was talking to the guy with the guitar. This was her chance to call Tony over. She waved at him. Then she headed to the entrance of the VIP. The crowd was thick in the VIP. This made it hard for her to get to the front entrance. She bumped into several people as she made her way to the entrance. Her pocketbook was small enough for her to hold it in her hand. Inside of it was her cellphone and her chrome twenty-two pistol. After seeing the guys with the guitar rush towards the stairs, she could feel that something was wrong with Tony.

Tony walked up the stairs slowly after seeing Geno go inside the office that was at the top of the stairs. There were two security men that were just as big as the other two men that were working the front entrance standing at the VIP door. They were watching as Geno was being escorted into the main office. After Tony reached the top of the stairway, he did a count of all of the security men in the building; there was a total of twenty men. The thought of approaching Valentina crossed Tony's mind when he reached the top of the stairs, but he changed his mind when he noticed more men coming out of the VIP in front of Valentina. He dipped into the men's restroom on the opposite end of the hallway. He looked out the crack of the door as Valentina and the crowd moved towards the stairway.

Valentina reached the bottom of the stairway and didn't see Tony. This sent her into a perplexed state. She thought that she was seeing things. She looked around the crowd for him. No Tony. Then, she made her way over to the main bar on the lower level. She ordered a shot of Dom Perignon liquor and then let her eyes roam the room for a sex victim. It was time for Valentina to feed.

Usher and Lil Jon's song came blasting from the speakers now. The drinks that Valentina had consumed in the upstairs VIP were taking a lethargic toll. The loud music was causing a thump in her head. She continued to look through the crowd for someone to help with her craving. She came across a white guy that was tall and built with black and blonde hair. He wasn't her type, but his feet were big. Her thoughts went wild again. Maybe he has a big penis? But this didn't mean that he was great in bed, Valentina thought as she thought about the last professional basketball player that had big feet that she had had sex with. Things didn't go too well that night, but Valentina managed to make the guy feel like a man-whore by leaving him ten brand new hundred dollar bills. The guy went on the internet looking for Valentina and even put out a reward for the person that had information about her whereabouts. Too bad he didn't have a picture. All he had was the fake business card that Valentina had printed up on her laptop.

The guy at the bar turned in Valentina's direction. She smiled at him as he approached her. It was time for some action. This was what Valentina thought as she introduced herself as Lisa from Charlotte, North Carolina. Then he said, "I'm Rick."

After Tony walked out of the restroom, he walked over to the office door. He could hear voices inside the room. Tony tried the knob, but it was locked. He whispered, "Damn." Tony decided to knock when he heard Sam shout, "I'mma get your money." A chubby faced wise-guy opened the door. He was one of the wise guys that had escorted Sam to the office. The guy asked, "What do you want?"

Before the men knew what was going on, Geno pulled out the Tommy gun. Tony asked, "Who's in charge?" Geno tossed the handgun to Tony. Tony walked inside the room, then he pointed the gun at the mob boss that was sitting behind a large wooden desk. "Now, turn Sam loose," he said.

The two men that had been working on Sam looked at their boss who was smoking a Cuban cigar.

The boss asked, "What family are you from?"

Tony responded, "I'm not a part of any crime family. I'm here, because Sam is my friend."

"Who are you?" the boss asked after placing the cigar inside his ash tray.

"I'm Tony Montana Jr!" Tony responded.

"Do you know who I am?" The boss asked.

"I don't care who you are. I just need to know how we can clear this problem up."

"You're stepping into no man's land. You will be dead before you can make it out of here."

"I didn't ask you what you can do to me. I asked you, what will it take to clear up the problem with Sam?"

"He owes me a hundred grand." The boss shouted as he slammed his fist on the desk.

Tony could tell by the suit that the man was wearing was worth more than a hundred grand.

"Can you give me some time to get the money?" Tony asked.

"I have already given Sam ample time to get the money. I will be the laughing stock of the city, if I don't do something about this situation." The boss said.

Tony could see that Sam was busted up bad. Tony spoke, "Give me a chance, I'll pay the money. I put my life on it."

"You sound like a man of your word Mr. Montana, but since you are not a part of one of the families, I can't do it," The boss said.

Tony didn't know Sam was in debt so deep. He thought it was a couple of thousand dollars. He knew he couldn't pay the debt, but life was like a card game. You have to play the hand you are dealt, Tony though. He said, "Maybe I can do something for you to pay the debt."

The boss asked, "What can you do for me that I can't have done?"

Tony hesitated and said, "Put some work in. I know how things work."

"This life isn't for you. It's best that you think about another path in life. I don't want to have my guys kill you for getting in my business. Now, I'm going to give you a chance to drop the gun and leave," the boss said.

Tony watched as the chubby boss slowly put his hands on top of a newspaper that was on his desk. He could see a lump under the paper. As the boss's hand went towards the lump, Tony watched. The boss continued, "Put your gun down and go now. Because if you don't, I will personally kill you myself."

After the boss finished his statement, he reached under the newspaper and grabbed a chrome pistol. Before he couldn't get the gun in full view, Tony pulled the trigger to his gun. The bullet caught the boss in the head. Blood and brain matter hit the wall. Then the boss's body hit the floor.

Geno fired three rounds. Quickly rendering the wise-guys useless forever. Then, he made his way across the office to un-cuff Sam with the machine gun still drawn to deliver more casualties need be if necessary. Tony was still looking at the boss laying on the floor with the gun locked in his grasp. He could see the golf ball sized diamond ring on the boss's pinky finger. He walked over to the boss and pulled it off his hand. Then Geno shouted, "We've got to go Tony."

Sam leaned against Tony to get his balance. After Geno put the Tommy gun back in the case, he opened the office door.

Valentina started feeling the effects from the drinks that she had taken out of Rick's hand at the bar. She had taken the drink down so fast that she didn't even know what the drink was until she finished it. Rick had spiked the drink with a date rape drug. He had been planning to give it to another woman but when he was approached by Valentina, he didn't stop her when she grabbed the drink out of his hand.

Valentina had been waiting at the bar for another drink when she heard gunshots. Rick, who had been conversing with her grabbed her and pulled her towards the door. Valentina worked her gun out of her pocketbook as she walked out behind Rick. The crowd was in a frenzy now. People were running towards the exit while the music was still playing.

Valentina tried to pull away from Rick as they got to the club's front entrance. Rick wouldn't let her go. He knocked the gun out of her hand and pulled her out of the door. The people in the crowd wasn't concerned with the couple. They were too busy trying to get out of the club. One of the security guards noticed that Valentina was struggling to get away from Rick. He rushed over and intervened. He shouted, "Let her go!"

Rick responded, "Get out of here! This is my woman!"

They were standing right at the front booth where most of the valet guys usually were standing. Valentina made a move towards the security guard, but she didn't have enough strength to get loose. She was too drugged up. The security guard said, "You're going to jail, sir."

Then he grabbed Rick by the neck, and the two struggled while Valentina looked on. More security guards joined in and wrestled Rick to the ground. Rick was handcuffed, then one of the security guards asked Valentina, "Are you okay?"

She said, "Yes."

The crowd was still trying to get out of the club. Valentina was trying to gain her composure when she heard more gunshots inside the club. This made her take cover inside the small booth. As the frantic crowd spilled into the street, she could see the emotional distress in their faces. This made her think about the drink that she had consumed while she was with Rick. She pushed her finger down her throat as far as she could. Then she threw up the drink and all the food she had taken in earlier. She wiped her mouth with a towel that she had found inside the booth.

Valentina knew she couldn't stay in the booth because she couldn't risk getting injured by a stray bullet. She stepped out of the booth and blended in with the crowd. She raced towards the garage with the crowd. Her mind was frantic now. She didn't want her grandfather to find out about her party girl lifestyle on the news. So she pushed the camera man out of the way as she entered the garage.

As she reached her car, she heard multiple shots, more people screaming and taking cover inside the garage. Mayhem wasn't new to Valentina. She was a trained assassin. He grandfather had introduced her to some of the best killers in South America when she was a kid. They had taught her to kill and then disappear.

After she grabbed her keys from the key booth inside the garage she made herself throw up again, then she made her way over to her car and got in.

When Tony, Sam and Geno stepped out into the hallway they could see that the club was in an uproar. People were in a panic, running towards the exits. The stairway to the main dance floor was blocked off by several security guards. Tony was still in shock from killing the mob boss. He had killed small animals in the past, but killing a person was different. He was numb, and his mind was racing.

Geno shouted over the crowd, "We've got to go Tony."

Tony was staring off in space. He gained his composure as he pulled the handgun from his waistline. He pointed the gun at one of the security guards as they reached the stairway. The security radioed for more help as Tony shot him and the guard's two partners in their chests. More screams came from the crowd. Tony turned and shot another security guard that was shooting from the balcony of the VIP. Then, he followed Geno and Sam as they were making their way to the front of the club. While they were making their way through the club, there were more shots. When they arrived at the front entrance of the club, there were several more security guards who were blocking the doorway. Geno pulled out the Tommy Gun, then he let off a few rounds. He cut them down like he was cutting down trees.

Once out in the street, Geno was looking for Lisa and Sandy. He tried Sandy's number. No answer.

Geno shouted, "They left us Tony! What do we do now?"

Tony said, "Go to the garage. We can get a car there."

As they made their way to the garage, there were groups of wise-guys pulling up in several black Cadillacs. Tony knew this wasn't good. It was time to get lost.

Valentina was sitting upright in her car after she had closed the driver's side door. She stuck her finger in her throat again, so she could throw up. Her head was spinning like she had been on a roller coaster. She hadn't expected her drink to be spiked, but it was. Lesson learned.

Valentina looked in her rear-view mirror, and she noticed three men were running towards her. She recognized Tony's face instantly. There were people running to their vehicles, but this didn't stop Valentina from thinking about finishing what she had set out to do. She turned her attention to seducing Tony. She had a change of heart about having sex with him. Her sense of reasoning was no longer in the equation. All that mattered to her was feeding her addiction. What would it hurt? Who would care?

As he walked up to the car, her face lit up. She was in the process of cleaning herself up in the mirror when he pointed the gun at her. He ordered her out of the car.

She spoke, "That is no way to treat a woman like me."

Tony shouted, "We need this car. Now get out!"

Sam and Geno were already getting in the backseat. Valentina spoke, "You cannot have my car. My grandfather purchased this car for my twenty-sixth birthday." Tony said, "I don't have time to fight with you over the car. You can go with us or you can stay right here where it will be safe for you."

She replied, "I'm not leaving my car."

Tony took a seat in the passenger seat. Before he could get another word out of his mouth about the car, Valentina put the car in drive and hit the gas. She shouted, "I'm the only one that's allowed to drive this machine." She maneuvered the vehicle through the tunnel inside the garage like an expert. Several men were blocking the exit of the garage as she looked ahead at the exit. She shouted, "Hold on. They've got guns." Then she smashed the gas harder, and the car took off like a rocket.

Several of the men didn't have time to get off shots, because Valentina drove right in between them. They almost didn't have time to react. She smashed the gas with her foot once she got to the main road. Then Valentina spoke, "We've got company." Several motorcycles were giving chase.

Tony responded, "Not for long."

Valentina watched as Tony turned and grabbed the Tommy-gun from Geno. She weaved through traffic while he loaded the gun. The motorcycles did the same. When Valentina noticed that one of the cyclists had a gun she shouted, "Get down!"

Tony ducked down in the front seat as several shots hit the back of the car. Valentina pushed the Maserati to a hundred and entered the freeway. The traffic on the freeway wasn't heavy from the club traffic. This made it easy for Tony to turn and point the Tommy at the cyclists. He sprayed a shower of bullets at the cyclist and watched as the cyclist weaved between two cars and a truck. Valentina looked over at Tony and could see that he was very tense while he shot the Tommy towards one of the cyclists. Her mind was racing. This wasn't the first time she had been in a car chase.

A couple of shots hit the rear of the car. This sent Geno and Sam ducking. Tony fired the Tommy in the direction of one of the cyclists that was on the right rear of the Maserati, and several of the bullets hit the cyclist in the chest. This sent the cyclist crashing into a pickup truck that was parked on the shoulder of the freeway. The motorcycle blew up after making contact with the truck.

Tony shouted, "Bingo!"

Valentina responded, "There's an exit coming up!"

Tony said, "Get off there!"

Geno shouted, "Left side!"

Another cyclist came up on the driver's side of the car. Valentina pulled the wheel towards the left with a quick and hard motion. And, the Maserati bumped the cyclist. The cyclist kept his balance. Tony aimed the Tommy at the cyclist, but he couldn't get a clear view of him.

Valentina shouted, "We're coming up on the exit."

Tony responded, "Slow up."

In Valentina's eyes, everything started moving in slow motion as the driver appeared next to her window on the motorcycle. Tony fired the Tommy as the cyclist raised his own gun. Tony was quick like Doc Holiday. Several bullets hit the cyclist in the head and sent the cyclist flipping in the air. When the cyclist hit the ground, the motorcycle blew up.

Valentina could see blood leaking from Tony's shoulder as she exited the freeway. She said, "You're hit."

Tony looked at his shoulder and said, "It's just a flesh wound. I'm okay."

Geno spoke, "Great shooting, Tony!"

Sam said, "You saved my life twice. I owe you big time."

Tony responded, "You don't owe me, Sam. Your debt was paid when you told me about my father."

Mr. Castro sat in the back of the store looking at Tony Sr.'s picture. He was having a drink like he usually did after work. He couldn't stop thinking about the day that Tony Sr. had shot him in the leg. Yes, he owed Tony Sr. money, but there was no need for Tony Sr. to shoot him in the leg like he had done. This was what Castro was thinking to himself as he stared at the picture.

Mr. Castro's mind turned to the day that he asked Tony Sr. for the consignment deal. During this time, Mr. Castro was making a lot of money in the northern part of Miami. This was in the early 80's when cocaine was a party drug. There weren't computers running everything during this time. It was much easier to get away with murder then. Cops could be paid off. Lawyers could get cases thrown out of court with a snap of a finger. Those were the good old days, Mr. Castro thought as he put Tony Sr.'s picture away.

Tony convinced Valentina to pull into a Days INN Hotel on the outskirt of the City. This hotel wasn't the best hotel, but it was clean. Valentina and Geno walked into the lobby area of the Hotel and asked for two rooms. Tony waited in the car with Sam, and while he was waiting, he took a look around the area. There was a dry cleaners on the right of the hotel and several other small businesses. There was a gas station down the street about a block away.

Sam broke up Tony's inquiring time. He said, "I have to tell you, Tony. We have to leave town."

"Why?" Tony asked.

"You killed a Mafia boss!" Sam shouted.

"So?" Tony said.

"So. That's major. They are going to come looking for us." Sam said.

"There were no witnesses."

"There were hundreds of witnesses. Someone saw us come out of that room."

"They don't have cameras there Sam."

"I know, but they have human cameras." Sam said.

"Can you fix this Sam?" Tony asked.

Sam said, "I don't think so Tony."

"So we have to leave town?" Tony said.

"Yes." Sam said.

"What about my grandmother?" Tony asked.

"They don't want her." Sam replied.

Tony asked, "What about this chick?"

"Valentina right?" Sam asked.

"Right." Tony said.

"She's going to have to report the car stolen just in case they got her tag number." Sam said.

Tony asked, "Then what?"

"Hope the guys don't kill her." Sam said.

"I'm not running Sam." Tony said.

"It's your choice Tony." Sam responded.

Valentina and Geno came walking out the front entrance of the hotel. Tony took a look at the dress Valentina was wearing. It was hugging her frame. There was a smear of some type of food on the dress. He dismissed his sexual thoughts about her when she opened the door of the Maserati. Tony asked, "Did you two get the rooms?"

"Yes. Connecting rooms." Valentina answered.

"That's great. We can take one and Geno and Sam can take the other." Tony stated.

"I'll pass, store boy. I told you that you have to hit the lottery first. And I can see that that will never happen." Valentina retorted.

All the men laughed. Valentina grabbed her head. Sam asked in a fatherly tone, "Are you okay?"

She responded, "My head is spinning. I think the drinks I had at the club are catching up with me." Then she passed out right on the seat of the Maserati.

Geno said, "I think she had too much to drink."

Tony stepped out of the Maserati, walked around to the driver's side of the car and picked Valentina up. He carried her to the room that she had rented out and placed her in the large bed. Then he walked out the door that connected the two rooms. Geno opened the door and Tony took one last look at Valentina. Then he closed the door. Then, he instructed Geno to go to the phone booth and report the Maserati stolen.

CHAPTER 10

Agent Tadeo had been a Federal Agent for the last 25 years. He came up through the ranks like all the other agents before him. There were even agents that he had trained with that were dead or retired now that weren't as driven as him. Whenever he had set out to get his man, he usually did.

Agent Tadeo had found out about "José Rivera" AKA: The Source, right before Tony Montana Sr.'s death. He started investigating one of Tony's street dealers after a street whore overdosed on the street dealer's product. The dealer that gave the whore the cocaine was Gallant Castro.

The first time Agent Tadeo had come in contact with Gallant was after the whore's death. During their meeting, Agent Tadeo offered Gallant protection from Tony, because Agent Tadeo knew Gallant owed Tony money for drugs. In exchange for protection, Gallant would have to testify against Tony after Tony was indicted for drugs. Gallant rejected Agent Tadeo's offer after he had found out that Agent Tadeo didn't have enough evidence to get an indictment on him for the whore's overdose death.

A few weeks after Gallant had met with Agent Tadeo, his leg was shot by Tony Sr. While Gallant was in the hospital, Agent Tadeo visited him and tried again to get Gallant to become an informant, but Gallant wouldn't cooperate. Agent Tadeo admired Gallant for sticking to the street code of "No Snitching."

After the visit, Agent Tadeo formed a theory about how Gallant got shot in the leg. He knew that Gallant owed Tony Sr. over half a million dollars. This was told to him by an informant. He also knew that Tony Sr. had sent men to Gallant to pick up the money on several occasions in which Gallant had never shown up for the meetings with these men. The shooting came down to Gallant not paying Tony Sr. the half a million dollars.

Agent Tadeo had continued over the months searching for information to trap Tony Sr. He even followed Tony Sr. to exotic places, expensive restaurants and fancy hotels. He finally caught a break after Lewis Baxton, a Cuban migrant was caught with ten kilos of cocaine and two high powered rifles. Under Federal law, Lewis was looking at twenty years for the drugs and the guns. Lewis had decided to become a federal informant after finding out that he was facing twenty years.

Agent Tadeo had set up an interview with Lewis and Lewis's lawyer. During this interview, Lewis told Agent Tadeo about Tony Sr.'s source and Tony's political connections. This interview had taken place two months before Tony Sr.'s death. Right before Agent Tadeo was going to serve Tony Sr. with a Federal indictment for distribution of cocaine, Tony Sr. was killed by The Source's hitman. Agent Tadeo noticed a lot changed after Tony Sr.'s death in the cocaine world. There were gun fights in the city of Miami almost every day and other cities suffered because their cocaine supply was cut short. This was all due to Tony Sr.'s death, and that The Source went underground.

Agent Tadeo had formed a file for The Source after he was assigned to find The Source. He had made charts about men who were linked to The Source and labeled each man that linked to The Source by their ranks. This chart was made up of Mafia men and street dealers. Agent Tadeo had gotten his superior to call Washington DC, to let the Attorney General know about this new drug lord. He gave his superior all the information that he had gathered about The Source in proper form, so the indictment could be written up.

Inside this package of information was all of Tony Sr.'s personal bank files, political connections, murders for hire and blackmail information on state and federal officials. All of this information could link The Source to Mafia men in which this would be used to bring down the Mafia. This had been Agent Tadeo's plan, until there was a leak in the department in which the leak informed The Source about Agent Tadeo's plans.

Agent Tadeo had found out about the leak and didn't think that his life would be in danger because of the leak. He thought that The Source had enough respect for the law not to come after him. This all proved to be wrong, after The Source ordered a hit on Agent Tadeo's wife and his first drug enforcement team. Agent Tadeo soon discovered that he would never be safe until The Source was dead. This was the conclusion that he had come to after his second wife was killed along with his two dogs and eight other comrades. These murders drove him mad. He didn't know if he was coming or going sometimes. Especially, when it came to looking for The Source.

Agent Tadeo often had flashbacks of his first wife's death, because he was there. They were attending a banquet that the agency had held for their efforts of taking down several corrupted politicians. These politicians had been feeding The Source information about America, plans to make laws to invade other countries to extradite people. After the banquet, there had been an after party in which it lasted until midnight. This party had taken place in the hotel's ballroom. There had been couples dancing out on the ballroom floor when Agent Tadeo slipped out of the hotel to get a gold watch that he had purchased for his wife for her 30th birthday. On his way back to the party, he had noticed a man dressed in Army fatigue that was holding a small device that looked like a bomb. This had sent his five senses rolling. He wanted to confront the man, but as he had turned to call out to the man the hotel exploded. The blast knocked Agent Tadeo ten feet from the building and knocked him unconscious. His superior had given him the watch that he was going to give his wife Susan Ann after he woke up in the hospital. This was after he was told by this same superior that his wife was dead along with his team.

Agent Tadeo had formed his second team a year later. Three months into searching for The Source, he ran into his second wife, in which she had been his high school sweetheart. They had married after six months and bought a house along with two dogs. He had been with her for ten years before she was killed at their home while he was in South Africa searching for The Source. His second team was later killed in a van bombing on their way to pick him up from the airport. He would have been inside the van if the van hadn't broken down right before the bomb went off at the entrance of the airport. The last attempt on his life was at a dog show. He had attended the dog show with a woman that he was interested in, and he had been introduced to by a friend. This time, a woman appeared in his presence with a small device that was a bomb. He had chased the woman by the exit of the building while he was shouting out to the crowd to get out of the building. Before the Brazilian looking female that was dressed in army fatigue hopped on a high priced motorcycle, she pushed the button on the device. The building exploded. Agent Tadeo had dodged death again.

It wasn't long before Agent Tadeo assembled another team. This time, he had told his superior that he wanted all his members to be unmarried and dedicated to his mission. Plus, he wanted this team to be off the record and have unlimited spending for resources that they needed for their mission to bring down, The Source. Approaching his mid-50's, Agent Tadeo wasn't showing any signs of slowing down. After his superior granted all his requests, Agent Tadeo built his body up for the task at hand. After three full months of weights, mountain climbing and gun range training, Agent Tadeo assembled a team of four that included himself.

The first person to join the team had been Josh McHall. He had served in the Army for four years before an honorable discharge. He took his call of duty after the World Trade buildings were blown up. There terrorist act had sparked a hate for terrorism in the 6'4, blonde haired, blue eyed son of a retired pastor. His mother and father were killed in one of the World Trade buildings. This was the main reason he went to war. After doing his duty, he returned to Raleigh, North Carolina where he got a job doing security for Big Rick's Strip Club.

Agent Tadeo had shown up at Josh's job on a crowded Friday night. He knew that Josh would be at work, because the famous stripper Goldie was hosting a party at the club. When Agent Tadeo walked inside the club, he saw Josh wrestling with a customer. While the wrestling match was taking place, Agent Tadeo walked over and introduced himself. The sound of Taylor Swift was echoing in the background.

Agent Tadeo spoke, "I'm Agent Terry Tadeo. I'm here to offer you a special job from the government."

Josh responded, "Hold on a minute."

Agent Tadeo watched as Josh flipped a customer to the ground and then pulled him by his hair out the club. Then he watched as Josh returned with a beer in his hand.

Josh had asked, "Have some?"

"No thanks. I'm on the job." Agent Tadeo answered.

"What does this special job offer from the government pay?" Josh asked.

"100,000 a year." Agent Tadeo responded.

"Wow. Never made that much serving my country. What do I have to do?" Josh said.

"Chase after a drug lord." Agent Tadeo responded.

"What country?" Josh asked.

"All over the world." Agent Tadeo replied.

"Sounds great. When do I start?" Josh said.

"When can you start?" Agent Tadeo asked.

"Right now." Josh shouted.

Agent Tadeo had handed Josh an envelope that contained one ticket to Miami, a hotel key and the address to Agent Tadeo's new office. Then he had headed out to Texas on a plane. The next day, he had shown up at Dean and John's ranch. The ranch was left to the brothers after both of their parents had been killed in a car accident. Dean, the tallest of the brothers had answered the door. He had been dressed in a large cowboy hat, T-shirt, cowboy boots and jeans. He asked, "How may I help you?"

"I'm special Agent Tadeo. I'm here to ask you and your brother to come help the government in the War on Drugs."

"You are not from around these parts?" Dean said.

"No. I'm from New York City, but I live in Miami."

John had shown up dressed in T-shirt, shorts and Michael Jordan Nikes. His hair was black like his brother's and his skin looked like he had a tan.

"You have to excuse my brother. He has no manners. My name is John. Would you like something to drink?"

"Showing your Southern Hospitality brother?" Dean asked.

"Shut up Dean and go take off those stupid cowboy boots before Special Agent Tadeo here think you really are a stupid cowboy." John said.

"As you can see Agent Tadeo, my brother John here is the totally opposite of me. I like country gals and country music. While he thinks wearing Michael Jordan shoes and listening to Rap music is gonna make him hip." Dean said.

"Guys, I'm not here to watch you fight. I know both of you served in the army, and you were good at what you did in the war. Now, with that being said, I want the both of you to let me know by Sunday night, if you two want to join my team." Agent Tadeo said.

Agent Tadeo had watched as the two brothers had consulted between themselves.

Dean spoke, "We can help."

John asked, "What's the pay?"

"A hundred grand a year." Agent Tadeo said.

"We've got money. Can you offer something besides money?"

"Yes. A thank you letter from the Attorney General." Agent Tadeo said.

John asked, "How about a letter from the President?"

"Maybe." Agent Tadeo said.

"We're in." Dean said.

Agent Tadeo had given them tickets, a hotel key and the address to his headquarters. Then, he had flown back to Miami. There was so much work to do at his new headquarters that he had stayed up all night getting the place ready for his men. He had installed all the tech stuff, like new computers, radios, face and eye scanners, walkie talkies, finger print scanners, motion detectors and remote control led cameras. Once all of the equipment was installed, Agent Tadeo had called his superior and gave him all the details about the new facility. It was time to start searching for The Source, he had thought.

CHAPTER 11

Valentina woke up inside the hotel bed feeling nauseated. She knew that she wasn't pregnant, because she hadn't had unprotected sex in about three years. As a matter of fact she hadn't had sex in about three months. And she hadn't missed her monthly cycle in these three months either.

Valentina could hear the TV playing in the next room. She didn't remember leaving a TV on, or how she was now lying inside this hotel bed in her thong and bra. She couldn't remember how she had gotten undressed. Her mind was racing with all kinds of questions, How did I get here? Where are my keys?

Valentina flipped the large blanket off of her beautiful body and rose up out the bed. She looked at herself inside the mirror that was stationed on the wall. She could see that her makeup was still on. She made her way over to the bathroom and entered it. Once inside, she grabbed a small toothbrush that was still wrapped in plastic. She brushed her teeth with the small tooth brush and some Close Up toothpaste she had. After brushing her teeth, she made her way to the area where her dress was hanging up. She checked her dress for her keys and found them there.

Then, she made her way back to the bathroom and took a shower. While under the warm water, she thought back over the night. She had remembered getting dressed at home and then seeing Tony at the club. Then it came to her. She remembered taking the drink out of Rick's hand. Then, she had remembered when Tony and his friends tried to take her car. Then, she recalled the shoot-out at the club and on the freeway.

Valentina hopped out of the shower and put on the robe that was hanging on the door inside the room. She made her way to the connecting door and started banging on the door. She knew Tony had put her in bed. What she didn't know was if she had had sex with Tony. When Tony opened the door, he had a smile on his face.

She asked, "Why are you smiling?"

"I'm just happy to see you." He responded.

"Did we have sex?" She asked.

"I'm not that type of guy." He replied.

"This wasn't a date you know." She said.

Tony said, "I know. Like you said, you have too much class for me."

"Now is not the time for jokes. Where are your friends?" She inquired.

Tony responded, "Geno went to get rid of your car. Sam is getting breakfast."

"Get rid of my car for what?" She shouted.

"You can't drive it anymore. The Mafia is going to be looking for it." Tony said.

"I don't have anything to do with what happened last night." She said.

"I know, but your car was involved so that makes you a target." He said.

"How am I supposed to get home?" she asked.

"They have cabs in Miami." Tony said.

"I hate you." She shouted.

"You can't hate me. I saved your life." Tony said.

"More like you put my life in danger." She said.

"I'm really sorry about the car. I know you have insurance." Tony said.

"Yes." She said.

"Well your problem is solved." Tony said.

"Not close. My grandfather purchased that car for my 26th birthday last year." She said.

"Maybe he can buy you another." Tony said.

"You have a smart mouth." She retorted.

"My boss tells me that all the time." Tony replied.

"Maybe you should try to change your way with words." She said.

"Look who's talking." Tony retorted.

"I should be going. Can you call me a cab?" she said.

"Where is your phone?" Tony asked.

"That's a question I should be asking you. You didn't take it to the pawn shop and sell it? Did you?" she said.

"No. I believe that guy you were hanging out with probably took it. He was trying to take more than just your phone." Tony retorted.

"What are you talking about?" she asked.

"You had a lot to say last night when the drug kicked in."

Valentina thought back about when she threw up inside the small booth at the club. She had thought that she threw up the drug that Rick had put in her drink.

"What did I say?" she asked.

"You went on and on how men were dogs and then you passed out." Tony responded.

"What happened after I passed out?"

"Nothing..."

"How did I end up in that bed?"

"I put you in that bed first. This was before the drug kicked in. I believe when the alcohol kicked in the drug kicked in too."

"Thanks for not taking advantage of me."

"I'm a gentleman. That's what gentlemen do."

"Can you help me find my phone?"

"Sure."

A knock at the door interrupted their conversation. Tony peeped out of the peep hole.

He said, "It's Sam."

Sam walked inside the room with a bandage around his head. In his hands he had McDonald's.

"Hotcakes or bacon and eggs," he asked.

Valentina said, "No time for breakfast. I have to be going." She went back to the other room and slipped into her dress and boots. Then she used the hotel phone to call a cab. Then she called her grandfather and told him about the car. When he spoke he reminded her that that was a 250,000 dollar car.

"I know Papi. I'm sorry." She responded.

"I saw the Miami News, Valentina. What is going on?"

"I was just visiting the new club, Papi."

"I clearly told you to handle all business affairs before you started partying."

"I'm handling business Papi. I only have one more store to buy before we can start building."

"I want you to know I have to call in a favor."

"I really do appreciate it, Papi."

"But I can't help the guys that were with you. This is going to cost me."

"I promise Papi, I will make it up to you."

Valentina could hear the anger in her grandfather's voice. "No more mess ups."

"Okay Papi. I love you."

The phone went dead in Valentina's ear. She didn't like when her grandfather was upset with her. She knew how he could change a person's life with the snap of his finger. She knew if it came down to it that he would put the bullet in her head, if she ever put his life or freedom in danger.

Valentina checked her face and dressed before she returned to the room where Tony, Geno and Sam were sitting around discussing last night's events. The news was playing on the TV in the background. All of a sudden a picture of the murdered mob boss flashed on the tube. At which time Sam said, "It's going to be trouble, Tony. I have to leave town."

Tony responded, "Here we go again."

Valentina interrupted, "I heard you all talking about me. I want you all to know that you don't have to worry about me. My grandfather has connections, and he's going to call in a favor."

Sam cut Valentina off, "What about us?"

"He told me that there is money on the guy's head who killed the boss. He didn't go into details. He was straight to the point after he asked about my car."

"I suggest we leave town Tony," Sam said.

"I think you should Tony," Valentina suggested.

Geno spoke, "We can't leave Tony's grandmother and my mother."

Valentina said, "I have to be going. You all will have to decide what you all are going to do."

Valentina started for the door. Tony joined her at the door. Then he spoke, "Will I see you again?"

"Only time will tell," she said.

Valentina walked out of the door and then she walked down the stairs. Tony watched as Valentina opened the door to the cab and got in. He returned to the room once the cab pulled out of the parking lot. Tony walk inside the room to find Sam and Geno picking over their breakfasts. The news was still showing the Mob Boss story. Tony picked up the remote and turned off the TV. Then he said, "We have a decision to make."

Sam responded, "What is it Tony?"

"Do we let Valentina live?"

Geno said, "There is no need to kill her, Tony."

"I'm thinking the same, but we don't know her."

Sam said, "I think if she was going to rat us out, she would have already done it."

Geno said, "We need to be worried about the Mafia."

Sam said, "It's best I leave town."

"Where will you go?"

"Tony… Don't worry about me. I have women in every state."

"Just keep in contact."

"I will. You two just keep your same routine."

CHAPTER 12

Agent Tadeo and his crew had arrived in South America after a week of training in Miami. They were in South America, because they had gotten a tip that The Source was back in Brazil at his new Compound. This Compound was the main distribution center for The Source's cocaine and heroin business. Agent Tadeo had been filled in about this Compound by another team that was helping in the investigation.

It took two whole days just to find the trail to the Compound. The terrain had made the trip hard, and the heavy rains had added to the hardship.

All of the workers that worked at the Compound had to wear black patches around their eyes. This was a mandatory mandate that The Source came up with after having this Compound built in the jungle. The reason for the eyewear was so the workers couldn't memorize where the Compound was located. There were metal detectors that scanned the full body of each worker when they entered the back of the trucks. Most of the time, these trucks would come to the local village and pick the locals up for work, if they wanted to work. Agent Tadeo knew all this through his investigation, and he had hired several locals and convinced them to become informants to investigate the drug Compound of The Source. To find the Compound, it took several informants to get the job done. Agent Tadeo had instructed the Informants to drop beans out of their lunch bags while riding in the back of the trucks to the Compound. Several informants were caught and killed on the spot. The last informant had made it deep into the jungle, before he had run out of beans. This frustrated Agent Tadeo because the informant was discovered and killed. This time Agent Tadeo had caught the break that he and his team had been looking for.

Agent Tadeo radioed, "Cain and Abel are you ready?"

"Yes Zeus," John responded. "Copy…." Dean said.

"How about you Bullet?" Agent Tadeo asked.

Josh responded, "Ten-four."

"They have ex-special ops. These guys are the best. I did a check on all ten of the guys that are leading the group up ahead, they are killers. Trained to kill in the blink of an eye." Agent Tadeo said.

"We've got the report," Dean responded.

Now at seventy-six years old, José Rivera looked more like he was 50. He had gone under the knife several times after seeing his face on the World News as a drug lord fugitive. His nose had been clipped about two inches, and his wrinkled face was now smooth like a baby's behind. His chin had been shaved down a little, along with the removal of his finger prints. His lips were smaller, and the tummy tuck made him look like he was fit. This was the life of the rich. Money was the key to a better life, even for someone José's age.

Life for José hadn't always been peaches, apples, jets and pretty women. He grew up struggling like most Brazilians from the slums. He had worked as a kid smashing coca leaves for two pesos a day. He had lost his mother because of her heart problem.

And, he had never known his father. After years of working in the jungle as a mere work boy, he found his way into a drug ring where he became the boss. This was ten years after working as a mule. Once José become the boss, he created his own drug empire. And he gained political power all over the world. When America declared the War on Drugs, a warrant was issued for José. This was why he changed his identity.

Looking out over his Compound now, he could see the local workers coming in from the South. What he didn't notice was the four agents a hundred yards away. José walked out onto the balcony of his large living quarters in his bathrobe. He waved to his men to take the workers to the back area of his Compound. Then he returned to his quarters and pulled out his special radio phone to call his granddaughter.

Valentina drove off of the imported car lot in her new Maserati. She didn't wait on the insurance check that was due any day now. She took action by going to the lot, and purchased a black machine with her black card. This vehicle was the same model as the one her grandfather had purchased for her, and it had more features like cameras in the doors. There was also a high-class sound system.

After pulling off the lot, Valentina picked up her phone when she heard it buzzing like a bumble bee. When she looked at the caller ID she knew the caller was her grandfather. He was the only person that knew her private number to her phone. She spoke, "Hi Papi."

"Hello, my princess."

"Is everything okay?"

"Yes."

"Why did you call?"

"I just was checking up on you. How is everything with the deal for the last store?"

"Mr. Castro is playing hardball."

"Did you need my help?"

Valentina knew what her grandfather was saying when he asked the question.

"No Papi... I can handle this one. I don't want to leave a trail."

"Well, get the deal done so you can come see me."

"I will Papi."

"One last thing. I saw that you purchased another car on your black card. You just couldn't wait for the insurance money."

"You grow money Papi. There is no need to wait."

"You are right, Princess. You deserve the best."

"Thanks Papi."

"Make me proud."

"I will."

Valentina pushed the end button to end the call and then her mind switched to Tony. She hadn't heard from him since the night to the club. The thought of killing Tony and his friends crossed her mind on several occasions, but she dismiss the thought after being reassured by her grandfather that everything was going to be alright. Valentina knew how to get away with murder, because she had gotten away with killing a team of Special Agents that were tracking her grandfather. The mission had proven her loyalty to her grandfather, and it had shown that she believed in her grandfather's cause. Her grandfather had always preached equality and loyalty for the people of his cause. These characteristics were traits that she took from her grandfather and used them to achieve the things she had needed in life.

After her mission, he grandfather introduced her to his business. And, he gave her a powerful position in his business because she had proven her loyalty and earned it. And it did help that she had a business degree in International Business. His whole objective for Valentina's life was for her to take his place at the head of his business after he retired. This would all take place after he built the biggest luxurious hotel on South Beach. This would be the place where he would live out the remainder of his natural life. Valentina knew all of this and she also knew why she would be given the power to her grandfather's business. Since she was his only heir, it was her birthright to inherit her grandfather's empire. Valentina turned on to South Beach strip after getting off the freeway. She pulled her Maserati right in front of Mr. Castro's store. The five Cubans were sitting out front playing cards. The smell of cigar smoke and food was in the air. Valentina stepped out of the vehicle after fixing her face in the mirror, and then she strolled pass the men as she made her way inside the store. She didn't pay the men any attention as she passed them, even though they did everything to try to grab her attention.

Mr. Castro was standing behind the counter taking an old hag's order, he looked up at Valentina who was dressed in a smoke-gray Prada dress with matching heels. Her toenails were painted the same color as her dress, and her hair was in a long ponytail. Mr. Castro was in his uniform, and his hair was under a blue baseball cap. The sound of the four fans in the store could be heard throughout the store. After the old hag left the store, Valentina spoke, "Hello, Mr. Castro. How are you today?" The name tag on his shirt was fading. He responded, "Who are you?"

"I'm Valentina Rivera," She responded as she stuck out her manicured hand. He shook her hand and said, "I heard you want to buy my place."

"We talked once right?"

"Yes."

Valentina looked around for Tony after Mr. Castro let her hand go. She didn't know Tony's hours, but she was curious to know what he had been up to.

Mr. Castro said, "So you want to buy my store?"

"I'm here to make you an offer that you can't refuse."

"I'm waiting, but first tell me why you want to buy the place."

Valentina made eye-contact and said, "I know you know about me buying up the properties around here."

"I heard."

"Well you should know I'm here to do business not play games. Let's just say I like to buy Mom 'n Pop stores."

"I like the way you do business, Ms. Rivera. Straight to the point."

"I don't know any other way."

"Well, if you are willing to pay the price than I'm willing to sell."

"What is your price?"

Mr. Castro grabbed a white rag that was sitting on the counter and wiped his hands with it. Then said, "A million cash."

"For this small place? I was thinking more like two-hundred grand."

"I know you need this place to build what you want to build."

"So you do know about the hotel?"

"Word travels fast."

"I'm willing to give half a million."

"If you can do half you can do a million."

"You drive a hard bargain."

"I'm a businessman Ms. Rivera."

"I can see that. What if I say eight-hundred thousand?"

"Like I said a million is what I need."

A customer entered the store and interrupted the negotiation. Valentina looked around for a sign of Tony while Mr. Castro was dealing with the customer. She walked towards the back of the store and looked inside the storage room where Mr. Castro's bed was in view. He touched her on the shoulder. She responded, "You must live here."

"Yes."

"I know it gets lonely here. You deserve to have a nice house with a beautiful woman and a dog."

"That sounds nice. That million will help with the dream you have for me."

"I feel good today Mr. Castro so therefore I'm going to make you a millionaire today."

"Seriously?"

"It's a deal."

"Thanks. When can you draw the deal up?"

"I will have my attorney send over the papers. I will write a check when the paperwork is signed by you."

"You have a deal Ms. River."

"You can call me Valentina."

"Nice name. Sounds like money."

"I come from old money."

"I have a question for you."

"What is it?"

"Can you help me find a house?"

"I don't work in that field. Sorry…"

Valentina turned to leave, as she turned she asked, "Where is your help?"

"He's off today."

"Where is the other guy?"

"Who, Sam?"

"Yes."

"I heard he left town. Why do you ask?"

"They were nice to me the last time I was here."

"Well, I can tell Tony you asked about him."

"No. I'd rather you not do that."

Valentina wanted to ask Mr. Castro for Tony's cell number, but she dismissed the thought after Mr. Castro said, "Tony will be here tomorrow."

Valentina picked up a set of flowers that were sitting on the counter. She asked, "Are these for sale?"

"Take them."

"Thanks."

"No problem. I'm a millionaire now."

"Don't spend it all in one place."

"I won't."

Valentina started towards the door but was interrupted, "One last thing. I will tell Tony that you came by."

"Don't do that."

"I can see it in your eyes that you have a thing for him."

Valentina smiled and walked out of the store. The smells of South Beach hit her nose. She walked past the men while waving and got inside her car. She pulled off from the curb thinking that she had shown Mr. Castro a sign that she was interested in Tony.

In her mind, she knew it was wrong but her heart was telling her that he was Mr. Right.

CHAPTER 13

Tony walked to his father's grave plot with the fresh set of flowers in his hand, and he inserted the flowers in his father's headstone slot. Right next to his father's grave was his mother. He changed the flowers in her plot too. Then he stood in front of his father's headstone and spoke, "Father, I have sinned. I killed a man."

Tony couldn't stop thinking about the mob boss that he had killed at the club, and even though no one other than Valentina, Geno and Sam knew about the murder, it was eating at his soul. Sam had schooled him about death when he was a young boy, and Tony took the lesson and ran with it. But the lesson wasn't helping with dealing with his guilt now. Tony continued, "I feel guilty about taking the man's life after finding out that he had a son. Now, his son will go through his life wondering how life would have been like with his father in it. The reason I bring this to you father is, because I know the feelings. There were many of the days I wished you were in my life, and there were times I wished we could have played basketball and baseball together, but we never did."

The sound of the thunderstorm took over the atmosphere. Tony didn't understand where the storm had come from, because it was sunny one minute and raining the next. Tony was used to the Miami weather, but he didn't like it.

Tony slowly walked towards the front entrance of the grave-yard after he touched both of his parents' headstones. He decided it would be best to take a cab instead of the city bus. While dialing the cab company's number, he noticed a black Maserati pulling up behind him. He couldn't see the driver because the windows were tinted on the car. Tony didn't know if the vehicle was here for the death of the mob boss, or just passing through. His heart was beating fast from the anticipation of being killed, but this didn't stop him from looking for a way out the graveyard.

The car pulled beside him and the driver rolled the window down. The driver spoke, "I hope it's not this easy for anyone else to find you." That's when Tony recognized the angelic voice of Valentina. He asked, "What are you doing here?"

She responded, "I had to visit a friend." The rain started to beat harder and the thunder was echoing as Valentina asked, "Need a ride?"

"Sure." Tony opened the passenger door and sat in the seat. Then he close the door as the rain increased and the lightning filled the sky. Valentina spoke, "You are a lucky camper. If I wasn't here you would have gotten wet."

"A little water wouldn't have hurt me."

"You must haven't had your bath?" Tony wasn't offended.

"I can see you purchased a new car. Did your grandfather buy it for you?"

"No...I purchased it with my black card."

"The life of the rich."

"It's a great life. It's better than being poor."

Tony smiled. Valentina continued, "Don't get any ideas buddy."

"I can see you miss me."

"Not even. I'm just being nice."

"Well, we can officially say this is our second date."

"Date… you call the night at the club a date?"

"It wasn't the perfect date, but it was a date."

"Don't flatter yourself, mister."

"Valentina pulled the vehicle into traffic. Then she asked, "Where to?"

"I was thinking dinner, movie and then to your place."

"No way. You're still a tyro."

"What does tyro mean?"

"Beginner."

"So, I scored some points?"?

"A-point. But you still are not in my class."

The sound of the rain beating against the vehicle took over the atmosphere when the two went silent. The tires were riding on the wet surface and they could be heard too. Tony broke the silence. "How about we go down town to this new burger joint and grab us some burgers?"

"How romantic." Valentina responded in a sarcastic manner.

"I'm not romantic?" Tony asked.

"Last time we were downtown you almost got us killed."

"Not that again." Tony said.

"How can I forget it?" Valentina retorted.

"Just give me a chance. I bet I can make you happy."

"Like I said, if you ever hit the lottery, look me up."

Valentina dropped Tony off at home. She didn't even wave to him when he got out of the car. She didn't show him that she was interested in him, because she couldn't risk falling in love. Not at this time when her grandfather needed her the most. She didn't want to jeopardize what she was trying to accomplish for her grandfather. This was why she didn't ask Tony what he was doing at the graveyard.

Valentina drove home, and when she got home she told Larry about picking Tony up at the graveyard. She even told him about the night at the club but left out the details about Tony killing the men on the motorcycles. After spending hours with Larry talking about Tony, she retired to her bedroom. Her thoughts were still on Tony when she looked at her clock on the nightstand. It was

12am according to the small clock, still enough time for her to go out and find a victim. Valentina decided that she would stay home and enjoy herself with her toy. It was best this way since there was no risk. Safe sex was the best sex, Valentina thought, as she pulled out her black vibrator from her walk-in closet. After pulling the device from her shelf out of a Prada shoe box, she positioned herself on her luxurious, extraordinary, extravagant queen sized bed. Her thoughts went back to Tony. She closed her eyes to get a visual of Tony, and she started caressing her body. She could see him cupping her breasts and kissing her deep. This aroused Valentina to the point of no return. The aroma from Valentina's love tunnel took over the atmosphere. Her juices were flowing to the point that they were dripping on to her exotic sheets. Valentina could no longer control herself because her mind was running wild. She needed Tony to be inside of her. She wanted to feel him. The foreplay that she was experiencing by massaging her quarter sized clit in a circular rotation with the toy, was out of this world. She pushed the toy inside her slowly and held her breath as she went deep. She built up a rhythm to the point where she climaxed all over the 10 inch toy. All of the stress that she had been carrying around was now gone, after she had released her juices on the toy. It was now time for sleep. This was something that she usually needed after visiting Brad's grave.

CHAPTER 14

M r. Castro hung up his cellphone after talking with Mr. Stein for about an hour. They talked about the deal that they both made with one another, and they talked about how Tony was catching onto their plan. This discouraged Mr. Castro, because Mr. Stein told him that Tony's grandmother had shown up at the board meeting at his firm. The meeting was a closed meeting, but several of the board members had invited Tony's grandmother because they were discussing her case. The board was aware that Tony's father had entrusted them with thirty-million dollars of Life Insurance money. Tony Sr. had left the money to his mother before his death. This was why she was invited to the meeting.

Mr. Castro was also told by Mr. Stein, that Tony's grandmother decided that she was still in favor of giving Tony the money when he turned twenty-one years old. This was after she had been told about the clause in the policy that said if there wasn't an heir, or any lineage that could receive the money then the money could go to any charity that the firm desired. Since Mr. Stein was a member of Stein and Family Charity, he thought he was entitled to the money because his father had been Tony Sr.'s attorney. Mr. Castro agreed with Mr. Stein's point, and this was why he was on his way to scare Tony's grandmother.

Turning on to the freeway, Mr. Castro thought back on the night that Tony Sr. shot him in the leg. He had been sitting in his living room of his Miami Beach condo when five men kicked in his door. Among these five men was Tony Sr., and he was holding a sawed-off shotgun. Tony Sr. was high on cocaine and death was in his eyes. A month before, Tony Sr. had given Mr. Castro ten kilos of cocaine on consignment and told him that he had two weeks to pay. The deadline came and the payment wasn't made. This was why the men had almost beat Mr. Castro to death before Tony shot him in the leg. The slug from the 12 gauge caused massive damage in which resulted in his leg being amputated.

Mr. Castro snapped back to reality once he entered the ramp that took him to Tony's grandmother's street. He picked up his cell phone off of his passenger seat and called his store. Tony answered, "Hello, Mr. Castro's store, how may I help you?"

"This is Mr. Castro, Tony."

"What's wrong, boss?"

"Nothing. I just called to tell you to lock up tonight, because I'm staying at a hotel."

"Is everything okay?"

"Yes."

Mr. Castro ended his call with Tony. Then he parked on the opposite side of the neighborhood of Tony's grandmother's house in an abandoned lot. This streetlight in the area was providing enough light for Mr. Castro to maneuver through the neighborhood without being seen. Before, he took on his mission he had opened the glove box inside of his Cadillac and pulled out a black mask to match his black outfit. He had checked his .22 pistol before he grabbed the tire iron off of the back seat. Then, he had stepped into the warm winter night.

Mr. Castro made his way down the block towards Tony's grandmother's house after he closed his driver's side door. While walking, he put on the mask and checked his gun again. Then he put the gun in his pocket and gripped the tire iron in his right hand. Once at the house, he entered the backyard where there was a small hole in the wooden fence. It didn't take him but a skip and a hop. Then he was at the back window of the house. He looked inside the window and didn't see a soul. The kitchen light was dim, and a glowing light was coming from the front room of the house by the hallway that connected the kitchen. Mr. Castro walked over to the back door and forced the tire iron between the lock and the door. Then, he put his weight on the tire iron just enough to pop the lock. He walked inside slowly as the rain began to fall. The smells of air freshener and leftover food were in the air. The food caused Mr. Castro's stomach to growl. It had been hours since he had a meal.

Mr. Castro gripped the tire iron as he made his way through the kitchen into the living room. He put a small device in his mouth to disguise his voice. Then he continued towards the living room. He could hear a game show playing on TV. When he got to the edge of the room where the two rooms met, he noticed Tony's grandmother asleep in her chair. A sweater was laying on her lap and the items on the floor next to the chair were evidence that she had been sewing before she fell asleep.

Mr. Castro tip toed behind.the recliner and bent down behind it. Then he pulled out the .22. He laid the tire iron on the floor, and then he put the gun to Tony's grandmother's head while he grabbed her by the back of the neck. She woke up and wrestled to get out of his grip. He was too strong. He spoke, "I'm not here to harm you. I'm just here to deliver a message." Tony's grandmother stopped kicking. She listened as Mr. Castro said, "I was sent here by a guy that needs you to sign the money over that you plan to turn over to your grandson when he turn's twenty-one. If you don't, I will have to kill you next time." Mr. Castro pointed the gun in Tony's grandmother' face after he let her neck go. He asked, "Do you understand?"

Tony's grandmother nodded her head up and down to let Mr. Castro know that she understood. Before Tony's grandmother knew what was going on, Mr. Castro brought the gun down over her skull. Instantly, a knot formed from the lick and blood leaked from the knot as Mr. Castro laid her body on the floor. Then, he took off his black gloves and pulled out his cellphone and dialed up Mr. Stein. When Mr. Stein came over the line, Mr. Castro said, "I took care of my part." Then he hung up his phone. Before Mr. Castro took off, he put back on his gloves. Then he laid a couple blows to Tony's grandmother's face. He did this out of hate for Tony Sr. He didn't care that she was old, he just wanted to get revenge for what Tony Sr. had done to his leg. She was just as responsible for him losing his leg as her son, because she birthed him, this is what Gallant thought as he left the scene.

Tony's cellphone vibrated inside his pocket while he was cleaning up inside the store. He pulled the phone from his pocket even though he didn't recognize the number. Then he hit the send button.

"Hello." A familiar voice came over the line.

"This is Sue, Tony. I'm calling your phone because your grandmother has been injured. She's in the hospital."

"What happened?" he asked.

"They think she was attacked," Sue answered.

"Is she alright?"

"No… She's in a coma."

Tony began to cry. He hung up the phone and rushed out of the store. He raced down the strip towards the direction of the hospital. He flagged a cab down when he reached the end of the strip. He hopped in the back of the cab and said, "Take me to Miami Hospital."

CHAPTER 15

Agent Tadeo picked up a bean that had been left on the trail by the informant. He smiled to himself when he looked up ahead to see that the informant was still with the pack of workers and the heavily armed guards. Off in the distance was the exotic Compound that he and his team had been looking for, for two days. Agent Tadeo spoke, "We found it! Look over there." Agent Tadeo pointed in the direction of the Compound while he looked through his night vision special eyewear. He continued, "We can build camp about a hundred yards from the Compound."

Josh spoke, "Terry, do you want me to do a recon now or when we get closer?"

"Do it now," Agent Tadeo responded.

It didn't take the team long to set up camp and pin point the Compound. Josh found a small creek deep in the brush area that was two hundred yards from the camp. He filled all of the canteens of the men after he filtered the water. Then, he returned to the camp to find all the men were sending information back to their computers to the camp that they had set up in town. Agent

Tadeo spoke, "There are five two story villas. The walls to the Compound are ten feet tall. There are four gun towers just inside the walls that have semi-auto weapons inside each tower. The Compound is stationed right in the middle of a dozen enormous tropical trees that hide the sky from the Compound.

Josh asked, "When do we go in?"

Dean said, "We're going to need more men."

John said, "First, we have to do a recon of the inside. I don't want the other team to get all the credit for this mission. I want to meet the President."

Dean responded, "We're going to meet the President, that's something you don't have to worry about. First, we have to take down the bad guys."

Agent Tadeo spoke, "Calm down ladies. We have to do this right. It's going to take some time to see what's going on in that place."

Dean responded, "I know what's going on in there, there are drugs being made. The Source is a drug dealer and drug dealers sell drugs."

Agent Tadeo spoke, "That might be true, but we still have to play this safe. That's why we're going to take turns on guard duty. We will have four three hour guard duties."

Josh spoke, "I'll start it off."

Dean said, "I'll go second."

John said, "I'll go after Dean."

Agent Tadeo said, "I guess I'm the last man." When Agent Tadeo took post as the guard duty officer, he did his own recon of the area and made notes while he was looking around. His handheld computer had a program where he could design a map on it. He drew a map of the Compound on the small device, and sent this information back to his computer at his camp in town. Then, he tried to get a signal for his military phone. No signal. There weren't any phone towers in the area. Agent Tadeo decided that he would just send more information back to his camp in town with his own computer. This was safe for him.

After returning to his men, he took a seat about fifty yards away from the camp and reflected back on the day when the young Brazilian girl blew up the building with Jill inside of it. Jill was a woman that he become interested in after losing his second team and his second wife. Jill had asked him to attend a dog show with her on her birthday and he had agreed after he returned from Africa, in which that trip had been for him to locate The Source. He didn't think that the young girl that looked like a high school student would be there to blow up the building that the dog show was being held in. The young woman had even greeted him right before the blast. Agent Tadeo came out of his trance when he heard the sound of a helicopter. His team were already on their feet when he looked over at them. He watched as all of the men grabbed their night vision eyewear and looked up in the sky at the approaching helicopter.

Josh shouted, "You think that's The Source?"

"Maybe." Agent Tadeo responded. Agent Tadeo could see the Blackhawk coming in from the North of their camp. The chopper was going to pass right over their heads. He could see that the chopper had large guns attached to both sides of it, and the artillery looked familiar to him. The eyewear that he was wearing could determine the speed, distance, height and weight of the machine. All of these features mattered because he could tell what he had to prepare for, if he ever had to go up against this machine.

Agent Tadeo hit another button on the side of his eyewear and this button turned the figures inside the chopper red. He could see that there were six men inside of the machine along with some cargo. This sent his mind wondering what was inside the chopper. He hooked his handheld computer to his eyewear and took pictures of the images that he was seeing. Then, he watched as the chopper passed over his head and landed by the flares that had been placed out on the homemade landing strip.

A crew of men appeared out of nowhere and started unloading the chopper. All of these men were dressed in black and looked like they worked out with weights for a living. As the men loaded the wheelbarrows that they were pushing out from the Compound, Agent Tadeo noticed a tall figure looking over to the landing strip. He couldn't make out all of the features of the man, but the one thing that his eye could make out was the height of the man. This man was the same height as The Source according to the eyewear.

Chapter 16

Tony walked through the sliding doors of the hospital and walked over to a nurse that was sitting at the check-in desk playing on the computer. The nurse looked up when Tony spoke, "I need to know what room my grandmother is in."

"What's her name?"

"Ms. Clara Montana."

Tony watched as the nurse typed his grandmother's name into the computer. Then the nurse smiled and said, "She's on the second floor in room 212. That's the Trauma Unit."

"Can I visit her?"

"Yes. After you show me some proof of who you are." Tony pulled out his ID and handed it to the nurse. She looked at it, wrote down his name and then handed it back to him along with a visitors pass. Tony pinned the pass to his shirt as the nurse said, "Have a nice visit." Tony walked slowly towards the elevator. While walking, he thought about who could have attacked his grandmother. Was it the Mob? Was it just a person that entered the house and didn't know that she was there? All of these questions flowed through Tony's head as he rode the elevator to the second floor. When he stepped off of the elevator he could smell the different scents of medication and feel the cool air that was blowing from the cooling system. These smells gave him the sense of death in the air and the smells reminded him of the night that he had killed the mob boss.

Tony stopped in front of a man that looked like he had AIDs. This man was in a wheelchair and he was about to be pushed by a nurse with a mask on her face. The man's hair was thin and he was wearing an air mask that was hooked to an oxygen tank that was connected to the wheelchair. The man had smiled at Tony as Tony had stopped at the nurse's station. A chubby white nurse was standing behind the M shaped counter and off to the side were two officers talking while they were sharing doughnuts and coffee. Tony didn't know if the officers were there to question his grandmother or just there for the safety of the hospital.

The nurse spoke, "How may I help you?"

"I'm here to see Ms. Clara Montana." The officers looked up.

"Let me see your pass." The nurse asked.

Tony turned so the nurse could see the pass that was pinned to his shirt. The nurse handed him a form that he filled out in front of her. After she looked over the form, she said, "You may go in and see your grandmother."

Tony walked over to the doors that the two policemen were sitting in front of still sharing doughnuts and coffee. He smiled and nodded his head at both officers as he opened the door. The Trauma Unit was large and dimly lit with large beds filled with patients that were hooked up to large machines. They were all unconscious, and the sound of their breathing machines were echoing through the atmosphere. Tony looked around the room, until he found his grandmother who was hooked up to two IV Machines. Her face was covered with bandages, and she was hooked up to a breathing machine.

There were large blue curtains that separated each patient's space and their machine. The curtains to Tony's grandmother's area were opened. Tony walked over to his grandmother and looked over her body. Tears formed in his eyes after he noticed the purple marks around her eyes. The only way he knew the woman in the bed was his grandmother was, because she was still wearing the ring he had given her for her 70th birthday. This had been the woman that cared about him when no one wanted him, and this was the same woman that taught him not to beat on women. Several questions popped into his head. Why? Who?

He slowly picked up his grandmother's right hand, while he was looking at it he was examining all the wear and tear on her hand. His grandmother had worked most of her, life and it was showing her hands. The veins were thick and looked like they were about to pop. While he was looking over his grandmother, she moved her hand.

He spoke, "Mama? Can you hear me?" He watched as her eyes opened slowly. There was still life in those sharp eyes. Tony continued, "Who did this Mama?"

Ms. Montana slowly whispered, "I was attacked Tony, some-one broke in." Tony couldn't fully understand his grandmother.

"Who?"

"He threatened to kill me."

"Who?"

Ms. Montana closed her eyes.

CHAPTER 17

Valentina decided to take a vacation after she instructed her attorney to draw up the papers for the deal with Mr. Castro. She decided it was best to go to Charlotte, North Carolina, because it was one of the safest cities in America. Plus it was one of the fastest growing cities too. After checking into the Westin Hotel in the downtown area of Charlotte, she drove her rental to a nice bar-n-grill spot three blocks away from it. She had been told by one of the clerks at the hotel that this bar-n-grill was one of the best in the city, and the reason being was because it was a mixed environment. There was great wine and music too. The dress code was modest, and there were all kinds of people who were upscale and middle class that attended. Valentina was dressed in a Fendi mid-cut dress with matching purple shoes, and her hair was wrapped in a three-thousand-dollar holder that made her look like a princess. She had had a manicure and pedicure before she had left Miami. Plus, a massage that had her looking as relaxed as ever.

The bar area was crowded and the dance floor was thick as some Down South barbeque sauce. There were two large screen

TVs mounted to the brick walls in the bar area of the large building. In a corner was a jukebox inside of the pool room area, and there were seven large pool tables to enjoy some pool. In one section of the building, which made the bar look more like an upscale restaurant than a bar, were dining tables. The waitress and waiters were dressed in elegant attire.

Valentina took in the delicious smells as she made her way into the restaurant area. There was roasted duck, apple cake, leg of lamb and any kind of dish that she could think of on the buffet. Celebrities like Michael Jordan usually ate in this exclusive night spot and usually enjoyed the cool sound of jazz with their meal.

Valentina wasn't in the restaurant to order a meal or listen to music. She was there because she wanted sex. She had seen a guy that caught her attention as soon as she had entered the restaurant. She took a seat a few tables from the guy that caught her attention. Then she made eye contact with him. The thrill of the chase was what she liked about getting new men to have sex with her. Especially, when she chased after married men.

The cold winter air didn't stop her from coming out without her panties and bra. She liked the thrill of walking around naked under her dress while her V-shaped bubbled like it was hot lava. This added to the hunt. She ordered a bottle of white wine after she waved at the guy to come over. She wasn't trying to get drunk, because she needed to be focused to get her catch. Most of the time her looks alone usually got the guy she wanted, but sometimes she had to seduce the guy with a little sexual conversation.

When the guy took a seat at her table she asked, "Are you from around here?" He responded, "Yes. I'm from the South Park area." South Park was known as the high society area in the city of Charlotte. There were judges, lawyers, politicians and other people that had influence in the city that lived there. She knew this, because she had dealt with some clients in the area in the past on business.

She asked, "Old or New money?"

"You are very blunt." The guy responded.

"When I want something I go for it." She replied.

"I guess we are in the same club."

It didn't take Valentina long to get Jimmy Blackwell to go to her suite with her. When they arrived at the suite, she took total control. She kissed Jimmy like he was the last man on earth. She stripped him down bare and ordered him to the bed. Then, she handcuffed him before he knew what was going on. He stared up at her with his blue eyes out of fear. He asked, "What are you doing?"

"Just relax."

"What are you doing?"

"What I want to."

"Freaky. I like Freaky."

"It turns me on to be in total control. The more you play, the victim the more I get turned on."

"Whip me mama! Whip me!"

Valentina grabbed her Fendi bag off of the floor that had all of her sex toys in it. She took out a small whip and hit Jimmy with it. He cried out in excitement. This turned her on. She took out a condom and a small bottle of KY Jelly. She bent over so Jimmy could get a clear view of her freshly shaved V-shape. She took out the leg irons, strapped them to the bed and his legs. Her firm nipples were pointing out like missiles as they touched Jimmy's face as she stood over him wide legged.

She spoke, "How about we have some fun?"

He responded, "Whatever you want to do."

She kissed him and gave him all tongue while she was massaging his penis diligently with her hands. It didn't take her long before she had Jimmy begging for more.

"Please... Please..."

She asked, "You sure you're ready?"

"Yes... Yes..." he answered.

She hopped up on his horse after she put the condom on it. She mouthed it with KY just to make it easy for her to ride it. She slowly inserted him into her hot spot.

"Oh…Ohh…" he said.

She used her hands to balance herself as she rode Jimmy cowgirl style backwards. She liked the fact that Jimmy reminded her of Brad Pitt the actor. This made the joy of sex more interesting because Brad was her favorite actor. She opened herself wide as she sped up her pace. She gave Jimmy all the sex faces that she could stand.

She shouted, "I'm cumming…"

He shouted, "Me too."

The orgasm started at her head, then filtered through her chest and on to her feet. This orgasm still didn't meet the tingling sensation that she had experienced like she had felt when she was with her ex. This upset her. Another meaningless sex act.

Valentina rose up and grabbed her clothes off of the floor and rushed to the bathroom. This was after she stuffed a rag inside of Jimmy's mouth. He was too exhausted to fight her. This was how she liked her victims after sex. After taking a shower and putting on her clothes, she returned to the suite and said, "Thanks for your services. I hope your wife doesn't find out about you cheating on her." Valentina took a picture of Jimmy as he tried to free himself. She continued, "Men like you need to lose everything you have."

She kissed him on the cheek, and then, she walked out of the room. Valentina didn't use her real name when she had checked into the hotel, or when she had rented the car. Her alias: Annie Baker was used only when she took trips like this. Her sex addiction was something her grandfather didn't' know about. This was something that she planned to keep to herself until the right man came along. Her secret was safe as long as her grandfather didn't find out about it.

CHAPTER 18

Tony was sitting in the lobby of the hospital when he noticed Sam and Geno walking through the sliding doors. They rushed over to him. Sam spoke, "I came as soon as I heard."

Tony asked, "When did you get back in town?"

"About an hour ago. Geno called," Sam said.

"Is it safe for you?" Tony asked.

"I don't know. I'm here for you." Sam said.

Geno interrupted. "I called him Tony, because I knew he would know [what to do]."

"It's okay Geno." Tony responded.

"What happened?" Geno asked.

"Someone beat up Mama." Tony said.

"Who?" Geno asked.

"That's what I'm trying to figure out Geno."

"Do you think it was the Mob?" Sam asked.

"I don't know. She couldn't tell me much," Tony answered.

"Is she going to be alright?" Sam asked.

"I don't know Sam," Tony answered.

"This is all my fault," Sam said.

"It's not your fault Sam," Tony said.

Geno interrupted, "I don't think it was the Mob, Tony."

Sam responded, "I don't either."

"What are you two thinking?" Tony asked.

Sam said, "The Mob would have killed her."

"That's what I'm thinking Tony," Geno said.

"Well, who could it be?" Tony asked.

Sam spoke, "That's what we have to find out."

Tony had been over at the hospital all night thinking about who could have hurt his grandmother. He didn't even think about calling Mr. Castro and telling him what happened. Tony spoke, "Mama doesn't have enemies."

Sam said, "We have to play this by ear."

"Where will you be staying Sam?" Tony asked.

"I have a woman on the Southside that I can stay with." Sam answered.

"Is it safe?" Tony asked.

"Yes Tony," Sam answered.

"Go there until I call you." Tony said.

"What's up Tony?" Sam asked.

"You don't need to be out in the city. If the Mob is behind this, they may be looking for you." Tony said.

Sam hesitated and said, "You may be in danger too."

"I know. I can handle myself," Tony said.

Sam said, "I have something for you Tony."

Sam handed Tony a small package that he took out of his pocket. Then he said, "That will help you stay awake."

Tony said, "You two go. I'll be okay."

Tony watched as Geno and Sam walked out of the hospital. It was time for him to do his own investigations. The police didn't know much. The neighbors didn't see anything and there were no other leads besides the Mob to go on. Tony walked to the restroom in the lobby area and took out the package that Sam had given him. He waited until the last guy walked out before he opened the package. Inside the package was cocaine. Tony knew this because he had seen it before. He took a fingernail amount put it up to his nose. Then, he snorted it. It took a few minutes before he could feel the drug. Tony liked this feeling. It made him feel like he was unstoppable. His senses were at an all-time high, he could hear clearly, see clearly, taste the dust in the air and feel the vibrations from the sound of people moving. These were the feelings Tony had been looking for. He felt alive.

CHAPTER 19

José walked slowly behind his bodyguards as they made their way to his drug lab. The head scientist who José had put in charge of the lab summoned him after discovering that the super Compound worked. Dan Dover had been a scientist for twenty years before he met José. They had formed a partnership after José found out that Dan was experimenting with different Compounds that could make plants grow faster and bigger.

José had brought Dan to the Compound after it was built and Dan had started experimenting with different substances that could make plants grow faster than the ones that he already had developed before he met José. Now that the new substance was in the final stage, Dan needed to see José. When José walked into the huge lab, he used his handprint to open the door where Dan was working. This was after he dismissed his bodyguards. The smell of the cocaine hit his nose.

José asked, "What's the problem?"

Dan responded, "There is a small problem with the formula, sir."

"What is it?"

"The leaves are growing extra huge, but the quality of the coca leaves aren't great. I'm having trouble making the right formula, so the plant can live in any condition."

"The bigger the better."

"It's affecting the quality, Sir."

"I want bigger and I want you to make the quality of the leaves better. That's what I want."

"I don't see that happening, Sir."

"Why?"

"I think I know where the problem is happening."

"Tell me, so I can fix it."

"Someone is spraying the area where these leaves are being grown with this chemical called: Flux-Flu. This chemical is used to damage the soil and the plant. It affects the plant's immune system. It's like giving the plant the AIDS virus."

"How did this happen?"

"Someone sprayed the area and the plants right before they were picked."

"I have men guarding that area twenty-four hours a day. There is no way that someone could do this. Maybe it's the climate change? Maybe global warming?"

Dan looked up from his work. He buttoned his smock up and said, "Let me show you something."

Dan walked towards the back door inside the lab, and planted his hand on the scanner and the door slowly opened. José walked inside the small room and let the scanner inside the room scan his face after Dan. A door opened to another lab where there were dozens of kids working while being guarded by armed guards. The kids inside the room couldn't see José or Dan, as Jose and Dan looked at them smashing mountain sizes of paste with their feet. Most of these kids were naked. This was a gruesome job for anyone to do. Kids had died from working in the lab and since most were orphans who died in the lab, it didn't matter. Dan hit a button inside this room on the wall and a small tray popped out the wall. On the tray was a large leaf that had spots in the middle of it. José took the leaf and asked, "How do you suggest we fix this problem?"

Dan smiled and then said, "There is this repellent that I want to create."

José interrupted, "Well, why haven't you created it?"

"I need this cactus root from South Africa to make it. It's called: Euphorbia Grandicornis."

"That's no problem. I will send for it. What else you need?"

"I need you to replace the men that are guarding the mountain region where you were growing both coca leaves and the H-leaves."

"I can do that. As a matter of fact, I will have all of the men killed."

"Thank you, Sir."

"Anything else?"

"No sir."

Agent Tadeo, Josh, Dean and John had been watching the Compound from the jungle for two weeks now. They were running low on food and most of their supplies were gone. They were now living off of the land by eating small insects, berries and animals. They decided not to go in for supplies, because they knew that The Source was on the Compound and they didn't want to lose track of him. They were keeping notes with their handheld computers and they were making maps out of everything around the Compound. They made sure every detail was enclosed in these maps, because when they decided it was time to call for backup to take down The Source, they wanted all of the teams to have this information.

The team had formed a voting system to solve problems. This system was used anytime a problem had come up that one person couldn't solve. Agent Tadeo had come up with putting numbers in a hat system. The number one was used for Yes and number two was used for No. This was the easiest way to keep the confusion down among the men. If there was a neck-tie vote, then Agent Tadeo used a coin to break the tie. Most of the time, it never got to this point.

Agent Tadeo put his eyewear down after looking at José walking back into the villa on the second floor of the Compound. He spoke, "He's having the time of his life."

Dean spoke, "You can say that again."

Josh said, "He's been with a different woman every day this week."

John said, "I'm jealous."

Agent Tadeo said, "Don't be. He's going to spend the rest of his life in prison."

Dean interrupted, "That's if we can get close to him."

"Don't worry, we will." Agent Tadeo said.

"I thought that we voted that we were going to wait until we could get another informant inside before we go in?"

"We did. But we haven't been to the town in weeks."

"I think we should take a vote," Josh shouted.

Dean asked, "For what?"

"To see who wants to go back for supplies and a fun night in town." Josh shouted.

Agent Tadeo interrupted, "I don't think it's a good time."

"That's why we should vote," Josh said.

"I veto the whole voting system."

After his statement, Agent Tadeo walked off and headed towards the creek area.

Dean spoke, "I think Terry is right. We need to stay put."

Josh said, "We need supplies."

John said, "You lose Josh."

"I knew you two weren't going to agree with me," Josh said.

Dean said, "It was worth a try."

Dean decided to follow Agent Tadeo to the creek. Agent Tadeo was getting undressed when Dean walked up.

He spoke, "Going for a swim?"

"Yes."

Agent Tadeo walked slowly in the water after he had slipped out his boots. The heat in the jungle was well over a hundred degrees and it was feeling more like hell on Earth. Dean jumped in the water after he removed his clothes. Both men were relaxing in the cool water until John and Josh had shown up ten minutes later.

Josh spoke, "It's our turn to enjoy some coolness."

Dean and Agent Tadeo got out of the water and put on their gear. They both had washed their Army fatigue uniforms and let their boots air out. Agent Tadeo spoke, "I'm going to do a perimeter check while you ladies enjoy the water. All three of the men looked at each other as he walked off in the opposite direction that they had come from.

Agent Tadeo got lost in his thoughts as he walked the perimeter that his team and he had set up. He thought back on the day when his team and him had hiked to the mountains on a one-day trip. They found Jose's plant farm where José was growing H-plants and Coca plants. When they found the area, they used the Flux-Flu that they had in their supply kit to poison the plants. They knew the poison wouldn't be detected right away. The operation was short and simple. The only hard part of the operation was when they had to trick the guards into believing that they were there because of José's orders. The jumpsuits they put on for the operations had the word "Scientist" printed on the back of them. These suits had helped with convincing the guards that they were there from the orders of José. After they sprayed the plants with the Flux-Flu, they hiked back to their camp in the jungle by José's Compound. They knew something was wrong with José's operation when they noticed him walking over to the lab a week later. This was after several loads of the plants that they had poisoned arrived at the Compound. Agent Tadeo snapped out of his daydream state as he heard the sound of Dean and John's voices. They were lip boxing over who was the strongest when he walked up on the camp.

He asked, "What's the problem?"

Dean responded, "He thinks because I'm the little brother that I'm the weakest."

John said, "You are. Ever since we were kids I've been beating you in everything."

Agent Tadeo interrupted, "You two are acting like kids."

Josh was cleaning his gun. He didn't say a word while Agent Tadeo scolded the brothers. The sound of a helicopter interrupted the crew.

Agent Tadeo spoke, "I think a shipment is coming in."

José closed the door to his living quarters after walking in his bedroom. He had just come from meeting with Dan after the new shipment had arrived. The new shipment was H and Cocaine. The shipment was labeled in two different packages. The H was labeled with the letter H and the cocaine was labeled with a skill head with bones crossing it. This was how most of José's packages were packed when they were sent out to different mules.

José wasn't worries about the packages, or the several hundred cactus that roots he had ordered from Africa because he had a bigger problem on his hand. Something had triggered the alarm on the west end of his Compound. He didn't know if there was someone trying to get in it or if it was another wild animal trapped in the fence. The alarm in his living quarters was flashing when he had walked inside it. He had already known the alarm had triggered from his watch. This is why he had rushed to his room and looked at all of the cameras inside his room. After looking at each camera, he noticed that it was another wild cat stuck in the fence. He called to his guards in tower four to handle the problem.

José pulled out his new GPX-4000 phone. He called several people and told them that the new shipment would be ready by the upcoming weekend. Then, he walked out on the balcony with the phone in his hand. He dialed Valentina's number and left her a voicemail. Then, he looked out over the jungle. All he could see was peace, and this was the way he wanted his operation to continue to be.

Agent Tadeo couldn't believe that José had a CPX-4000. There were only a hundred of these high powered phones ever made. This is why he couldn't believe that José had one. These phones were made by the U.S. Military and they were displayed at an international convention in Paris, France.

Agent Tadeo had attended this convention and purchased several items at this event, that's how he knew about this high-powered phone. These phones were banned after several terrorists used two of them to plot another terrorist attack on the United States. With the help of the United States FBI Services, these plots were discovered and the men that were planning these attacks were apprehended. Then, they were given life sentences. Two GPX-4000's were confiscated and the FBI were labeled as the heroes.

Agent Tadeo spoke, "I know why José has been ahead of us."

Dean asked, "Why?"

"He has a GPX-4000 phone."

"And."

"This phone does everything, except use the bathroom for you."

John asked, "What does the phone have to do with him staying ahead of us? He hasn't even left his Compound."

"My point," Agent Tadeo responded. He continued, "This phone had a radio frequency that made it easy for the person that owned the phone to tap into any phone in the world. As long as the person that owned the phone has the number they wanted to tap into, he or she can do this"

Dean asked, "You think he knows we're here?"

Agent Tadeo responded, "I don't know."

John said, "I don't think he knows, because if he did we would all be dead."

"Not necessarily," Agent Tadeo responded.

"How do you know?" John asked.

"Because if he had our radio number then he could listen in on my conversations with my superior, in which I doubt he has the number, because this mission is private," Agent Tadeo said.

Dean asked, "What about your theory of José letting us live?" John said.

"My theory is really a hope of faith," Dean said.

Agent Tadeo ended the meeting with his team and went over to his tent. And, then he made notes of his new discovery. He wanted to have everything in order when he got back to camp in town, so he could send it off to his boss. The information that he was planning to send was evidence that someone had purchased the phone for José. The convention in Paris was for top ranking government officials only, and it was a private convention for official services people too. Everyone that had attended the convention had to sign in. This gave Agent Tadeo the assumption that this person that purchased the phone for Jose, he or she were in the U.S. Database.

CHAPTER 20

M r. Stein sat quietly in his office waiting on Mr. Castro. It was time for their monthly meeting. Every 2nd of the month, the payment for babysitting Tony was due. Usually, Mr. Castro would meet Mr. Stein out at a public place, but after the assault on Ms. Montana they decided it was best to meet at Mr. Stein's office.

Mr. Stein instructed Mr. Castro to rough Ms. Montana up but not to the point where she was stuck in a coma. This wasn't a part of his plan. Neither was giving Mr. Castro a million dollars, if the money was signed over by Tony. Mr. Castro had threatened Mr. Stein by saying that he would go to the police if Mr. Stein didn't give him a million dollars. This was one of the reasons that Mr. Stein decided to hold their monthly meeting in his office.

Mr. Stein didn't need Ms. Montana's death to lead back to him, because he knew that the police would know the motive after his partners at the firm found out. Mr. Stein knew about all of the provisions in Tony Sr.'s policy after he received Tony Sr.'s file. This was done after Mr. Stein's father had passed away from cancer. Tony Sr. had made his wife the sole benefactor of the thirty million dollar policy, but there were stipulations in the contract that said that she had to stay clean in order to receive the money. Mr. Stein had made sure that Tony Sr.'s wife wasn't clean so the money would go to the next of kin in line for the money. He did this by hiring a dealer that he represented on several occasions to give Tony Sr.'s wife bad drugs. He even arranged for this male dealer to meet with Tony Sr.'s wife after Tony Sr.'s funeral. This dealer even had sex with Tony Sr.'s wife and tried to claim the baby that she had been carrying around Tony Sr.'s death was his. Mr. Stein told the dealer that there was a clause in the contract that said the money could go to the baby if she was dead.

The dealer that he hired to poison Tony Sr.'s wife tried to blackmail Mr. Stein which lead to the dealer's death. Mr. Stein contacted one of his mafia clients and paid twenty thousand to have the dealer killed. But this added to his problems because the mafia client had dirt on Mr. Stein. He had recorded the whole conversation of Mr. Stein and him discussing the murder for hire deal. Mr. Stein had to pay ten thousand a month to keep his secret under wraps. This payment was due every month.

Mr. Stein had been relieved when he found out that Tony Sr.'s wife was dead, but he was shocked when he found out that the doctors saved the baby. This sent him into a rage because the baby had been placed in state custody. Mr. Stein had already gotten Tony Sr.'s mother to verbally say she was going to sign the money over to him. This deed had been done before Tony Sr.'s wife was even in the ground. Mr. Stein knew that Tony Sr.'s mother didn't like drug money and she had considered the money a curse because of her own beliefs. Mr. Stein told Ms. Montana that she had a grandson and if she signed over the money that he would help her gain custody of him. She didn't agree to the deal, but he still brought Tony Jr. to her.

A knock at Mr. Stein's office door brought him back to reality. He spoke, "It's open."

Mr. Castro walked inside the office using his wooden cane. He was dressed in his store uniform and he looked worried. He spoke, "I hope I'm not too early?"

"You're on time, Gallant."

Mr. Stein reached in his desk and pulled out a white envelope. Then he asked while he tossed it to Mr. Castro," You think she's ready to sign now?"

"Yes."

"I'm going over to the hospital later."

"Make sure you take the policy, she's dying to sign it."

"How about Tony?" Mr. Stein asked.

"He's missed two days of work." Mr. Castro responded.

"You think she's told him about the money?"

"I don't think so."

Mr. Stein lit up a cigar as Mr. Castro took a seat right in front of his desk. He took a pull and blew the smoke into the air. Then he hit the button on his cellphone that was laying on the table in front of him. Mr. Castro didn't know that his conversation was about to be recorded. "Tell me Gallant, What did you do to Ms. Montana?"

"I put the gun to her head. Then I gave her a few face blows for good measure. I know Tony Sr. is rolling around in his grave."

"Tell me Gallant, did she scream for help?"

"She couldn't because I was choking her."

"You know it's a crime what you've done?"

"I know… but my mouth is sealed."

"How about the leg?"

"This new leg is perfect."

"Do you still think about the guy that took your leg?"

"Why are you asking me these questions?"

"I'm just curious, Gallant. You are a friend and friends look out for each other."

"Every time I look at my leg I think of Tony Sr. I wish I could go dig up his bones and burn them to ashes, that's how mad I am at him. Maybe I will."

"Life is too short to hold a grudge. I'm Jewish, Gallant. My people suffered at the hands of Hitler, I don't hate him."

"What are you getting at Stein?"

"Nothing." Mr. Stein paused the recording. He had the evidence that he needed to get Mr. Castro locked away for the assault on Ms. Montana. He had let Mr. Castro talk long enough to for him to dig his own grave. If Mr. Castro didn't go to prison, surely Tony Jr. would seek revenge if he heard the recording. Mr. Stein walked Mr. Castro out of the office after their meeting. Then, he called the hospital where Ms. Montana was housed at and asked about the visiting hours. After getting the hours, he returned to his desk and grabbed his briefcase. Then he headed over to the hospital. It was time to get Ms. Montana to sign the money over to him.

Mr. Stein walked inside the Miami Hospital with his briefcase in his hand. He looked around the semi-packed lobby and spotted a chubby nurse at the front desk. Mr. Stein introduced himself as Ms. Montana's attorney and got the nurse to give him a visitation pass. Once he received his pass, he made his way over to the elevator. Inside the elevator he gave his business card to two African American men after they asked him if he was the famous attorney, Stein! He told them he was. Then he stepped off of the elevator onto the second floor. He was nervous because he didn't know if there was anyone at the hospital that could identify him if Ms. Montana decided to scream for help. However, this didn't stop him from asking the nurse on the second floor at the nurses' station for the room number for Ms. Montana. "How may I help you sir?"

Mr. Stein responded, "I'm here to see Ms. Montana."

"Are you family?" the nurse asked.

"No… I'm her attorney."

Mr. Stein didn't see when Tony walked out of Ms. Montana's room and walked in the restroom on the corner of the hallway. He was too busy watching the nurse check the computer. The nurse handed him the visitation pass back and pointed to the Trauma Unit.

Once inside, Mr. Stein located Ms. Montana's bed by looking at the names at the bottom of the bed. Each bed had a chart on it with the patient's name on it. There were flowers and cards on the side of Ms. Montana's bed. Several were from Tony. When he noticed a basket of red roses and a card with Gallant's name on it, he wanted to throw up. This was after he had looked over Ms. Montana's body.

CHAPTER 21

Tony walked into the restroom on the second floor of the hospital. He looked in the five stalls inside the restroom before he pulled out the small bag of cocaine that Sam had given him. He had been using the substance for the last two days. He hadn't had much sleep because he was too high to sleep. And, he was afraid if he went to sleep that he would awake and his grandmother would be dead.

Tony took a snort of the cocaine after making a line on the sink. The drug gave him a rush, but not like the first time when he had used it two days ago. He put the package back in his pocket, and then he looked at himself inside the box shaped restroom mirror. He looked older than his twenty-one years. The last two days had been hard on his body. He couldn't eat or sleep. In his mind, he couldn't stop thinking about who did this to his grandmother. The only conclusion that he could come up with was, the Mob had ordered the attack on his grandmother. There was doubt in his mind about the incident because there were rules and codes that the Mafia operated by that wouldn't allow these men to hurt innocent people. But there could have been a clause in the rules when people outside of the families killed a mafia member. This would apply to outsiders in a sense where it didn't matter who was killed.

Tony opened the first stall and took a seat on the toilet. He needed to be by himself for the moment. There were so many different things running through his head, like if his grandmother was going to live or die. He didn't have anyone to talk to about the situation other than Geno and Sam. Mr. Castro wasn't an option, because Tony didn't trust him after finding out that Mr. Castro knew more about Tony Sr. than he had been leading on to him. Once again, Tony opened the bag back up. He snorted some more of the cocaine while sitting on the toilet thinking about his next move.

Mr. Stein was shocked when Ms. Montana opened her eyes when he touched her hand. She asked, "What are you doing here?"

"We need to talk." He answered.

"Where is Tony?" she asked in a weak tone.

"I have no idea."

A nurse that was checking on other patients inside the room looked over at Mr. Stein. He flashed his visitation pass and then he closed the yellow curtains to the area that Ms. Montana was stationed in. He spoke in a whisper, "I'm here to talk to you about the money."

"I don't want to talk about the money," she said.

"The money is going to get Tony hurt next," He said.

"Where is Tony?" she asked.

Mr. Stein could hear the panic inside of Ms. Montana's voice. He looked over at her hand that was close to the red help button. The sound of the machines were echoing through the room.

He whispered, "Don't do it if you want your grandson to live."

Ms. Montana removed her hand from the button and turned her full attention on Mr. Stein. He continued, "There are some people that want to kill your grandson because he owes them money. You can solve the problem by signing the money over to me."

"I don't care about the money. I'm too weak to even be thinking about money. Where is Tony?"

"Tony will be back here, that's why I want you to hear this recording."

Mr. Stein turned on the recording and then watched as Ms. Montana listened to Mr. Castro voice on the recording. Panic filled her body.

"That's the guy that assaulted me?"

"Yes. That's Gallant."

"Why?"

"Your son shot him in the leg."

"Tony Sr. did that to him?"

"Yes."

"Just, please leave sir."

"Not until you sign the papers."

"Just leave them with me. I'll do it later, right now I'm too tired."

"I'm going to leave a copy of the paperwork with you. Remember that people are watching Tony Jr."

Mr. Stein dropped the paperwork on the small table that was next to the bed. Then he smiled and walked out of the room. His missioned had been accomplished.

Tony turned the water on in the restroom and used his hands to splash some on his face. He used some tissue from one of the stalls to wipe the water off of his face. Then he walked back to his grandmother's room. His grandmother was awake when he returned to her bed side. She was reaching for the documents that had been left by Mr. Stein. Tony spoke, "Let me get that for you." He could see that his grandmother's eyes were filled with tears. After Tony handed her the papers, she spoke, "I'm happy you're here Tony. There's so much I have to tell you."

Tony couldn't understand his grandmother, because her words were slurred. The medication was the cause.

"Do you know who did this to you Mama?"

"Yes. Gallant…" Tony didn't understand the name.

"Who?"

"The guy had on all black."

"Do you know his name?"

"You are not safe Tony."

"What are you talking about Mama?"

"We have to tell the police."

"Who was it Mama?"

"The lawyer Tony. He played me a recording."

"What lawyer? Did he do this to you?"

"There's something I have to tell you Tony. It's about your father's past." Tony didn't understand why his grandmother wasn't getting around to who attacked her. It was clear she wasn't in her right frame of mind. "Your father had a life insurance policy on himself. You need to get the box from my closet."

"What does this life insurance policy have to do with you getting assaulted?"

"It's thirty million dollars."

"What are you saying?"

"Your father left the money to me."

"Where is the money?"

"It's in a trust fund. I don't want it."

"We can use that money, Mama."

"No…"

"Why?"

"It's blood money Tony. Your father made that money from selling drugs." Ms. Montana began to cough.

"Take it easy Mama."

"I don't want the money Tony. That's why I put the money in your name."

"Where is this money?"

"The lawyer Mr. Stein has it."

"You're talking about the lawyer that got me out of Child Services when I was a child?"

"Yes."

"I know something wasn't right about that guy."

"Listen Tony... I need you to promise me that you won't take the money."

"I can't promise you Mama..."

"Well, promise me that you will never be like your father."

"Why do you want me to promise you this?" Ms. Montana began to cough again. Tony reached over and grabbed some tissue. Blood came out of her mouth. She spit it out in the tissue.

"Promise me, Tony."

"I can't Mama. I don't know what the future holds."

"Hand me those documents on the table." Tony picked the documents up off the table. He could see that his grandmother was too weak to read or hold the papers.

"Read them to me, Tony."

Tony started reading the documents out loud to his grandmother in Spanish. When he came across the amount of the policy, he stopped and noticed that his grandmother's eyes were closed. He stopped reading the document and put it in his pocket. He now knew he would be a millionaire on his twenty-first birthday. The thought of getting revenge on the people that brought harm to his grandmother entered his mind. He knew that Mr. Stein knew the person that had assaulted his grandmother. This made him want to get revenge on the person that did the assault and Mr. Stein as well. But first he had to go home, change clothes, and inform Geno, and Sam about the new information that he had received from his grandmother.

Tony took a cab home after making sure that his grandmother was comfortable and stable. When he arrives home, he noticed that there was crime scene tape still there. He removed the tape and walked inside the house where there was more tape. The inside of the house smelled like stale blood. This came from the house being closed up for two days. Tony looked over the room with anger in his eyes. He could see how the person that assaulted his grandmother had come through the hallway that lead to the kitchen. The footprints were in plain view. The police had told Tony that they had evidence, but they hadn't arrested a suspect or even got back in contact with him after his interview with them at the hospital.

Tony whispered to himself, "This is something a psycho would do." In Tony's mind he knew it had to be something mentally wrong with the person that assaulted his elderly grandmother. When he came across the dried blood by his grandmother's recliner, he began to cry. There were spots and stains all over the recliner and the carpet. There were different patterns in which this gave Tony a clue on how the assault took place.

Tony envisioned the attacker creeping up on his grandmother from behind grabbing her by the neck and then choking her. He knew from the information he had received from the doctor that his grandmother's windpipe was damaged by her attacker. When he first heard this, it sent chills up his spine and a squeamish feeling through his body. Tony wasn't the type to get easily nauseated, but knowing that his grandmother had been kicking, squealing, crying, squirming and fighting for her life made him disgusted. His grandmother didn't have anything for anyone to take that was valuable inside the house. This was why Tony was perplexed. There were pieces missing from the puzzle.

Tony reflected back on the conversation that he had with his grandmother at the hospital. She had told him that her attacker was wearing all black, and the guy had big hands. This wasn't enough information for Tony to come up with a suspect, but as he looked over the scene, he envisioned a theory about what happened in the house the day his grandmother was attacked. As he walked into the kitchen, he replayed the intruder's movements after looking over the footprints. The footprints lead to the back door where there were wooden fragments on the floor inside the threshold of the door.

Tony looked close at the prints and noticed that the shoe prints were different sizes. When he first made this discovery he thought it was two intruders but he had dismissed this theory after he looked at how the shoe prints matched the same directions. Tony made a mental note of the prints, and then he pulled out his cellphone. He called a locksmith. While waiting on the locksmith, he did some more investigating. He walked back into the living room and noticed an embedded name print in the carpet. It was the make of the shoe that the intruder had been wearing. Tony made another mental note to check the shoe stores for the Rockport Orthopedic shoes. The intruder had provided evidence of a foot problem, but the police had missed it. This disturbed Tony because the police hadn't done a good job with their investigation. When the police had given Tony their facts about their investigation, they left out the facts that the intruder had a problem with his foot and the size of the intruder's feet.

After looking over the entire house, Tony turned his attention to the box that his grandmother told him about. This box had been left by a federal Agent months before Tony was born. This box contained items that belonged to his father. Tony didn't' know about the box until his grandmother had told him about it at the hospital. Tony took the box from his grandmother's shelf inside her closet and he sat the cardboard box on the bed. Then, he stared at it for a moment. Then, he opened it. His emotions began to run wild when he saw a wallet that had his father's name on it. The wallet was leather, and it was filled with pictures of his parents. He placed the pictures all over the bed, and he then pulled out the other items inside of the wallet. There was an old receipt of several purchases of Armani dress suits and shoes. The cost of these suits were two thousand dollars, and the shoes were one thousand dollars apiece. My father had class, Tony thought to himself as he folded the receipts and put them back inside the wallet. He turned his thoughts to what Valentina had said about class when he first met her. He was pretty sure that he was in her class now, since he was a millionaire.

He decided after looking over the pictures that he was going to accept the money. He loved his grandmother, but he believed that he was entitled to the money because his father had left it to him. Even though it was blood money, it was his money. And, he was going to do something good with the money. Tony smiled to himself after he put the wallet back in the box and took out a gold necklace that was at the bottom of the box. The necklace had a Virgin Mary charm that was the size of a large grape. It had a picture of his aunt Gina inside the locket. The picture showed only her pretty face and jet black hair. Tony admired the heart shaped charm that his father had worn under his exclusive dress shirts. The charm represented his father's love for his aunt. He decided to put the charm on and wear it. After he put the necklace on, he walked over to the large mirror inside of his grandmother's room. He smiled and admired the necklace once again.

The necklace made Tony feel like he was finally connected to his father and aunt. He kissed the charm and walked back to the box. Then he pulled out a notebook. The notebook was the size of a small size reading book. It had yellow pages that were filled with his father's handwriting. He looked over some of the pages and recognized that the writings were in codes that his father had made up. The codes were mostly numbers. It took Tony hours to figure out what the numbers meant. When he figured out that the numbers were the letters, he turned the codes into words. The first word he recognized on the page was cocaine. The whole notebook was made up of names of people that his father had dealing with in the cocaine business. Tony came to this conclusion after he had decoded Gallant's name. He was shocked that the Feds hadn't decoded this notebook.

He was also shocked to learn that Gallant was on his father's debt list. There were four other men on the list, but Gallant stood out because this was Mr. Castro's first name. Tony knew this was Mr. Castro's first name, because Sam had always called Mr. Castro by his first name. This new revelation sent Tony's mind into a whirlwind. He felt like he had been betrayed by Mr. Castro. When Tony made out the amount that Mr. Castro owed his father, he couldn't believe that it was so much. Tony decided to see if these other men that were on the list were still alive. He did this by running their names through a search engine inside his bedroom.

All four of the other men were alive but living in different states. Most of these men had criminal records and had been to prison.

Tony decided to call Sam after his discovery. During this call, he told him about all of their men and the debt. He even told him about Mr. Castro being on the list. Before Tony hung up with Sam, he said, "I'm going to collect that money from every single man that owed my father."

Sam had responded, "That was 21 years ago. Let it go Tony."

"I can't Sam." Most of the men were in their fifties, and they were well established. This was what made Tony want to make good on collecting the debts for his father. He also wanted to know why Mr. Castro had deceived him for years. Tony called Geno and instructed him to come over to the house. This was after he took a shower and put on slacks, snakeskin dress shoes and a white dress shirt. Then, he laid out the rest of the cocaine that Sam had given him at the hospital. He did a line while he called Sam again. He instructed Sam to come over and bring some cocaine. When both men arrive, Tony opened the front door with a smile.

"You both are on time," Tony said as he waved them in. Both men were dressed casual.

Geno asked, "Is everything okay, Tony?"

"Yes. I just need both of you two to help me collect the money that these five men own my father."

Sam spoke, "Have you went crazy?"

"Like you taught me Sam, a debt is a debt until it's paid."

"You're going too far with what I taught you."

"Something else you taught me Sam that has stuck with me, you said a man's word is only good when he does as he says. In my book, the men that gave my father their words to pay, should have given the money to me or my grandmother."

"You sound crazy, Tony. I think that cocaine is getting to you."

"Where is the cocaine I told you to bring me?"

"I don't think you need anymore." Sam had a small sack of cocaine in his pocket.

"You are not my father Sam."

"I'm your friend Tony…I don't want you to go down the same path your father went down.'

"Then why did you teach me the mafia way of life? Why did you teach me about the streets?"

"I don't know Tony."

"Give me the cocaine."

Sam pulled out the cocaine after Tony pulled out a small .22 pistol. Sam tossed the cocaine on the living room table. Then he spoke, "Your father would be disappointed."

Tony picked up the cocaine and put out a couple of lines on the glass table. He snorted both lines and said, "I'm rich. I can do what I want. The world is mine."

Sam asked, "What are you talking about Tony?"

"My father left me thirty million dollars."

"I think you had too much Ya-yo. That stuff can make you feel like superman."

"It's not the cocaine. I'm really rich. I just have to wait until my birthday next week to pick up the money."

Geno said, "Are you serious Tony?"

"Serious as a heart attack."

"Who told you about this Tony?" Sam asked.

"My Grandmother told me everything."

Sam said, "Now, what's this about Gallant?"

The cocaine kicked in. Tony spoke, "I have to show you two something." Tony opened the notebook that was sitting beside the cocaine residue on the table. He spoke, "These are codes."

Geno asked, "What do they say?"

"It took me a while to make out everything inside the notebook, but I did. It's like my father was talking directly to me. I figured out the numbers are people's names and what they owe."

"Your father was brilliant," Sam said.

"I know."

Tony watched as Sam pulled out a cigar, lit it up and took a pull. Then Sam said, "These people that owe your father are probably dead."

"No they are not. I Googled them."

"Those damn computers."

"What's your problem, Sam?"

"Some things you just need to leave alone."

"Not until I find the guy that killed my father."

Sam took another hit of the cigar and said, "The guy that killed your father is a powerful man. He hasn't been seen in years, but he still supplies America with cocaine."

"So you know this guy?"

"Not on a first name basis. I just heard your father say his name a time or two."

"Who is this guy?"

"His name is Sosa. He's also knows as The Source."

"So the story that Mr. Castro told me is true?"

"I wasn't there when Gallant told you the story."

"He told me about the deal my father made with Sosa."

"I heard stories, but I didn't take all of them as truth."

"Was my father a hitman or a drug dealer?"

"Your father was neither. He was a businessman. I wouldn't classify him as anything but that."

Tony changed the context of the conversation when he asked, "Did you ever see my father wearing this necklace?" Tony unhooked the necklace from his neck and reached it to Sam. Sam opened the charm and said, "This is your aunt, Gina."

"I know. What I really want to know is why my father have a picture of her inside of the necklace."

"Your aunt Gina was your father's heart. In my opinion, I believe that your father looked at Gina as the purest thing in his life. You have to understand what type of world that he was living in to understand your father." Sam took a pull from his cigar and dumped the ashes in the ash tray on the table. Then he continued, "Your father trusted Gina, but he found out that Gina had gone and got married to his right-hand man. This was after he told his right-hand man not to even look at your aunt."

"Did my father really kill her?"

"No!"

Tony Jr was told that his father had killed his aunt from his grandmother. She had told him one afternoon after she had come in from visiting Gina's grave.

"Why did my grandmother lie to me?"

"She may have felt like your father was responsible for Gina's death, because Gina was killed at your father's mansion."

This information was new to Tony.

"Family secrets."

"Your grandmother holds grudges, Tony. She's a woman that doesn't forgive easily. Your father told me that she didn't want his money, and she didn't want him to ever come to her home again."

"Mama can be hard at times."

"Just say she's protective. I guess your father got that character from her."

"Why do you say that?"

"He was protective of your aunt Gina. This is why he killed his right hand man."

Sam took another pull from the cigar, and then he blew the smoke into the air. He looked off into space like he was searching for the right words to deliver to Tony. Geno interrupted, "Is it okay for me to fix us drinks?"

Sam continued to look off in space while Tony said, "Come back to Earth, Sam." Geno disappeared into the kitchen.

Sam spoke, "Sorry, Tony. I needed a minute to gather my thoughts. Now, where were we?"

Tony reached his hand out to Sam for the necklace. Sam placed it inside his hand and said, "Your aunt Gina was a casualty of war Tony. Your father didn't know that Sosa was going to send men to his house."

"I see the big picture now. My father killed his right hand man and then took my aunt to his house, the day Sosa sent men to kill my father."

"That's what happened Tony."

"How did my aunt get involved with the nightlife?"

"Once she turned eighteen, she started living. It was the 80's, drugs and clubs were the thing to be doing. Your father didn't like the fact that his sister was becoming a woman at a fast pace. There were times when your father had to pull Gina from the clubs."

Tony watched as Sam put the cigar out in the ashtray. He could see that Sam was searching for his own thoughts again. Geno returned to the room with lemonade, then he set the pitcher on the table. As Tony watched, Sam continued, "Mannie was your father's right hand man. He started spending time with your aunt Gina. Your father didn't know." Tony laid out another line of cocaine on the table and snorted it up. Then he asked, "What was so special about Mannie? Why did my aunt marry him?"

"He was a ladies man Tony, like your buddy Geno."

Tony looked over at Geno, who was now sitting on the love seat smiling. Sam continued, "Mannie helped your father make millions only to be killed, because your father felt like Mannie betrayed him."

"Did my grandmother ever meet Mannie?"

"I'm not sure. Why do you ask?"

"Because, I used to ask my grandmother about my father's friends. She always told me that she didn't know any of my father's friends."

"There is your answer."

Geno was taken in the whole conversation like a sponge. It was like he was watching a good tennis match, because Tony and Sam started going at each other about the codes of the streets. They both had different views on why Mannie had been murdered by Tony's father. Tony thought that his father shouldn't have murdered Mannie and Sam thought opposite, because he was from the old school and lived strictly by the old trust codes. Sam believed if someone broke the code, then, they were entitled to death. Tony's new school principles were based on the situation. He thought that his father was wrong, because his aunt Gina was her own woman, and should have been able to choose whom ever she wanted to be with. Tony believed that love didn't have a code.

Tony closed the notebook and said, "I have what I've been looking for. I now know my purpose in life."

Sam asked, "What is that Tony?"

"To find my father's killer."

"You sure you want to go looking for the big bad wolf?"

"I now see why you were put in my life to mentor me. You did good, Sam."

"The reason I've been mentoring you Tony is, because I like you. I look at you like a son."

"Why didn't you tell me about the situation with my father and Gallant?"

"That's a good question."

"You know the story. You know about the half million dollars that Gallant didn't pay my father."

Sam relit the cigar and took a few pulls. Then he said, "There is a code that I live by Tony, I don't get into someone else's business unless they ask me to."

"You knew all these years, you could have told me."

"I didn't mean any harm Tony. I wanted the past to stay in the past."

"What's Gallant paying you?"

"Nothing…"

"I don't believe you. You are the one that taught me that everyone has a motive. What's your motive with me Sam?"

"I swear Tony… There is no motive. I really do love you like a son."

"If you have loyalty for me then help me take care of Gallant." Tony was feeling like Gallant had betrayed him.

"I don't know Tony. I just can't kill someone that's been helping me over the years."

"I saved your life Sam, I could have let the Mob kill you."

"I'm not in the clear, Tony. They still want my head."

"You are breathing now. That's what counts."

"Let me think about it, Tony."

"Just remember you owe me, Sam."

"What are you doing, threatening me Tony? After all I have done for you."

"I'm not threatening you Sam. I don't make threats; I make promise that I don't break. My word is all I have, and that's what I live by."

"I taught you the streets, Tony. I taught you how to be a gentleman. You are not your father."

"But I am my father's son. I do have his blood."

"There is no need of stirring up new trouble. We're safe on the murder beefs."

"Can I trust you Sam?"

"Yes, Tony."

"Then, when the time comes for Gallant to go to the next life, make sure you are available."

Sam stood up, fixed his shirt and walked over to the door. He looked at Tony after he opened the door, then he stated, "I know your pedigree, Tony. I don't want anything to do with Gallant's past transgressions."

Tony watched as Sam walked out of the door and disappeared down the walkway. He picked up the glass of lemonade that Geno made for him. He took a drink and said, "We might have to kill Sam."

Geno said, "No problem Tony. No problem."

Tony smashed his drinking glass against the living room wall. He was upset that Sam had created a dilemma that could have been solved, before he left out the door. Tony didn't understand why Sam was showing distrust towards him after all he had done for Sam. Tony didn't know if he was overreacting to the situation or if the cocaine was the cause of his emotions to be running wild. Life was too short to be worrying about things that he couldn't control, but there were things that could be controlled that Tony wanted to control and planned to control. He knew that he had to use Sam to get to Gallant, because Gallant was smart and Gallant was always on point when he was around. It was going to take a mapped out plan to kill Gallant, Tony thought as he looked at Geno and smiled.

CHAPTER 22

Tony and Geno noticed Pablo Martez walking out of John-ny's Used Car Lot building. They were sitting across from the lot in a stolen Cadillac that Geno had taken from a law office in the downtown area of the city. Geno was behind the wheel, while Tony was in the passenger seat with a .38 special in his hand. Tony told Geno to get a car with a large trunk, because the trunk was needed in order to carry out their plan.

Both men watched as Pablo got inside a blue minivan in front of the main office of the building. Tony spoke, "That's our guy."

Geno spoke, "He's a Mexican."

"Sam told me he was a Mexican."

"A Mexican making drops for the Mafia?"

"This is how they throw the Feds off."

"I don't get it."

"They tricked you, didn't they?"

"You've got a point Tony."

"When he pulls off the lot, get behind him."

"He has cameras on the van."

"Don't worry about the cameras."

"We have to. This is murder."

"Did I say we were going to murder him?"

Geno pulled the Cadillac out of the parking lot behind the van. Then he said, "You think he's got the money in the van?"

"I know the money is in the van. You don't remember that he drove up in an orange Nissan."

"What are we going to do with the money Tony?"

"Keep it."

"I thought this was revenge on Big Paul?"

"This is the only way we're going to get him to come out on the streets. He's old school, remember, he's not out in public much."

Tony and Geno rode in silence while eye-balling the van. They were two blocks from Paul's Bar-N-Grill when a red light caught them. Geno sped through the intersection and after, he got the Cadillac through the intersection he looked through the rearview to see if the police were anywhere in sight. Tony was deep in thought. He still had his mind set on the van.

When Pablo pulled the van into a gas station a block from Paul's Bar-N-Grill, Geno pulled in after him. Geno parked on the opposite side of the building. Tony and Geno watched as Pablo went into the building and paid for gas. Tony spoke, "This might be our only chance to kidnap Pablo."

"I thought we were just taking the money."

"Change of plan."

"There are too many cameras Tony."

"That's what makes it fun."

Pablo came walking out of the store with a small bag in his hand. Tony spoke, "When he starts to pump his gas I want you to walk up and get his attention. I'm going to come from behind with the Taser."

Tony pulled the Taser out of the glovebox of the Cadillac and a chrome .45 pistol.

Geno spoke, "Let's do it."

Geno opened the driver's side door and stepped out into the sunshine. Pablo was looking around like he was searching for someone when Geno walked up on him and asked, "Do you have a light?"

"No English…"

As soon as Pablo turned to put the pump back into the pump holder, Tony shot him in the chest with the Taser. Then, he watched as Geno caught Pablo. Tony quickly removed the keys from Pablo's pockets and opened the van sliding door on the passenger side. Geno and Tony stuffed Pablo in the back of the van. Pablo was still shaking when Geno turned the engine over in the van. This all happened in a matter of seconds.

CHAPTER 23

Agent Tadeo decided it was time for him and his team to take a break from watching José. He decided this after realizing that there was a possibility that José knew they were there. Plus they were running low on their food supplies and needed to load back up. It was dark out when they started their trip back to where the Hummer was hidden at the bottom of the jungle.

The trip was going to take a day and a half, since they knew where they were going. The team had been travelling for ten hours when Agent Tadeo began to think about when he attended the convention in Paris. He had remembered seeing a beautiful young female that was bidding for one of the hundred GPX 4000 phones. She was surrounded by several bodyguards, and she wasn't acting like all of the other military people at the convention. When Agent Tadeo found out that this young woman was from South America, he wanted to know more about her. He was sure that she knew José Rivera, because she was made up of money. Plus, Agent Tadeo had witnessed a similar woman with José in Africa a year before the convention. Agent Tadeo got an

Ex-Delta Force guy to introduce the young woman to him. When he met Valentina and looked into her eyes, it seemed like he had seen her before. He couldn't place where he had seen her, but he knew those eyes. Agent Tadeo snapped back to reality when he and his team heard footsteps in the distance. He spoke, "Everybody be still."

They all stopped and turned off their flashlights. They listened to see if there was anyone coming.

Agent Tadeo said, "We have to split up."

He pointed for Dean and John to go in the opposite direction of him and Josh. The little power they had in their radios was enough for them to keep in contact with one another while they tried to lose the men that had been following them for the last ten hours. After getting off the main path where the guards and the workers travelled to get to José's Compound, Agent Tadeo cut a path through the thick brushes that ran close to a lagoon.

He spoke, "We can hide here."

Josh and Agent Tadeo camouflaged themselves with mud and grass. They watched as the men that had been following them ran right past them. Agent Tadeo said, "That was a close call."

Josh asked, "How many were there?"

"I think about ten."

"Do you think there's more?"

"I don't know. We have to radio Dean and John and see."

Agent Tadeo pulled out his radio and called Dean. Dean came over the radio, "This is Cain."

"What's your location?"

"I think about five miles off the path."

"Do you have anyone following you?"

"No…"

"Is Able ok?"

"Yes."

"We found a lagoon about two miles off of the path. We're going to set up camp here. I want you two to come to the lagoon."

"Copy."

The sun was coming up when they all took rest at their new camp. Josh took the first guard duty. Agent Tadeo couldn't sleep, but he closed his eyes anyway to get some rest. While lying in silence, he thought about Valentina again. He never learned the young woman's last name because as quick as he had met her, she was gone. But her eyes were a trait that he would never forget about the young woman. A couple of months later, he had realized where he saw those eyes at. Those were the same eyes that he had seen at the dog show. Valentina was the person that murdered Jill.

A crying sound from an animal brought Agent Tadeo back to reality. He opened his eyes and noticed a black jaguar in a tree over top of him and his team. The tree was thirty feet tall with huge limbs that the cat could walk on. The cat looked mad, because his bluish-gold eyes were glowing.

Agent Tadeo knew he had to keep his composure in order to keep the cat calm. He did his best not to make direct eye contact with the cat. His heart was racing, and his arm pits were filled with sweat. The sound of the crying animal was getting louder by the second. Agent Tadeo noticed that the sound wasn't coming from the cat in the tree. It was coming from a hole that wasn't too far from where they were laying. There had been bushes covering the hole but the bushes were lying off to the side of the hole. Now, a small cub's head was sticking out of it. Agent Tadeo grabbed a hold of his gun that was lying beside his sleeping bag and then he noticed Dean and John looking at him. Josh was coming up from the rear of the box shaped area that they had made the camp out of. Agent Tadeo put his finger to his mouth while holding the gun to his side. The jaguar, then positioned himself in attack mode. Before he leaped towards Josh, Agent Tadeo squeezed off three shots. All three hit the animal in the head. The cat landed two feet from the hole. Dean and John scrambled to their feet. Agent Tadeo couldn't believe what he had done. He spoke, "Is everyone okay?" Everyone shook their heads indicating they were fine. He continued, "Let's pack up. It's time to go."

CHAPTER 24

Valentina decided it was time for her to go see a sex therapist. This was after she had told Larry how much she couldn't stop thinking about having sex with every man that she came in contact with. Larry suggested that she go see his friend Jerry Brown, a sex therapist that operated out of his home in Atlanta. Valentina hopped on a plane and landed in Atlanta on Friday morning. She checked into a hotel downtown and called Jerry.

It didn't take Valentina long to find Jerry's house two blocks from Peachtree Street on North-West. She had used the GPS in her rental car to accomplish this. Jerry was standing on his large porch when Valentina pulled into his driveway. There were two BMWs in the driveway along with an SUV. She hugged Jerry and introduced herself. Then she told Jerry that Larry didn't come, because he had a funeral to attend. Jerry invited her in a showed her to his office.

There were a million things running through Valentina's head as she walked down the narrow hallway of Jerry's beautiful home. She couldn't stop thinking about Tony. This was one of the reasons that she had come to see Jerry. Even though she hadn't had physical sex with Tony, she had thought about him almost every time while using her sex toys after meeting him. She was sure she was an addict when it came to sex, because it didn't matter if it was with a man, woman or toy, she wanted it. Most of the times it wasn't just about sex, it was about the hunt and the chase. Being an addict was someone she thought was addicted to drugs, but when she learned about the psychology part about sex in college she knew there was more to sex than just the physical attraction.

This is what made her come to the conclusion that she could be addicted to sex. She took psychology and sociology in college and she learned about the philosophies and theories that people came up with about sex. She disregarded some of the information that she had received from these classes as trash-facts, because she had experienced sex on all levels. Her philosophy about sex was mind over matter and matter over mind. This was how she looked at how she solved her problems in life. Sex was her answer to most of her problems.

Hunting humans had become a part of her life after Brad was killed. There were signs before Brad, but Valentina didn't recognize them until she did some soul searching after Brad's death. When she thought back to the times, she started having sex with grown men after her parent's death, she thought about the gardener that her father trusted so dearly. The gardener raped Valentina one afternoon while her parent were away. She never told her parents, because the gardener told her that he would kill her parents if she did. A few months after her ordeal with the gardener, her parents were killed in a fake police raid. Her grandfather was outraged when he heard about the fake raid and had the men murdered after he found out who was behind the murders. Valentina moved in with her grandfather after her parents were murdered, and she was groomed to be the person that would run her grandfather's empire once he had retired.

Valentina took a seat on the small couch in Mr. Brown's office after she walked in. The room was modest. Mr. Brown closed the door and asked, "How was your flight?"

She responded, "Okay."

"Where are you staying?"

"Downtown... It's a nice suite."

"Larry didn't tell me that you were so beautiful."

"You are a hunk yourself."

Mr. Brown was an African American, 50ish, smooth skinned guy that looked young. He was dressed in an Armani suit and alligator shoes that matched his gray suit. This was a sign to Valentina. She loved a man that loved fashion like her. Her thoughts started to run wild, and she started sizing Mr. Brown up. He asked, "Where did you get that Prada one piece jumper suit and those shoes are fabulous..."

"Thank you... Larry orders my clothes. He knows me like the back of his hand. He's been working for me for the last two years."

"Well enough about fashion... let's get started."

"Well, I have a problem with sex... it's like I think about it all the time. Lately, I've been having fantasies about this guy named Tony..."

Mr. Brown interrupted, "I don't mean to cut you off, but I need to write down a few things about you before we get started. How old are you?"

"Twenty-six... My birthday is in May."

"Taurus."

"What do you do for a living?"

This question caught Valentina off guard. She didn't want Mr. Brown to know that she was running dummy companies for her grandfather to hide his drug money so she said, "I'm currently doing some work for my grandfather."

"What kind?"

"I'd rather not talk about it Mr. Brown."

"Call me Jimmy."

"Okay, Jimmy. I'd rather not talk about my work."

"I need to know a little about it so I can help you find out what's your problem."

"Sex is my problem."

"Usually I would agree with my clients when they come out and say this, but you are a special case. Being that I'm a therapist and I have helped hundreds of people I know best so therefore you need to be truthful when I ask you questions."

"I'm not hiding anything."

"You're jumping to a defense already."

"No…I'm just nervous."

"Relax… You are in good care. Now, I want you to know something about me. I'm gay…"

Valentina had heard all the rumors about Atlanta being the homosexual capital of the United States. She asked, "What does that have to do with you helping me with my sex addictions."

"I just like people to know who I am so they can understand where I'm coming from. I can see things from both worlds…"

This comment made Valentina laugh to herself.

"You are funny, Jimmy."

"Did Larry tell you that I used to be a sex addict too?"

"No…"

"It's a disease Valentina. Just like most drug addicts we have the same disease they have, but we are sex junkies."

"How do you deal with it?"

"I take it one day at a time."

Valentina didn't think that she was going to get anything out of her session but after an hour with Jimmy, she realized it was more to her addiction. There were things in her past that she needed to address in order to work on dealing with her addiction.

CHAPTER 25

S am couldn't stop thinking about why he had given Tony the information on Big Paul's drug money drop. Sam knew that Tony was going to pay Big Paul a visit after Tony had found out that Big Paul had owed Tony Sr. money. Sam had left Tony's grandmother's house perplexed the day that Tony had discovered that Big Paul owed Tony Sr. The debt was 21 years old, and it had been made before Tony was born. This was why Sam was perplexed, because he knew the guys on the list were well in their 50's and these debts were far from their minds.

The 80s had been all about no cameras and money. Murder was necessary. Especially, when cocaine prices increased like stock. Sam had always lived by the street code, and he had believed in Karma. This was why he had always played fair and went by the old school rules. But, times were changing and the new breeds of predators in the street were different in which it was making it difficult for Sam to stick to his old school mentality. This was the real reason that he had given Tony, Big Paul's drug money drop information.

Sam was still contemplating whether he should tell Gallant about Tony's discovery of the black notebook. This was why he was on his way to Gallant's store. While walking down the South Beach strip, his mind reflected back on the years that he had been schooling Tony. It had started the day that he had met Tony at Gallant's store after Tony started working for Gallant. It didn't shock Sam that Tony like all the philosophies and rules that the Mafia went by. This was in fact Tony Montana Sr.'s son, and when he had given Tony Mafia books to read, Tony would read them within a two day period. These books were mostly written by Mario Puzo. This was Sam's favorite author.

Sam had educated himself while doing a bid for armed robbery back in the later eighties. After serving his time, he returned to Miami and hooked up with Gallant. They were already friends before Sam starting working at Gallant's store. Gallant had given Sam money to get on his feet when he had gotten out from serving his bid. And,he gave him a place to stay. This was why it was hard for Sam to leave Gallant in the blind about Tony's new findings.

In the past, Gallant and Sam had discussed the issues that Tony Sr. had with Gallant, but they decided it was best to leave the past in the past. When Tony Jr. started working at the store, these issues came up again and Gallant told Sam that when the time was right that he would discuss those issues with Tony. The time never came. Now that the notebook had been found, Sam was in the middle of a big betrayal scheme.

Gallant was standing behind the counter of the store when Sam walked in. There were no customers inside the store. Gallant asked, "How is it going Sam? Didn't know you were back in town."

"Got back a couple days ago."

"Have you seen Tony?"

"No…"

"The reason I ask is, because he hasn't been to work and he isn't answering my calls."

"That's weird. That's not like Tony."

"I was thinking the same thing." Sam could see that Gallant was a little jumpy.

"I heard that his grandmother was in the hospital."

Gallant didn't blink.

"I didn't know."

Sam turned and walked over to the beer cooler and grabbed a Budweiser. Then he said, "Tony has been staying at the hospital with his grandmother."

"Maybe I should send flowers?"

Sam didn't know that Gallant had already sent flowers.

"That would be nice."

Gallant changed the subject when he said, "You know the word on the street is that you had something to do with that Mob boss's death?"

"I know…"

"A few of the Boss's men came by. I told them I didn't know where to find you."

"Thanks."

"There is a heavy reward on your head."

"How much?"

"Half a million. Dead or alive." Sam could see the devil in Gallant's eyes.

"I'm worth half a million?"

"Yes…"

Sam noticed Gallant had his hands under the counter. He spoke, "I think I'm going away for a while."

"That's a good idea Sam."

"Are you still going to sell the store?"

"Yes. Then I'm going away too."

"What about Tony? You're just going to leave him?"

"He's a big boy now."

"I always knew you had a cold heart, Gallant, but I never thought it was ice cold."

"What are you talking about?"

"You know you messed up."

"What are you talking about Sam?"

"I've got to go Gallant…" Sam walked out of the store without saying another word. Once he got in a cab, he felt safe. He knew Gallant would have turned him into the Mob. This was why he made his decision to help Tony kill Gallant.

CHAPTER 26

It had been over an hour since Tony and Geno had arrived at the storage building on the outskirts of the city. They brought Pablo to the building after they had kidnapped him at the gas station. Geno had already set up the place to look like a torture chamber by laying out grip pliers, a large razor blade, brass knuckles, butchers knives, steel hammers, steel rods, and a fire torch.

Geno picked up the large razor blade and grabbed Pablo by his neck after sitting him down in the chair that was stationed beside the van that Pablo had been driving. Tony walked in front of Pablo and said, "Where is the money?"

"No English."

Tony asked Pablo in Spanish about the money. Pablo didn't answer. Tony waved Geno out of the way after checking the rope that Pablo was bound with. Then, Tony grabbed Pablo by his jet black hair and whispered the same question in Pablo's ear. Pablo responded, "Big Paul is going to kill you two."

Geno was staring at Tony.

Tony grabbed one of the butcher's knives and cut Pablo across the face. Pablo screamed out in pain. Tony shouted, "Shut your mouth."

Geno spoke, "We have to hurry, Tony."

Blood was leaking from the long line Tony had created with the knife. Pablo was naked. Geno had made Pablo get naked at gunpoint and Pablo had complied without resisting but now he was resisting.

Tony spoke, "Cut his balls off."

Pablo shouted, "No… No… Please!"

Geno grabbed the brass knuckles and hit Pablo in the nuts while Tony held him. Pablo screamed out in pain as Tony pushed him to the concrete floor. Pablo shouted, "Please…. Please… I'm just a runner."

Geno said, "We have to go, we don't have time to keep playing with him. Let me put a bullet in his head, Tony."

Tony smiled to Geno when Pablo shouted, "I'll tell you where the money is if you let me go."

After Pablo told them where the money was in the secret compartment inside the bottom of the van, they let him go. Before they let him go, they told him to tell Johnny to tell Big Paul that he was in debt to Tony Montana Jr., and that the debt had to be paid.

CHAPTER 27

J ohnny was sitting at his desk inside his office on the phone when he noticed Pablo walking in front of his car lot without any shoes on. He blinked his eyes twice to make sure that he was seeing what he was seeing. Johnny's two bodyguards stood up and walked out of the office and met Pablo in the front of the building.

After the bodyguards searched Pablo, they escorted him into Johnny's office. Johnny had been on the phone with his uncle Big Paul when they walked in. Paul and him had been talking about why Pablo hadn't shown up at Big Paul's Bar-N-Grill will Paul's money. Johnny spoke, "Where have you been? And where is the van?"

Pablo answered, "They took it."

"Who?"

"Tony Montana Jr. and his crew."

"Who is Tony Montana Jr.?"

"I don't know sir I was thinking you could tell me."

"How did they know about the drop?"

"I don't know sir."

"It seems to me that you don't know anything."

"They had me blindfolded."

"Tell me how did they get you?"

"They kidnapped me at the gas station a block from your uncle's place."

"I don't believe you."

Pablo had bandages on his face and chest area. His bandage were covered in blood and the blood looked dark rose red. The evidence of a beating was in Johnny's face, but he still didn't believe that someone had the balls to steal from his uncle. This was why he called his uncle back while Pablo was in the room. When his uncle came over the line, his uncle said, "Where is Pablo?"

Johnny answered, "He's here."

"Where is my money Pablo?"

Johnny had turned the phone on speaker, so Pablo could hear. Pablo said, "Tony Montana has it."

"Who is Tony Montana?"

"I don't know sir."

"How many guys are in his crew?"

"I'm not sure. They had me blind folded."

"Where is the van?"

"Tony told me to tell Johnny that he needed to see you sir because you owe his father money. This is the reason he said he was taking your money."

"The only Tony Montana I ever knew was killed in the mid-eighties. That could only mean, it's his son."

"He said something about you owe a debt to his father."

"You're busting my balls right?"

"No sir…"

"Tony Montana has a son and he said that I owe him for a debt that I owe his father?"

"That's correct, sir."

"If you're lying to me Pablo, you are a dead man."

Johnny noticed tears in Pablo's eyes. He didn't want his uncle to kill Pablo but he knew if his uncle didn't get the money back then Pablo would have to die, because his uncle would be the laughing stock of the city.

Johnny spoke, "Let me take care of everything, Paul."

"Get my money back Johnny or Pablo's dead. Bring it to my bar."

Johnny listened as his uncle hung up on him. Then Johnny said, "Pablo I love you like a brother, but if you're lying then you are a dead man walking."

Geno and Tony sat listening to the conversation that Johnny and Pablo had with Big Paul. They couldn't believe how lucky they had gotten from listening to the call. The listening device that Tony had purchased from this online company had helped them find out the location of Big Paul. They knew from the call that Big Paul was hanging out at his own bar.

Tony didn't want to start a war with Big Paul, but he knew the only way to get the rest of the money that big Paul owed was to start a war. This was why he attacked Paul's crew. After turning off the listening device, Tony instructed Geno to drive them to Big Paul's Bar-N-Grill in the downtown area. This was after they returned to the storage building where the money was at and picked up a few weapons for their mission.

Tony had done his research on Big Paul. He knew that Big Paul had been the owner of the Bar-N-Grill for over ten years and Big Paul had purchased the place after Big Paul had become a made man. The place was purchased to cover up all of the dirt that Paul was doing in the streets of Miami. Tony knew that Paul was still doing dirt in the streets but was using Johnny as a cover man. Tony had found all of this out from Sam. Sam also told Tony about how Big Paul had climbed up through the ranks in the Mafia.

Big Paul had started out as a Picci Otto: a lower ranking soldier enforcer also known in the streets as the "Button Man." Then he worked his way to become a Cap: boss/don. He met many "Giovaned 'honore'": Mafia associates typically non-Sicilians and non-Italian members. One of those associates had been Tony's father. When Big Paul was a Capodecina AKA-Lieutenant of his mafia family he met Tony Sr. at a night club. Then they had begun doing business. They met through a mutual associate and after a sit down a week later, Tony Sr. had given Big Paul a million dollars' worth of cocaine on consignment. When Tony Sr. was gunned down at his home, Big Paul decided he wasn't going to pay the money that was owed for the consignment deal. This had all taken place over 21 years ago when Big Paul was in his late 40's. Now in his late 60's he was still built, a little chubby in the stomach area but desirable to the ladies his age. He was full Italian with gray sideburns and black hair that looked like it was wet when the sun hit it. His face was wrinkled in the corner of his eyes, and his cheeks were smooth as a baby's rump. He had changed dramatically since the deal with Tony Sr., but he was still as mean as a lion. Now semi-retired, Big Paul was preparing his nephew to take over his business affairs and the Family. First, his nephew would have to make his bones. This would take place in front of a Capodittutti AKA: Superboss, but first the family counselor had to do a background check.

Tony and Geno walked inside Big Paul's Bar-N-Grill. They noticed two men that they made out to be Big Paul's bodyguards. They were standing at the bar with a built older man that was nursing a drink. Geno was carrying Tony's guitar case with the Tommy and two 9 mills. The two bodyguards turned their attention on Tony and Geno as soon as they had entered the building. There were only four people inside of the bar. There was a bartender in which was a white young female with big breasts, the two bodyguards and Big Paul.

Tony and Geno didn't know who Big Paul was when they walked in the bar, but when Big Paul asked, "I'm Big Paul, the owner! Who are you?"

Tony responded, "I'm Tony Montana Jr."

"You have balls coming here after taking my money."

Geno opened the guitar case and pulled out the Tommy gun. Tony pulled a 9 mill, then he spoke, "We can do this the hard way or the easy way."

Big Paul asked, "What do you want Tony?"

"I want a million dollars cash."

"I don't have that kind of money here."

"I guess you want to die." Tony pointed the gun at Big Paul.

"Please Tony… Just give me some time. I'll get the money," Big Paul begged.

"You have about a minute to tell me where the safe is at in here," Tony responded.

"There is no money here, Tony."

Tony clicked the 9 mill. Big Paul said, "If you point that gun at me, you will be a dead man by morning."

Tony pointed the gun at Big Paul, then he spoke, "Your minute's up." One of the bodyguards went for his gun inside his right shoulder strap. Before he could get to the gun, Geno put two bullets in his chest.

"You see what you made him do? Now, where is the money?" Tony said.

"There is no money here, Tony," Big Paul said.

Geno asked, "You want me to kill him?"

"No… I'm going to do it," Tony said.

Big Paul made a move for his gun. Tony shot him in the center of his head and then took out the other bodyguard who reached for a weapon that was in a shoulder strap. The bodyguard's body hit the floor right next to Big Paul. There were blood splatters all over the floor and the bar counter. Tony looked at the bartender, who was crying standing over at the bar. She was a drop-dead doll with blonde hair and blue eyes. She looked like she was in her early twenties.

Geno asked, "What do you want to do with her?"

The bartender said, "I know where the safe is at. It's in Big Paul's office. The money is there."

Tony said, "You are a smart woman."

Tony decided to let Sue live after she gave him the combination to the safe. There was 1.2 million in the safe. Tony took a million and left the two hundred grand, because he only wanted what was owed to him. The two hundred grand he took from Pablo was the interest for the money that was owed. After Geno and Tony packed the money into several bags, they called Sam and told him to meet them out front in the rental van that he had rented for this occasion. Sam helped Tony and Geno load the bodies and the money into the van after he tied Sue up. They went to this abandoned house right outside the city limits after they took the money to the storage building. Once at the house, they dismantled the bodies of Big Paul and his bodyguards. Sam did most of the chopping of the bodies. After they put the bodies back inside the van, they took them to the ocean. Then they dropped them in the middle of the ocean after they tied large rocks to each body.

Tony returned to his grandmother's side at the hospital after he had dropped Sam and Geno off at their hotel room's downtown. He wasn't worried about Geno or Sam stealing the money from the storage building because they knew he had the means to hunt them down if they decided to take the money. Tony pulled out the black notebook once he was alone by his grandmother's side. He marked off Big Paul's name. Then he looked at Toby Red Firm's name. Toby was the next man on Tony's hit list.

CHAPTER 28

Valentina watched as the forty-ish old man worked out with a set of dumbbells inside of the YMCA. She had been working out by herself for over two hours. Usually, she would hit the shower after an hour, but Doctor Martin had caught her attention when she entered the weight room area. He was tall, slim and his eyes were the color of the blue sky. His body was toned from head to toe, and his short haircut gave him the boyish Tom Cruise look.

Valentina watched as Doctor Martin made his way to the shower area after placing the dumbbells on the rack in the weight room. She decided it was time to make her move on the Doctor after putting the weights she had been working out with back on the rack. She followed him into the shower area after she grabbed her towel off of the bench, that she had been using during her workout. When she arrived at the shower door, she could see that Doctor Martin was in one of five showers alone. His back was towards her. He didn't even know a vampire had arrive in the room.

Dinner and a movie was never in Valentina's equation when it came to sex. Her philosophy about sex was plain and simple. Just do it when you can, whenever you can. She loved having sex. Especially with strangers.

Valentina could smell the VO5 2-in-1 shampoo as she tiptoed over to the steamy shower that Doctor Martin was in. He didn't even know that she was inside the shower area. This was how she liked it. The anticipation of having sex inside a public shower had Valentina's walls leaking like water faucets. Watching her prey was what she liked most about the hunt and smelling its body scents too. This was what made her senses heighten and want to seduce her prey in the weirdest way.

Valentina didn't have her sex kit with her, but she knew that there was more than one way to seduce a man without the right equipment. She noticed Doctor Martin's shoes sitting on a bench a few feet from the shower. She grabbed the tennis shoes and unlaced them quickly. Then, she moved over to the shower, and stripped off all of her clothes while holding the laces inside her hands. Then, she used the laces to make a lock for the door to the shower, so her and Doctor Martin wouldn't be interrupted.

When Valentina turned around after making the wedge for the door, Doctor Martin was stepping out of the shower. She spoke, "Are you ready to operate on me Doctor?"

Valentina watched as Doc's penis rose for the occasion. It brought out the wild side in her, so she grabbed ahold of it and began to suck it viciously. He asked, "What are you doing to me?"

Valentina continues her vicious attack on his penis. Doctor Martin closed his eyes and enjoyed the moment.

CHAPTER 29

Agent Tadeo and his crew returned to their camp by José's Compound, after the phone call with Agent Tadeo's superiors. While in town, Agent Tadeo received a package from his superior. Inside the package were fly sized bug put in. These devices were made by the United States Military, and they were sold at the same convention in Paris where José's granddaughter purchased the phone. With the package was information on Valentina. Agent Tadeo spoke, "I have classified information about José's granddaughter that I need to brief everyone on."

Dean responded, "José has a granddaughter? I thought he didn't have any known relatives."

"I had my superior to get classified information on José, and this is what they came back with."

Agent Tadeo opened a folder and pulled out a picture of Valentina. He handed it to Josh as he said, "She's beautiful."

John said, "Yes... A real doll."

Agent Tadeo said, "That doll is a killer and very smart."

Dean responded, "Who did she kill?"

"My girlfriend and team."

"Why isn't she in prison?"

"I don't have enough evidence that proved that she did the bombing."

Dean stated, "I'm confused."

"Let me explain why she isn't in prison. Her grandfather has connections in the United States government. When I started trying to find out who she was before I formed this team, I was shot down by Washington. I was never given a formal answer why, but I was taken off of the case."

"We can kill two birds with one stone."

"Why do you say that?"

"Because, it says here that Valentina is working for her grandfather's company in the United States. When we get him for the Rico Act, we can include her in the indictment."

"It's not that easy guys."

"We work for the government right?"

"You guys are under me; no one but my superiors know about this mission."

John said, "I'm confused. I thought we were agents just like you?"

"You are, but you are special in a way that no one can know that all of you exist. It's for your safety."

Josh said, "As long as I'm getting paid it doesn't matter."

Dean responded, "We were promised a visit to the President's office."

"I'm still working on that."

John said, "We know you're going to come through."

Dean said, "I hope the new guy becomes the President. He's fit for the job."

"Mr. Obama?"

"Yes."

"He would be a good president."

Agent Tadeo interrupted, "We've got to focus on getting into the Compound."

Josh said, "What about Valentina?"

"We can get her after we get José."

"What if we don't get José?"

"We are going to get him."

Dean said, "If Valentina's anything like her grandfather, it's going to be hard to set her up."

John said as he looked into Agent Tadeo's eyes, "Do you think we can really build a case on her without building one on José?"

"Yes. But there's more to Valentina than you think."

John asked, "Like what?"

"She isn't directly connected to her grandfather's drug business. Her role is to run his legal businesses."

Dean said, "She's like the front guy?"

"Yes."

"So, what are we going to do?"

"We wait until she slips."

John said, "What if she doesn't slip?"

"Trust me. She will."

José watched as the crew of men packed hundreds of stuffed animals with large amounts of cash. They were putting ten thousand dollars in each stuffed animal. All of the bills were in hundreds and fifties. The only thing José didn't like about this process was that he had to be inside the room when the money was packed in the stuffed animal. It took time and patience to make sure that every animal was packed right to be shipped to the United States.

José and his inspectors stood over the crew of men during the whole packing process because each stuffed animal had to be weighed on the large scale inside the room. Before this process could take place, the money had to be washed to make sure there was no cocaine residue or any other substance that could set the alarm off at the airport. If the bills didn't meet the standard that José was looking for, then they had to be placed in a bin where they would be washed or destroyed.

Most of the crew of men used small razors to cut the stuffed animals open in the back area, where most of the cotton inside would be removed through this opening, and then reused once the money was stuffed inside the stuffed animal. The money was wrapped in plastic, before it was stuffed inside the stuffed animal. Most of these workers were women, and they were treated better than the men's crews because they were women. They got two large meals a day in which the men received only one large meal.

José watched as three men sealed up the large wooden boxes that the animals were put in. These boxes were nailed shut and labeled as fragile. The signs were painted on each box in red paint, and the letters were larger than stop sign letters. After this process, the boxes were put in the loading area where they were picked up by a crew of men and taken to the helicopter landing strip. Then they were loaded onto the chopper.

José called Valentina after he got all twenty boxes on the chopper. He had used the GPX-4000. She came over the line after three rings.

She spoke, "This is Valentina Rivera's office, how may I help you?"

José responded, "This is your grandfather."

"Hello…"

"I just called to tell you that the shipment is on it's way."

"I'll be looking for it."

"No need to look. It will be there tomorrow morning."

"Thanks, Papi."

"You are welcome, my Princess."

José ended his call and walked back to his bedroom. He was tired from all of the work that he had done in the last six hours. It was time for bed, José thought as he slipped out of his clothes. He didn't know that he was being watched.

CHAPTER 30

Tony sat inside the abandoned building parking lot in downtown, Miami. He was several blocks from the police station and two blocks from Mr. Stein's law office. He was in the lot waiting on a guy that was connected to one of the Mexican Cartels. Sam had set up a deal for Tony so that Tony could purchase a hundred kilos of powder cocaine for a million cash. Tony was looking to double his money and purchase more. He was planning to do this with the help of a compressor machine and Sam. Sam knew most of the dealers in the city that needed the product, and he knew how to take one kilo of powder and turn it into two kilos.

Geno arrive fifteen minutes before Tony, and he stationed himself on the other side of the street of the lot. He could see cars coming and going from the T section where he was parked. The older lot where Tony was stationed was shaped like a large E. There were three ways in.

As the white van with two Mexicans and Sam in it pull up in the lot, Tony watched. They pulled the van right in front of Tony's white van that he had rented in a fake name. Tony watched as the two Mexicans stepped out dressed in blue business suits. Sam was sporting a Polo outfit that was perfectly fitted. Tony was dressed in Polo shorts and shirt. His shoes were Nikes. When the Mexicans walked over to Tony into the Miami sunlight, Tony greeted them with a hand shake apiece and said, "It's nice to be doing business with you."

The small Mexican with big eyes said, "I'm El Chapo. I heard good things about you, Tony." Tony looked at the AR-15 in El Chapo's hand.

"I heard good things about you. Now, let's get down to business."

"I like your style, my friend." Tony put his nine mill in his waistband, then he waved to Sam and radioed Geno after he told El Chapo that he was calling help to move the money. Sam watched as Tony waved Geno over from the other lot. Geno pulled the Cadillac inside of the lot and popped the trunk from the inside. Inside the trunk was the million dollars wrapped in plastic bags inside large trash bags. Tony spoke, "Where is the coke?"

El Chapo looked at his man and nodded his head for him to open the back door on the van. El Chapo spoke, "I do good business. Pop the compartment." Tony watched as El Chapo put the AR-15 in the backseat of the van after his right hand man opened the secret compartment that was located in the floor of the van. El Chapo said, "It's a hundred kilos, Amigo."

"I need to check it," Tony responded in Spanish. Tony pulled out a knife after looking back at Geno and Sam, who were both armed with handguns. He punched a hole in one of the kilos after El Chapo handed it to him. Then he taste it with his pinky finger. The cocaine instantly numbed his tongue. The smell of the cocaine hit the air and it was so loud that Sam and Geno could smell it. They both fanned their hands by their noses after Tony busted open the package.

Tony spoke, "This is pure Ya-Yo."

El Chapo and his right hand man smiled. Tony said, "We got a deal." Then he shouted, "Bring the money, Geno." Geno pulled the Cadillac right behind the van. Geno and Sam loaded the money into the van after they loaded the kilos inside Tony's van. After the deal was done, El Chapo said, "I have plenty more Tony. You will be a very rich man in the future if you deal only with me. Just call when you need more."

Tony smiled. He knew this was the beginning of a good relationship.

Tony, Geno and Sam drove straight to the storage building after the deal. Sam went straight to work on mixing the cocaine with baking soda with the compressor machine. They turned each kilo into two and the power of the drug was still strong. Tony liked this because he knew he was going to take over the city in a matter of weeks. With El Chapo as his source, there was no stopping him now.

Chapter 31

Valentina signed the fake name on the papers after the old, pale faced truck driver handed them to her. She had been using the alias: Kim Kash for a month now. She smiled at the driver after she handed the papers back to him. Then, she watched as the driver got back into the truck and pulled off.

Valentina had watched this same driver unload twenty wooded boxes filled with stuffed animals in the warehouse that she rented just to receive the boxes. She knew the stuffed animals were filled with cash that she had to clean up for her grandfather. She didn't mind cleaning the money, but she didn't like when Fred, the owner of the trucking company that delivered the boxes, sent a new driver instead of coming himself. She didn't like to deal with new people, especially people that had undercover cop demeanors.

Valentina let out her breath as the truck pulled out the parking lot of the warehouse. She pulled the warehouse door down and looked at the large wooden boxes. They were filled with stuffed animals that was filled with cash. Getting her hands dirty wasn't new. Her grandfather had taught her that almost every rich man has gotten his hands dirty a time or two. This was a reminder to her that life was real, and not a game.

Valentina took off her expensive sweat jacket and laid it on one of the tables that were stationed inside the large box-shaped warehouse. The table that she laid it on was in the center of all twenty boxes. It was large enough to hold twenty briefcases, a money machine and a money scale. It was going to take hours to count four million cash. Each box contained twenty stuffed animals, and each animal contained ten thousand dollars. This added up to be two hundred thousand in each box. All of the boxes together total added up to four million. This was the first of five shipments for the month. This job wasn't new to Valentina. She knew the job like the back of her hand. That's why she had hired different women for the job, and most of the women were college students in need. They were hired to count the money, and then help put the money in the bank. This was done by using fake ID's. Most of these women were hand-picked by Valentina and Larry. They didn't even know that Valentina had had someone hack into the school's computer and see that they were in debt to the school. Valentina had been doing this for four years now. She had never gotten caught or had never witnessed one of her girls that she had hired getting caught. Breaking the law gave Valentina an erotic feeling, but it wasn't as good as an actual sex act.

Valentina picked up the crowbar that she had laid on the table and pried open one of the twenty boxes inside the room. After opening the box, she pulled one of the twenty stuffed bears out of the box. The bear was wrapped neatly in plastic and didn't give off any sign that it contained U.S. currency.

Valentina sat the bear beside the scale on the table. Then she grabbed the razor that was sitting on the table and used it to cut open the back of the bear. She had made a cut from the back down to the butt area. Then, she pulled the cotton out of the stuffed animal so that she could reach the money. After pulling the money out of the first bear, she called her assistant Mary at her office and told her to send the girls over. After the five girls arrived, she watched as they counted the money and put the money in the briefcases. Then, she instructed them that it was going to be a ten day job to put the money in the bank. This always drove her crazy, because she had to stay at the warehouse with the money. Even though there was an alarm on the building, Valentina didn't feel safe knowing that she could be robbed or even killed for the money. This was the most vulnerable part about the job. But it had to be done.

CHAPTER 32

Sam pulled the curtain back at the new stash house that Tony purchased through his new attorney. This house was made up of three bedrooms, two bathrooms, a den area, a large kitchen and a big backyard. The location was on the outskirts of the city. It was perfect for it's duty.

Sam liked the fact that Tony took the time to buy the house being that Tony never had time to do anything now. Money and power was changing Tony, and Sam could see this. He wanted to say something to Tony about his behavior, but he didn't want Tony to have a change of heart about him. This is why he just kept his mouth closed and enjoyed the time he was getting to spend with Tony.

Sam let the curtain go and went back to sitting on the large, white leather couch inside the living room of the house. He turned on the surround sound system to some Pop music and got lost in his thoughts. The first person came to mind was Gallant. He was still concerned about Gallant, because Tony was planning to kill Gallant soon. In his heart, he felt like Gallant's life should be spared because the debt was so long ago. But, on the other hand Gallant had been linked to Mr. Stein and the attack on Tony's grandmother.

Sam knew it was his doing of polluting Tony's mind with the Mafia's way of life. He felt guilt about doing this, but there was nothing he could do about it now. The street life was the only life he knew, because he had never gotten a formal education or had the opportunity to be taught how to live by the proper rules to life. He had always broken the law to make a living and had never found a way to live by the law without breaking it. This information was what he had passed on to Tony.

Mafia non-fiction books had become the diet of Tony's education from Sam. This was all a part of his plan to prepare Tony for the street life, but he didn't think Tony would enter the life so quickly. He never had any doubt that Tony would take in all the values, morals and principles that Tony had read about in these books that he passed off to Tony. He never doubted that Tony would pass the street academic test. He knew Tony made notes of all the real-life gangsters in the books, and this was what intrigued him about Tony. Especially, when Tony displayed some of the real life characters etiquettes in front of him.

Whenever Tony conversed about the sentiments of the characters, Sam listened closely, because Sam wanted to see how diligently Tony could dissect the characters. The only thing he didn't like about Tony's conclusions were the different philosophies that Tony formed about each character. These philosophies disturbed him because some of them went against the Mafia's rules and philosophies. Like one rule about the Public Safety workers that Tony didn't like was that they were given immunity and were not to be killed even if they were not in the line of duty. This bombarded him, because Tony told him that if it came down to it that a judge, DA and other powerful figures would be killed if they got in his way. This was what Tony told Sam while passing the book "Omerta" back to him. In Tony's eyes, these were crooks too, but this didn't sit right with Sam so Sam asked Tony for an explanation. Tony told him that Law Officials used their pens like guns. They were paper gangsters and paper gangsters were more powerful than street gangsters. This was when the debate started about the paper gangster and the street gangster. Tony had said, "It's a shame how many people are letting Law Officials live off their entities."

Sam had remembered saying, "That's an opinion." Tony had gotten offended, because he thought Sam was taking up for the police. This was what made him say, "We all are created equal in God's eyes. He's the only one that can judge us." The statement had caught him off guard, because he knew Tony knew he didn't believe in God. This ended the debate. There was no love lost after the debate. In fact, this debate had made their bond stronger. Sam snapped back to reality when he heard the computer beeping in the den area of the house. He quickly made his way down the hallway to the room. When he walked in, he could see that the inbox had a message. He briskly made his way over to the computer and took a seat in the small steel chair. The message was from the hospital. It was for Tony.

CHAPTER 33

G eno drove as Tony messed around with his cell phone. He was looking for the number the nurse had given him on his last visit at the hospital. He wanted to call and check up on his grandmother and see if she was getting better. On his last visit, he had learned after the visit that his grandmother had a mild heart attack. This sent Tony's emotions into a fluctuating state. He was constantly in between mad and unsure most days. He couldn't grasp the fact how his grandmother's condition went from fair to serious all in a matter of minutes.

Tony knew that Mr. Stein's visit had something to do with her heart attack because just before Mr. Stein had shown up, she was fine. The nurse told him that Mr. Stein had been there. This was after Tony did his own investigation of the people that came to visit his grandmother. When he saw Mr. Stein's name, he knew this was the guy that had left the documents for his grandmother to sign. And, this was also the person that told his grandmother that his life was in danger. This sent Tony in a rage, but he had managed to keep his rage covered up.

The box his grandmother told him about helped get him some closure about his father. But it also opened up Pandora's Box to other dilemmas that Tony was trying to figure out. Like for instance, the death of his aunt Gina and Gallant's debt to his father. He wanted to know all of the who's, what's and why's to these dilemmas.

Tony switched his mind to Toby Red Firm after sending Sam an email. He knew Toby was a career criminal from all of the information that he had gathered from court records at the Miami Courthouse. He even had the clerk at the courthouse click on to the new website that was called: International Criminals, in which the clerk told him that Toby Redfirm had been in fact on the Most Wanted list five years earlier. But, taken off the list after he was captured. This led to Tony doing some more research of his own, in which he found out that Toby had served three years for a gun and was now back on the streets.

When Geno pulled the rental Cadillac up in front of the stash house, Tony noticed Sam standing on the porch smoking a cigar. Tony spoke, "Something is wrong Geno… Sam is smoking."

Tony hopped out of the front seat of the Cadillac and walked briskly up to Sam. Sam spoke, "It's your grandmother, Tony."

"What's the problem Sam?"

"They want you over at the hospital."

"Why didn't you call?"

"I knew you were close by. The hospital sent an email about ten minutes ago."

"We've got to get going."

Nightfall had come quickly. The heat was still in the high eighties. The jungle made Agent Tadeo feel like it was hotter than it really was. He was used to the high humidity, and how the heat made him sweat through his clothes. This was the least of Agent Tadeo's worries. After looking through his military eyewear to get a closer look at the Compound, he placed the eyewear with his gear and said, "I think José is sending more drugs out tonight."

Dean responded, "What gives you this assumption?"

"The boxes. They were large."

Josh said, "All of the boxes that go in the place and go out the place are large."

John replied, "You've got a point there, Josh."

Agent Tadeo said, "Me, being an agent gives me the sixth sense to know when there are drugs being moved."

Josh said, "We all have a sixth sense."

"Just trust me on this one."

Dean said, "I object."

"This is not court."

John said, "Let's take a vote on what we think is in the boxes."

Josh said, "That's a great idea."

Agent Tadeo asked, "What do you all think are in the boxes?"

"Dean said, "I thought you would never ask. We think that U.S currency is in those boxes."

"What made you all come to this conclusion?"

Josh spoke, "Just think about the color of the boxes. They are light brown and they only leave out five times a month."

"The other boxes are brown."

Dean responded, "But they are not light brown."

"Maybe we need to get a closer look at those boxes. I'm going to fly the spy bug in on the next load."

John said, "That's about two days from now. What are we supposed to do until then?"

"Wait," Agent Tadeo stated.

Dean said, "This waiting stuff is starting to get on my nerves."

"What do you suggest?" Agent Tadeo asked.

"How about we pretend to be inspectors like we did when we went to the mountains and destroyed the plants," Dean said.

"Too risky Dean." Agent Tadeo said.

John said, "How about we kidnap one of the guard duty guys and Dean takes the guys place?"

Agent Tadeo interrupted, "I veto that. We all have to make it home safe."

"What do you suggest?" John asked.

"Just wait." Agent Tadeo said.

Tony's thoughts were running wild, as he sat in the back seat of the Cadillac. Geno and Sam were talking amongst themselves as Tony wrestled with his thoughts. The person that kept appearing in Tony's mind was Mr. Stein. He was the reason that Tony's grandmother was in the hospital. Tony knew that the guy that had attacked his grandmother knew Mr. Stein. He learned this from his grandmother. But Tony was still trying to digest the fact that Gallant was the person that attacked his grandmother. He came to this conclusion after he had checked the shoe patterns inside of his grandmother's house.

Tony pulled out a gold case that held a small amount of cocaine. He took several snorts. Then he said, "I've been thinking, Geno and Sam."

Geno asked, "What's on your mind, Tony?"

"The notebook brought light to my life," Tony said.

Sam asked, "What light Tony?" Geno exited the freeway with the Cadillac.

"That I've got to kill Gallant and Mr. Stein this week."

"We don't need to discuss this now Tony," Sam said. Tony ran his hands through his hair, and then he took another snort of the cocaine. He wiped his nose with the back of his hand. The suit he was wearing looked like he had it on for days. His hair was all over his head. Geno, on the other hand looked decent and Sam looked like a wise guy in his slacks and dress shoes.

Tony spoke, "Gallant deceived me for years."

Sam responded, "You know the rules of war, Tony."

"That's why I'm going to have you kill Gallant," Tony stated.

Sam said, "You know how I feel about him Tony."

"I know that's why you have to prove your loyalty to me," Tony responded.

"I already did that Tony when I introduced you to El Chapo," Sam said.

"Business is good with El Chapo. I have to give it to you, you've done great," Tony said.

"Thanks Tony," Sam responded.

"I must say that you've done so great that El Chapo is even talking about fronting me a thousand kilos. A deal that will make me the Cocaine King," Tony said.

"I'm happy for you, Tony. Your father would be proud," Sam said.

"Speaking of my father, I pledged my loyalty to him. That's why I'm asking you to do the honors of killing Gallant."

"You're asking me something that I never thought could be asked of me."

"Like I told you before, either you're with me or against me."

"I'm with you Tony."

Tony snorted some of the cocaine out of the small case. He knew his habit was getting worse, but he didn't' care because he could support it.

Geno said, "We're almost at the hospital, Tony. Clean yourself up."

Tony spoke, "I have a question for the both of you. I am my father's son. Do you both agree?"

Geno and Sam shook their heads indicating that they meant yes.

Tony continued, "My father left me thirty million dollars to pick up where he left off at and to kill the people that betrayed him."

Geno said, "The hospital is five minutes away. Can we discuss this some other time? Your grandmother needs you Tony."

"We're going to discuss this now." Tony responded in a casual tone. In his mind, the world was his and people were going to play to his tune.

Tony continued, "The world is mine."

Sam turned around and took the small case out of Tony's hand as Geno pulled the Cadillac up in the hospital parking lot. Tony didn't put up a fight. He checked his nose by wiping it with the back of his hand again. Once in the parking lot, Geno parked the car in a handicap spot. He hopped out of the Cadillac after Sam opened the back door for Tony. Then he helped Tony out of the car.

Tony spoke, "I can see that you are loyal, Geno. I can see this by looking through your windows."

Sam spoke, "My loyalty is for you Tony. Please don't ever doubt it. I wouldn't be here now with you if I wasn't loyal."

"Your windows say different, Sam."

When Tony, Geno and Sam walked inside the hospital, they were met by several nurses. The chubby, African American nurse pulled Tony to the side and asked, "Are you Tony Montana?"

"Yes."

"I don't know how to tell you this, but your grandmother passed away a few minutes ago."

Tony couldn't believe what he had heard. It had been two weeks since his grandmother had entered the hospital. There was no sign of her dying from the assault. In fact, after the heart attack her health improved.

Tony asked, "Can I see her?"

The nurse said, "Sure. But only family."

Tony followed in behind the nurse to the room where they were keeping his grandmother. When he entered the room, he noticed it was cold and that his grandmother looked asleep inside the hospital bed. Someone had combed her hair and made it look decent. The dim light added color to her pale skin.

Tony spoke, "Please leave us alone."

The nurse turned and walked out the room. Tony walked over to the bed and stood beside it. He stared over at his grandmother for a full five minutes before he said, "I let you down, Mama. I'm sorry..." The tears rolled down Tony's face as he grabbed his grandmother's hand. He continued, "I will get the people that did this to you. I promise, Mama."

Agent Tadeo and his crew were shocked to learn that they had been relieved of their duties to follow José Rivera. This was after they returned to town for supplies. Agent Tadeo and his team were upset about the news, but they knew they couldn't do anything about it. An order by his superiors had been sent with the team to inform him and his team that they had to return to the United States immediately. There was no reason on the order. This was why Agent Tadeo was confused about the order.

After informing the other team about the past week's events on José's Compound, Agent Tadeo and his team caught a flight back to Miami. They arrived the next morning at the Miami Airport where a government van was waiting on them. They all got in the van after a short debriefing of why they were called in to the Miami Headquarter. After arriving at the Headquarters, Agent Tadeo and his team were informed that they were needed on another matter. Agent Tadeo was furious about the new assignment, but when he heard that it had to do with a Mafia killing and El Chapo, he thanked his superiors and promised them that he would do what they were asking.

They informed Agent Tadeo that El Chapo had been spotted in Miami. El Chapo was on the FBI's Most Wanted list, and he had been on the list for years. Instead of being loathe about his new assignment, Agent Tadeo embraced his new task. He looked over all of the new cases while they rode along Washington Avenue after leaving the FBI Headquarters.

When he looked at the information about El Chapo, several statements stood out that caught his attention. El Chapo had been seen in Miami over the last month and had even been seen with Cuba Sam, a known associate of the Miami Mafia. This shocked Agent Tadeo, because he thought El Chapo was in South America and he thought that Sam was out of the drug business.

Agent Tadeo looked at the two mafia figures' files and found out that big Paul and Demiles had been killed. There were several witnesses in Demiles' case, but these witnesses had changed their stories when the FBI interviewed them. This gave Agent Tadeo the assumption that someone had interfered with the investigation. But who and why?

Dean pulled the van in front of their headquarters and noticed that there was a letter stuck in between the front entrance door. The grass on the outside of the place looked like it needed to be trimmed and the building looked abandoned from a distance. Agent Tadeo spoke, "We have work to do here. It's been months since we've been here, so be careful when you all enter."

All the men in the van cracked smiles at Agent Tadeo after his comical comment. Agent Tadeo pulled the letter that was addressed to him out of the door and opened it in front of his team. Then he said, "I'm going to need a couple of minutes alone." The team excused themselves and left him alone. He read the letter quietly to himself after taking a seat on the front steps of the building. The letter was typed up on white paper in computer ink. It said:

Dear Agent Tadeo,

First off, I would like to say that I'm sorry that I had to take you off of José's case. I know how much that case meant to you and your team, but I have other issues that need to be solved. I know that you and your team are the only people I know can get answers. I know you have looked over the files by now and know about El Chapo arriving in the United States and the two mafia bosses' deaths. I don't know if these cases are connected, but I need you to find out. I believe there is a link and the link will give you all of the answers that I need. There is something that I've been meaning to tell you for years, but I never found the time to tell you. Big Paul helped me get in position to become head of the Miami FBI. I know this is shocking news to you, but Big Paul worked for me for twenty years and Demiles did too. They were my best informants. That's why I need to know who murdered them. Do this deed for me. I really do appreciate your help, and I will make sure you return to your mission of catching José in the future.

Thank you,

Agent Woodard

Agent Tadeo put the letter in his pocket and walked in the building. He was ambivalent about the matter, and he couldn't see how Agent Woodard would have allowed himself to get caught up with such corrupted people. In Agent Tadeo's eyes, this was like making a deal with the devil.

Agent Tadeo knew he didn't have a choice in the matter because if he didn't, he would have been advised of his choices when he was still in South America. Quitting the force wasn't an option, because he knew he couldn't track Jose unless he had the government resources. Agent Tadeo didn't want to disappoint Agent Woodard, because Agent Woodard had always had his back when things looked bleak when he as chasing after José. This was why his loyalty was with Agent Woodard. It was time to find out what was going on in the city of Miami and then return to his mission of Capturing José.

CHAPTER 34

Tony woke up feeling like his life was in a bad state after a long night of drinking and snorting cocaine. The day before, he had watched as his grandmother was put in the ground. It was still hard for him to grasp the fact that his grandmother had died in the hospital after her assault. Geno convinced Tony to get a suite instead of staying in his grandmother's house because of the memories of staying in the house with his grandmother.

After taking a shower and putting on a new Armani suit and shoes, Tony walked in the front room of the suite where Sam and Geno were watching the news. The sun was shining brightly through the windows of the room, and the smell of McDonald's was in the room too. Both Sam and Geno were dressed in nice suits too, and they were wearing matching blue shoes that looked like they cost a pretty penny.

Tony spoke, "I have decided I'm going to pay Mr. Stein a visit."

Geno said, "Today is your birthday, Tony. We should celebrate."

Sam responded, "Yes Tony. We should celebrate."

Tony said, "Not until Mr. Stein and Gallant are dead."

Sam said, "I heard Gallant has closed his deal on selling the store. He's leaving town any day now."

"He's not going to make it out of town."

Sam interrupted, "You are under a lot of stress Tony. I think it's time you get some rest."

Tony shouted, "Not until the roaches that killed my grandmother are in the ground. Now, I don't want to talk about nothing but getting these two roaches. When they're dead, I'm happy. If I'm happy, then we all will be happy."

"There is bigger business Tony. El Chapo wants to front you a thousand kilos. He only wants ten million for these kilos. There isn't any cocaine on the East Coast because there is a drought. The U.S. isn't letting any drugs in."

Tony interrupted, "Shut up Sam... I don't want to hear anything about drugs."

Tony pulled out his small gold case out of his front pocket of his suit. Then, he laid out most of the cocaine inside the case on the glass table in the room. Geno spoke, "Tony, it's too early to be getting blasted."

"This is my coca... I snort it when I feel like. You two had McDonald's for breakfast, I'm having coca for breakfast. And if I want it for lunch and dinner it's my prerogative."

Sam said, "You have been going a little hard on the coca, Tony."

Tony interrupted, "My grandmother just passed. I need this to help with my pain."

Geno said, "We are here Tony, because we care about you."

"I know you are loyal, Geno. That's why I need you to go with me to Mr. Stein's office to get my thirty million. I also need you to do me a big favor."

"What is it Tony?"

"When the time comes I will let you know."

"I've got your back, and your front Tony."

"What about you Sam?"

Sam responded, "I'm with you Tony."

"I need you to go check out a warehouse. We're going to need a large one, because I'm going to buy the thousand kilos from El Chapo after I get my money from Mr. Stein."

"Okay, Tony."

"It's Boss Tony…"

"Okay Boss Tony."

"Geno, get the car ready. We have to go see Mr. Stein. Today is the day I pick up my lottery money."

"Okay, Boss." Geno walked out of the suite as Tony said, "One last thing, Sam. I need you to get some men to help guard my thousand kilos and I want you to see how much my father's old house cost."

Sam responded, "Those properties in that area cost in the millions, Tony"

"I don't care how much it costs, I want my father's old house."

"I will take care of that Tony, and the men."

"The world is mine… I'm Tony Montana Jr."

Tony put the small case back in his pocket and walked over to the door after Sam opened it for him. Geno was behind the wheel of the Cadillac. The fresh Miami air hit Tony in the face as he walked out of the room and got in the Cadillac. He waved to Sam as he and Geno pulled out of the parking lot. Fifteen minutes later, they pulled up at Mr. Stein's office building. After getting his Armani briefcase out the trunk of the vehicle, Tony told Geno to stay in the car. After he explained to Geno that he needed to talk to Mr. Stein alone about the money. He even told Geno how Mr. Stein had been invited to his grandmother's funeral and didn't show up. Tony didn't like the fact that Mr. Stein was acting like a prevaricator. He knew why Mr. Stein lied about coming to his grandmother's funeral, but he didn't want Mr. Stein to know. This was why he had shown up unexpectedly at Mr. Stein's office.

Tony walked inside the beautiful brick building with large windows that over looked the downtown Miami area. It was a Friday morning, so business wasn't busy like mid-week. The smell of car engines and food hit Tony's nose before he had entered the lobby of the building. Once inside, Tony took the elevator to the fourth floor where Mr. Stein's office was located. Tony had learned about Mr. Stein's office through the internet and even looked over the different exits of the building on this same web page.

Tony knew the bank was right across the street from the office and that there was a parking garage that most of the attorneys in this building used for parking. There were blinds spots in this garage that Tony had discovered while looking at the map of the garage. This was how he had formed his plan to kill Mr. Stein.

Tony walked inside the lobby of Mr. Stein's office. He smiled at the white twenty-ish woman behind the desk that was dressed in a blue business suit. Her hair was in a long ponytail with a gold ribbon holding it in place. Her face was filled with make-up, in which made her look like she was about to go on air in a TV show. Tony waited until the young woman hung up the phone before he approached her at her marble and wooden desk. As he had approached her, he noticed her taking notice of his two thousand dollar briefcase and his thousand dollar matching gator shoes. He had ordered the collection off of the internet after seeing a runway show on the internet.

Tony spoke, "I would like to know if Mr. Stein is here?"

The chubby faced secretary responded, "Do you have an appointment?"

"No… but I really need to talk to him."

"What's your name?"

"I'm Tony Montana Jr."

"Let me see if he's busy."

Tony watched as the secretary dialed Mr. Stein's extension. He could tell that she was pious to Mr. Stein because she turned in the opposite direction after she had said his name. This was rude in Tony's book. He knew Mr. Stein wasn't going to talk to him because Mr. Stein had been dodging his calls. Tony watched as the secretary became evasive after she got off of the phone. When she said, "He's busy, come back some other time." He knew he was going to have to take action like he had already prepared to do. He asked, "When can I see him?"

"Not today. He's full all day."

"I guess I will have to come back another day."

"You have a nice day, Mr. Montana."

Tony turned to leave after the secretary exposed all thirty something of her white teeth to him. Then he texted Geno. In the text, he had instructed Geno to camp out at the garage where Mr. Stein's BMW was parked. Then Tony turned back around in the secretary's direction and asked, "Excuse me. Is there a restroom I can use?"

The secretary had picked the phone back up and was attending a call. She said, "Yes. Right down the hallway on the right."

Tony walked slowly down the hallway while looking at the names that were on the doors of the offices of the lawyers. When he came across Mr. Stein's office, he gathered his thoughts and grabbed the door knob before, he looked to see if the secretary was looking from the lobby. He could see that she was still talking on the phone non-stop. Tony opened the door and quickly stepped inside. Mr. Stein was on his office phone looking out his office window. As he turned to hang up the phone, he was startled by Tony's presence."

Tony said, "Hi there, Stein."

Mr. Stein reached for the phone. Tony pulled out the nine mill that he had tucked in his briefcase. Then he asked, "Why haven't you been answering my calls?"

"I've been busy Tony... You have to forgive me."

"God forgives... I don't Stein..."

"What is this about Tony?"

"You know Stein. Cut the act."

Tony could see the sweat forming on Mr. Stein's forehead.

"No act, Tony. I swear to God that I was going to contact you about your grandmother's will." Mr. Stein reached for a file that he had on the desk.

Tony responded, "Why didn't you come to my grandmother's funeral?"

"I was busy, Tony. I'm really sorry."

"You're not sorry, Stein. I believe you are one of the reasons that she is dead."

"No… No…"

"What did you say to her at the hospital?"

"I didn't say anything Tony… I swear."

"My grandmother told me that you wanted the money. Now, I want to hear it from you."

"I swear Tony, it wasn't me."

Tony raised the gun, so it was pointing at Mr. Stein's head.

"Just tell me Stein… Who is the other guy that helped you?"

"I swear Tony… I didn't do anything. It wasn't me." Tony aimed the gun directly at Mr. Stein's head. Mr. Stein shouted, "Please… I have kids."

Tony knew Mr. Stein could see the hate in his eyes. His demeanor told him this. The way Mr. Stein was trying to avoid eye contact told Tony this.

Tony continued, "Was it Gallant?"

"Yes… It was Gallant. I didn't know he was going to do it."

"She trusted you, Stein."

"I swear Tony it wasn't my idea."

"Does Gallant know about the money?"

"Yes… Please listen Tony. Your grandmother didn't want the money. She said it was blood money."

Tony interrupted, "How did the money end up in my name?"

"Your grandmother decided to put it in your name after she decided that she didn't want it. The way the policy was written up before your father's death was for you mother. She was the person that was supposed to receive the money, but when she died after your birth, your grandmother became the person that received the money."

"How did you find me?"

"I tracked you down after I found out that your mother birthed you at the Miami Hospital. This was after my father passed from cancer and I became a partner. I did this hoping that your grandmother would give the money to my father's foundation for cancer research."

"I don't believe you."

"You've got to believe me Tony."

"I looked over all the fine print. I know the money goes to you if I don't want it."

"It's not what you think, Tony."

"I see the clear picture, Stein. Your greediness has gotten you caught up."

"It's more to it, Tony."

"I know that's why I'm going to give you a chance to correct your wrongs. I want you to go over to the bank and put the thirty million in my account.

"I can't do it today."

"If you want to live, you will."

"It might be too late for such a big transaction."

Tony looked at his gold Rolex and said, "It's 3:30pm. I'm sure you can pull some strings."

"If I don't? Then what?"

"Then you die."

"Really Tony, I didn't mean for this to turn out like it did."

Tony put his finger to his mouth indicating to Mr. Stein to stop talking. Mr. Stein did just that. Tony said, "Now, I'm a man of my word. I promise I will not kill you for what you have done if you make this go smooth."

Then minutes later, Tony and Mr. Stein walked over to the bank and had the money transferred into Tony's account. They returned to Mr. Stein's office two hours later. Back in the office, Tony texted Geno and told him that he had the money. Mr. Stein offered Tony a drink after making himself one. Tony declined and then said, "There is one more thing. Who assaulted my grandmother?"

"You are a very rich man, Tony. You shouldn't be worried about past events. It's time you enjoy life. We should celebrate."

"I wouldn't celebrate anything with you."

"Why are you being so rude? You have your money, Tony."

"Money isn't everything. My grandmother is someone that I loved dearly."

"I didn't want to get involved, but seeing you here today made me realize that I did the right thing when I recorded Gallant."

"What are you talking about?"

Tony watched as Mr. Stein turned the recording on after he hit a button on his phone. Tony listened as Gallant told Mr. Stein in detail about the assault. Gallant's voice was unequivocal on the recording in which touched a nerve in Tony.

Tony spoke, "Why did he tell you this?"

Mr. Stein took a drink of hard liquor before he said, "He wanted me to be his lawyer."

"Are you his lawyer?"

Tony watched as Mr. Stein opened his arms like he was about to catch something out of midair and said, "Tony, it's never personal. It's business." Mr. Stein sealed his own fate by saying that he represented Gallant.

Tony responded, "I see your position. I understand."

"Please Tony, you must understand… Gallant threatened to kill me."

"You broke your client privilege with Gallant."

"I know, Tony."

"This is why I don't believe you, Stein. You will do anything to stay alive."

"You have to trust me, Tony. You trusted me when we walked over to the bank! I didn't try anything."

"You are not in a position to try anything, Stein. You lost that when you played the recording."

"What are you talking about Tony? You promised me you wouldn't kill me. You promised…"

Tony knew he promised Mr. Stein that he wouldn't kill him but he didn't promise him that Geno wouldn't do it.

Tony turned to leave, and then he stopped by Mr. Stein. And, Mr. Stein said, "If you ever need me Tony, call me." Tony smiled and walked out of the office. He didn't even look at the secretary as he walked through the lobby to leave the building. Once outside, he noticed Geno pulling up in the Cadillac. Tony opened the passenger door and got inside the car. Geno pulled over the curb as Tony spoke, "Mr. Stein must die tonight."

Geno asked, "What happened in there?"

"He's the guy that's pulling Gallant's strings. They conspired to assault my grandmother."

"I'll take care of him, Tony."

"Make sure you leave a hundred dollar bill by him with blood on it."

Tony pulled a few bills out of his pocket and handed them to Geno. Then he continued, "Make sure you put these bills in his mouth."

CHAPTER 35

Agent Tadeo decided it was best to go back to his old stomping grounds to try to get some answered about the two murders and El Chapo. It had been nearly a year since he had ridden down South Beach Strip. Even thought he had grown up in North Carolina, he knew the city of Miami like the back of his hand. His familiarity with the city came from his days of tracking Tony Montana Sr.

While riding the strip, Gallant Castro's face popped into Agent Tadeo's mind. It had been about two years since he had seen Gallant. Whenever he was close to South Beach, he had always ridden past Gallant's store just to see if it was still open. He did this because he knew Gallant had been a witness in helping with Tony Sr.'s drug case and he knew he was going to have to use Gallant as a witness if he ever caught The Source.

Agent Tadeo pulled the Range Rover along the curb in front of Gallant's store. He was shocked to see that the five Cubans that were on the store front had aged just a little. He knew most of these men, because he had been in contact with them during his investigation of Tony Sr. He stepped out of the Range Rover after checking his nine mill, and his throw away pistol that he had strapped to his ankle.

The sun was cool, and the summer heat wasn't as hot as it was usually. Dressed in Ray Bans, blue shorts, Polo shirt and black Nikes, Agent Tadeo was fit for the weather. He was even fit to take care of himself if need be. He had let his team have the day off. He decided it wasn't a sin to question old witnesses about new cases.

Looking more like a tourist, instead of an FBI Agent, Agent Tadeo walked up to the store front and greeted all five men with a wave. As he made his way into the store, he noticed Gallant was standing behind the counter watching TV. When Agent Tadeo had entered the store the smell of fresh roasted peanuts was in the air along with the smells of all the different foods that South Beach had to offer.

Agent Tadeo removed his Ray Bans after looking over the store. Then he asked, "What's going on, Gallant?"

Gallant recognized Agent Tadeo instantly. He responded, "What are you doing here?"

"I was just passing through."

"It's been years since you've been here. Have you caught The Source?"

"No… but I'm still working on that case."

"What brings you here?"

"I just wanted to ask you about the Mafia murders."

"I don't know anything."

"Sure you do, Gallant."

"I promise you I've been a clean man and I don't hang out in the streets." Gallant looked at his Bible on the counter.

"What about El Chapo?"

"Is that the Mexican Drug lord that's wanted by the government?"

"Yes. He's been spotted here in Miami."

"You think he killed those Mafia bosses?"

"That's what I'm trying to find out."

"Well I can't help you."

"Didn't I help you, Gallant?"

"Not really… I lost my leg before you came along."

"Just give me a name, Gallant."

"I don't have a name…"

The news on the TV caught Gallant's attention. He held his hand up to stop Agent Tadeo from talking. He listened to the news reporter as the news reporters described how Mr. Stein was found dead inside the downtown garage with a hundred dollar bill with blood on it in his hand. And, there was before several hundred dollar bills stuffed in his mouth. Gallant spoke, "That' my friend… he's dead."

"Do you know who did it, Gallant?"

Gallant turned the TV off, and then he walked over to the cooler where the Budweiser's were located. He pulled out a six pack and popped open one of the cans. Then he swallowed the liquid like it was the last beer on earth. Agent Tadeo felt like he was onto something. There was something in Gallant's demeanor that gave Agent Tadeo this thought. He asked, "Was he your lawyer too, Gallant?"

"Yes… I knew him for about five years. He was a great man."

"Who do you think did it to him?"

"You wouldn't believe me if I told you."

"Test me."

"Tony Montana's kid."

"I don't have time for games, Gallant."

"I'm serious. The kid is just like his father."

"Why would he kill your friend?"

"I don't know for sure, but one thing I know is I'm not safe."

"Why do you say this?"

"He knows that I had a problem with his father."

"How does he know that?"

"He used to work for me."

"What? Are you kidding me Gallant?"

"No… I did it as a favor to my friend."

"The one that was killed last night in the garage?"

"Yes…"

"What's the motive, Gallant?"

"Money. Mr. Stein owed him money. A lot of money."

"Do you owe him money?"

"No…"

"Well why would he come after you?"

"I owed his father money."

"What does that have to do with him?"

"Do you remember how vicious his father was?"

"Yes. What does that have to do with Tony Montana Jr.?"

"He's much smarter and vicious."

"Why do you say these things about a young man that doesn't have a criminal record?"

"Word on the street is that he had something to do with those Mafia boss killings. The Mafia has sent men here asking questions."

"What did you tell them?"

"I told them that I didn't know Tony!"

"You lied for him… why?"

"Tony hasn't been here since his grandmother passed away several weeks ago. Well, I was going to sell the place right before I heard the news, but the deal fell apart because I forgot to sign one of the deeds."

"What does this have to do with Tony?"

"Word is he stole the lady's car that is buying my place. This took place the night one of the Mob bosses was killed."

"Now I'm lost. You're telling me that Tony Montana Jr. killed a Mafia boss?"

"Two Mafia bosses."

"The two murders that I'm investigating?"

"Yes… He's your man."

"What's your proof?"

"He hasn't been here. That's proof that he did it."

"That's not enough…. I need evidence that links Tony to the murders. All three of them if you want me to arrest him."

"I'm going to need some time."

"I don't have time, Gallant. The Source is in South America and he's still making drugs."

"I promise you, I will get some answers by the end of the week."

"I'm counting on you, Gallant. Don't let me down. I hate to have to bring those old murder charges that I dropped for you, back up."

Agent Tadeo winked at Gallant, grabbed a bag of cheese crackers off the front rack that was in front of the counter, then said, "Put this on the house…" Gallant made a disgusted face gesture as Agent Tadeo walked out of the store. He watched as Tadeo got back in the Range Rover and pulled off. He picked up his phone and dialed Sam's cell phone number. The phone went straight to voicemail. It had been weeks since he had talked with Sam. He didn't understand why Sam hadn't been by after the day he was talking in riddles. This was why he was perplexed at the moment.

Gallant decided to call Valentina to see if she had gotten the deals done with the other store owners. When she answered the phone he said, "Good afternoon, this is Mr. Castro."

She responded, "It's nice to hear from you."

"I called because I haven't heard anything from you since the day I forgot to sign my name on one of the contracts."

"I hear desperation in your voice. What's wrong?"

"There is no desperation… I was just thinking it was time to get out of town."

"How can I help?"

"Write out a check. We can handle the paperwork later."

"You know I'm a woman that's about her business. I have the new contract written up. I can hand deliver it myself today."

"That would be great…"

"Do you need anything other than your money?"

"Yes. I need a first class ticket to Boston."

"I can arrange that too."

"We'll see you soon."

"I'll be there by three pm."

"Fine."

"Make sure you have the deed to the property."

"I have it. I will sign it over to you once the check is in my hand."

Gallant ended the call after he said goodbye. Then, he walked to the back of the store and started packing. There wasn't any time to waste. The 4th of July was in two days and there was going to be a large celebration all over the city. This was going to be the perfect time to slip out of the city.

CHAPTER 36

Tony turned off the large screen TV inside of the hotel suite after seeing the news about Mr. Stein's death. He was satisfied at the fact that Geno had done exactly what he had instructed him to do. Mr. Stein was found with a mouth full of dead presidents and a bill with blood on it in his hand. This was the death sentence that Mr. Stein deserved, Tony thought as he poured some cocaine from his gold case on to the table inside the suite living room area.

Tony didn't think he had a habit, but Sam and Geno did. They were constantly asking him to slow down on the powder cocaine, because he was snorting almost a half an ounce a day. When he started out snorting, he just was using it to help him cope and stay awake at the hospital when his grandmother was in a coma. Now, he was snorting every hour on the hour. It was like cocaine was his life.

Tony was making a name in the underworld because the hundred kilos that he turned into two hundred kilos were gone in a two week period. The money was rolling in so fast that Tony had to rent another warehouse to stash the cash. The men Sam had hired were guarding the place twenty-four hours a day. This worked out for Tony, because he had always wanted to own his own business.

Tony took a snort form the small mountain of cocaine that he had put out for his enjoyment. This product wasn't cut like the cocaine that he was selling in the city. This was the pure stuff that El Chapo had sold him. This was the product that he had cut and turned one kilo into two. The cut stuff was being sold at twenty a kilo. The mid-dealers were paying twenty-five thousand a kilo. Everyone was making money, even the runners. Life was great for Tony and his crew, but there were a couple of loose strings that he had to tie up.

Toby Red Firm, Mr. Castro and the man that killed his father, I have to kill them Tony thought as he ran his nose across the glass table once again. After letting the cocaine drain, he took a drink of the wine that he had taken from the mini bar. Then, he laid down on the couch inside the room and thought about who he would murder first between the three men. First, it would be Mr. Castro on the 4th of July. Then, Toby and then the search would begin for the guy that killed his father.

Tony picked up his cell phone and called Import City Car lot. This was one of the largest Imported Car lots in Miami. They catered to anyone that had the money to buy their cars. Their cars were Maybach's, Maserati's, Range Rovers, Batman Benzes and any other kind of car that was on the market that could be ordered. Tony placed several orders. The guy on the phone thought Tony was playing, until Tony instructed him that he wanted to do a cash purchase. And, he didn't want the cash purchase to be on record. The guy hung up the phone on Tony. Tony laughed to himself because he knew the guy would be excited when he showed up at the lot with a million in cash. This transaction was going to take place right after he had taken out Gallant, Tony thought as he called El Chapo. Then he placed the order for the thousand kilos.

❖ ❖ ❖

Agent Tadeo was excited that he had found a name for a possible suspect in the Mob murders. In his heart, he didn't believe that Tony Montana Jr. could be the man that had taken out two mob bosses in a three month period. This just wasn't making sense to him. There was no motive. Not at the moment, Agent Tadeo thought as he pulled back up at his headquarters.

His team was in deep conversation when he entered the building. They were all sharing how they felt about being pulled off José's case to work on the Mob murders. The conversation ended when Agent Tadeo walked in after standing at the door listening for a full minute. He didn't say a word as he made his way upstairs to his office. The glass windows in his office gave him access to watch over the downstairs area like he was a Greek god. He closed his blinds to his office when he noticed his crew looking up towards his office. A few seconds later, Dean came knocking at the door. Agent Tadeo was checking his emails when Dean walked inside the office.

Dean asked, "Is everything okay, Boss?"

Agent Tadeo continue to look at the screen as he ran his fingers over the keys like he was working for a computer company. He spoke, "Yes. Everything is fine."

"Any leads?"

'I'm not sure. The name that I received, I'm not sure if he's the guy."

"Well, we're going out to get beer. Do you want to come?"

"No thanks. You all go ahead."

"You sure?"

"Yes… I have research to do on Tony Montana Jr."

"That's the guy's name?"

"Yes."

"How old is he?"

"He's twenty-one years old."

"That's too young to be a mob boss killer."

"You only have to be eighteen to go into the Army."

"You have a point. Age doesn't matter when death is at hand."

"Go get beer. I'll be here when you all return."

Dean didn't hesitate before he walked out of the office. Agent Tadeo watched as his team piled inside the Hummer V and disappeared off the lot. He wanted to tell his team about the letter that he had found the day they had returned to their Headquarters, but he didn't want them to know that they were looking for a mob informant killer. This would've caused them to doubt his judgment when it came to fighting the right cause. Agent Tadeo knew this because he knew his men like the back of his hands. They had been a team for five years now and had confided in each other over the five years. They had built bonds and these bonds led to them trusting each other with each other's lives.

At the moment, Agent Tadeo felt like his trust was being tested because at the briefing with his superiors he felt like this wasn't the right cause. In his mind, he felt like the Mob bosses got what they deserved because of the life they had been leading.

Agent Tadeo remembered all of the great speeches that he had given to his team about being true to self and having integrity. These speeches were delivered over the years while they were out all over the world chasing José. These speeches kept his team intact with their mission, especially in times of stress.

After answering the emails, Agent Tadeo turned his attention back to Tony. He decided he would call in a favor and see what he could come up with on Tony. While waiting on the friend from Washington to call, Agent Tadeo thought back over the conversation he had with Gallant. He knew that Tony Montana Jr. could be responsible because of Tony's lineage. Tony Jr.'s father was a killer and he had killed when it was necessary. Was Tony Jr. in this class just because of his lineage? Or was he intelligent and vicious like Gallant was proclaiming? These were the two questions that were flowing around in Agent Tadeo's head the whole time his team was out having drinks. When they returned he was creating a chart with the two mob bosses' pictures at the top of it. The two mob bosses members were under the bosses' heads on the chart. Demile had twenty members and Big Paul had thirty members.

Josh interrupted Agent Tadeo, "We are back… What's going on?"

Agent Tadeo continued to write. Dean said, "Man, we had fun. It's been a long time since we've enjoyed ourselves like he did tonight."

John said, "We brought some beer back for you."

Josh said, "We know you are trying to crack these cases, but you deserve to have some free time too."

Agent Tadeo turned around after writing the last note on the chart with a black marker and said, "I believe these cases are related."

Dean asked, "How so?"

"When I went to visit an old criminal earlier today, I found out through him about Tony Montana Jr. I know that I haven't told you all the whole story about Tony Sr. but I believe it's time. Tony Sr. is the reason I'm chasing José. When I was investigating Tony Sr., he was killed by José's men. Tony Sr. was my main target and he was powerful back in the mid-eighties. Back then, he was controlling the drug trade on the whole East Coast. He came from Cuba after the criminals were cast out of the country. Tony Sr. managed to bully his way into the cocaine business after being almost killed in a drug deal. I heard during this drug deal that Tony was tied up in a hotel bathroom and beaten half to death until his right hand man Mannie decided to show up."

Dean interrupted, "What does this have to do with the Mob murders?"

"Can't you see it's a takeover and revenge plot?"

John asked, "How did you come up with this?"

Agent Tadeo rubbed his hands together and continued, "When I was investigating Tony Sr., I found out there were a lot of people that owed him money before his death. One of the men was Big Paul. Tony Sr. never got to collect the money because he got murdered. As Agent Tadeo was looking through Big Paul's file, he found a statement from the bartender that she had stated a million dollars was taken from the safe in the building. But, she didn't know or see the men that did the murders or robbed the place."

Dean asked, "Do you think she had something to do with the murders?"

"No… But I do believe that she knows more than she is telling."

"Where is she now?"

"She left the city."

"Do you know where she went?"

"She has a grandmother that lives in South Carolina. I think she went there."

"Anything else that we need to know about in this case?"

"Yes… Tony Montana Jr. is the number one suspect for now."

"Do we have enough evidence to bring him in?"

"No…"

John injected his input, "I think we need to beat the streets. A Little foot work won't hurt."

"Good idea."

Agent Tadeo was satisfied with the outcome of the meeting. He still felt uneasy about searching for the Mafia bosses' killer. His position while on the force had always been to take down the bad guys. Not to protect or serve the bad guys.

After the meeting, all of the men hit the streets. They figured that they could go after the low level drug dealers to get them to talk about what was going on about the murders. In the past, this had worked for Agent Tadeo, but times were changing and crime was becoming harder to solve. Plus, the system was running out of funds to house criminals. Mass incarceration was already the American people's problem, because the United States had become a police country overnight. Agent Tadeo knew this, that's why he did things his way when it came to catching criminals. If he had to break the law to get his man, so be it. He would rather be judged by twelve than carried by six, this was his motto.

It was close to 9:00pm according to Tony's Rolex. This was the perfect time to enter Gallant's store because everyone was waiting on the fireworks show that was supposed to take place at 9:00pm. The strip was filled with kids and parents that were waiting on the show. There were people coming and going up and down the strip as the fireworks started. The smells of the ocean and the food were in the air. Tony knew that Gallant usually closed his store up on this night because he didn't want anyone to get hurt inside his store and file a lawsuit. The past two years Tony had watched the fireworks from the strip himself along with Geno by his side. This night, Tony was alone. This was how he wanted it to be. This is why he told Geno to stay at the suite until he returned.

Tony blended in with the crowd until he reached the strip where Gallant's store was located. His heart was pounding inside of his chest from the excitement of knowing that he was about to confront the man that had attacked his grandmother. And the man who had stolen money from his father. He had looked at killing Gallant like taking care of two birds with one stone. This was something he had to do, and he wanted to do it.

Tony approached the back of the store where a light was on in the storage room. He looked around before he approached the backdoor, where most of the supplies were carried in at. He knew the lock on the door was loose enough to be pulled off the door with a little help. There was a large two by four by him that blocked the door. Tony removed the two by four and used his pocket knife to open the lock. Tony watched a couple walk by before he entered the building. Once inside, he looked around the room for any signs of Gallant. No Gallant… The place had been cleaned up and Gallant's personal items were missing. The bed that Gallant took rest to was even missing. This put Tony in a perplexed state.

As Tony made his way to the dimly lit front area of the store, he noticed a shadow at the front entrance. He was watching as the shadow at the door unlocked the door and walked inside the building. He waited until Gallant locked the door back before he came out of the shadows. Tony spoke, "I thought you had left the city?"

Gallant was startled by Tony. He responded, "What are you doing here?"

"I was just about to ask you the same thing."

"I knew you would come Tony."

"Why didn't you run?"

"I planned to do that, but Valentina didn't write the check out until today."

"So you sold the place?"

Tears were forming in Gallant's eyes. "Yes…"

"Why?"

"I've got one leg Tony and I don't have long to live."

Tony shouted, "Stop your bloody crying. Be a man…"

"You think the world loves you Tony? You are a fool if you think that. This world is cruel. It's a give or take world."

"You proved that people could be cruel when you took my grandmother."

"I tried to help you, Tony."

'By beating my grandmother into a coma?"

"Did Stein tell you this?"

"He recorded you talking about it."

"I knew he wasn't worth a penny. I should have known he was going to sell me out."

Tony noticed the gun in Gallants front pants by his zipper.

"Toss the gun, Gallant."

"No… You know I can't do that, Tony."

Tony slowly moved his hand to his gun on his side, while keeping his eyes on Gallant. Gallant went for his gun as soon as he saw Tony going for his. Tony managed to get a shot off to Gallant's chest. Gallant fell to the floor. His eyes were blinking out of control. Tony walked over to Gallant and stood over him.

Tony spoke, "Why?" There was pure hate in Tony's voice.

"Your father ruined my life Tony when he took my leg."

"Why my grandmother?"

"It wasn't my idea, Tony."

Gallant coughed and blood came spilling out of his mouth. Tony knew it wasn't Gallant's idea. He just wanted to hear Gallant say it was Stein.

"Why did you go along with it?"

"Greed and revenge," Gallant responded.

"Why should I spare your life?"

The fireworks outside the store were getting louder by the second. There were people standing by the windows of the store, but they weren't paying Tony and Gallant any attention. The gunshot to Gallant's chest had blended in with the fireworks.

Gallant said, "There isn't a good reason you should spare my life. You have a justified reason to kill me."

"I trusted you, Gallant…"

"Jesus trusted Judas."

"You're right."

Gallant started laughing a taunting, wicked laugh. He even smiled a wicked smile at Tony as Tony pulled out his pocket knife. Tony grabbed Gallant by his neck and looked him in his eyes and said, "This is for my grandmother and father." Then he pushed the knife in Gallant's throat until he couldn't push it in any more. Blood spilled all over Tony's hands as he watched the life fade out of Gallant's body. He twisted the knife as he squeezed the handle to get more grip. He made sure that he looked into Gallant's eyes until Gallant's last breath. This was pure satisfaction for Tony.

CHAPTER 37

Valentina decided to take a trip to Vegas after she had finished putting all of her grandfather's money in the bank and closing the deal with Gallant. This was her reward to herself for all of the hard work that she was doing for herself and her grandfather. When she arrived at the airport she noticed a slim, mixed breed young woman dressed in the latest Prada collection. Her blonde hair was cut in a short style that brought out the woman's blue eyes. From the woman's demeanor, she was looking for a good time.

In front of the airport was a group of men that were passing out flyers that said, "What goes on in Vegas, Stays in Vegas." Also on the flyers were naked women that were for sale. Valentina watched as this exotic woman took one of the flyers out of one of the men's hands. Then, she watched as the woman got in the back of a black Lincoln that was waiting by the curb. The exotic woman noticed Valentina eye-balling her and winked at Valentina before she got in the back of the Lincoln. This gesture from the woman heightened Valentina's sexual senses. This was what Valentina loved about seeing new prey. The hunt and the chase were what turned her on the most.

Valentina grabbed one of the flyers and looked at it. The words, "New In Town" were printed on the inside of it. It showed several women in full-color, incredible explicit photos of exotic, mix breed girls on top of a waterbed and nude. One of the girls were laying back on the bed while one was in between her legs. The bed was filled with satin pillows and silk sheets. Printed at the bottom of the picture was the name "Diamond" and a phone number along with the words "I will come to your room tonight!"

Valentina wasn't surprised at how brazen the ads were. She knew how Vegas operated, and she knew the motto was what most people adopted when they came to Vegas. This was what she liked about Vegas. Valentina stuffed the flyer in her Prada bag and thought to herself. "What would it be like to be Diamond for one night?" No matter how much any woman might deny it, every woman has had a fantasy of being a hooker one time or another. Knowing that a man or woman wanted you so much that he or she is willing to pay for sex was an incredibly wonderful feeling. This was what Valentina was thinking as she was flagging down a cab.

She instructed the driver to follow the woman in the black Lincoln. This brought on Valentina's sense of awareness in her sex pot. Her juices were brewing like beer in a factory. As the black Lincoln turned into the MGM Hotel parking lot, she didn't know that she had come so much inside the back of the cab. Because she had been too busy caressing herself. The black driver of the cab didn't even know what she was doing in the back seat because she had a towel over her lap.

After getting out of the cab and instructing the driver to bring her luggage inside the hotel lobby, Valentina looked around the lobby for her prey. Her prey was standing at the check-in counter. She walked over to the woman and introduced herself. "Excuse me, my name is Annie Jones. I was wondering if you could join me for a drink later?"

The woman looked into Valentina's eyes like they were the only two eyes in the lobby and said, "Sure." Then reached her hand out to shake Valentina's hand. Valentina asked, "What's your name?"

The woman answered, "Is that important?"

Valentina could have put her hand on the Bible and sworn that this woman was fermenting right in her presence. The smell was fruitful mixed with body sweat. This gave Valentina permission to investigate the woman's full physical body. She loved what she was looking at, after she had arrived at the fresh manicured toes of the woman.

Valentina spoke, "Is it okay if I call you Diamond?"

"Sure. We are in Vegas."

It didn't take Valentina long to get checked into her suite. She unpacked all of her clothes and took a hot bath. She wanted to be clean and relaxed before she met up with Diamond. When she got the call from Diamond, she was already dressed in a Fendi dress with matching red heels. Her sex kit was sitting on the living room leather white couch. Inside of it was a large black dildo, handcuffs, a rabbit, sex-hole cream that tingles like Halls coughs drops and leg irons.

After her call with Diamond, she went to Diamond's suite. When she arrived at Diamond's suite five minutes later, she could hear the smooth sounds of jazz flowing inside the suite. The smell of lemon and cinnamon lingered in the hallway along with the hotel's food. Valentina waited patiently at the door after she knocked twice. The smells were starting to get to her. The mixtures of lemon and cinnamon turned the sex side on in her.

Diamond opened the door after looking through the peephole. Valentina spoke, "You look nice." Diamond was dressed in a purple one piece dress with noodle strings holding it in place. The dress looked more like something a woman would wear to bed. Her white heels were open toed with straps that reached up to the calf area. Her makeup was flawless.

Diamond asked, "Would you like a drink?"

"Sure." Valentina walked in with her sex kit in her hand. The suite was one of the most exclusive, extraordinary, extravagant places that she had ever set foot in. There was a large bar with all kinds of liquor and beer to choose from. The view was so beautiful that it was breathtaking. The whole strip was live and looked like a world inside a world. The furniture was white leather like Valentina's suite. There were high priced pictures on the walls and glass everywhere. The soft white carpet looked like a large pillow and felt just as soft.

When Diamond handed Valentina the drink Valentina responded by planting a kiss on Diamond's lips. Diamond responded back by sticking her tongue down Valentina's throat. They kissed for several minutes before they made their way into the large bedroom of the suite. They both quickly stripped out of their clothes. Then they went at each other like two porn stars. This was the sensation that Valentina had been looking forwards to. The chase was over.

CHAPTER 38

Tony walked into his new home that was once his father's. He couldn't believe he had gotten the owner to sell him the house for ten million, when it was market priced at twelve million. When he walked inside the house, he felt a sense of his father's presence. It was something about the house that had him feeling like he was in the right place. He had been told stories about how his father was gunned down inside the house. There were no signs that a gun fight had ever taken place. All of the walls were filled with high prices art work that Tony couldn't pronounce. There were even other items that came with the house like a statue of the Virgin Mary.

Tony tried his best to picture his father twenty-one years ago inside of the large estate. He looked over the French stairway when he reached the top of the stairs. He held out his hands and shouted, "The world is mine!"

Geno interrupted Tony's moment when he walked inside the room with Sam on his trail. He spoke, "Tony... I have El Chapo on the phone. He's ready to do business."

Tony smiles and said, "Who put this shit together… I did! Tell El Chapo I said wait."

Sam said, "That's not good business, Tony."

"I'm the boss, Sam."

"Sorry, Tony…"

"Don't be sorry Sam. You don't get paid to be sorry. You get paid just to be Sam."

Geno said, "What do you want me to do, Tony?"

"Tell El Chapo, we do business in two weeks. I have something I need to take care of."

Sam interrupted again, "You can't put a man like El Chapo on hold, Tony."

"I'm the man with the money. He wants my money, so therefore he moves to my beat."

"This is the wrong approach. You're asking for trouble."

"El Chapo doesn't want war with me. I'm the King of the jungle right now. I run the East Coast and I'm planning to take the West Coast when El Chapo sells me the thousand kilos. Now, Geno end the call and call the Import Car lot. I have to pick up Valentina's Maserati."

Geno responded, "Anything else, boss?"

"Yes… make plans for a trip out of the country."

"Where to?"

"Where do you think Valentina wants to go for our date?"

Sam said, "You think she's going to go out with you, Tony?"

"Didn't she say she would, if I hit the lottery? Well, I hit the lottery. I'm worth thirty million."

Tony dismissed Geno and Sam from his presence after he finished his statement. He was serious about making Valentina his first lady. There was no other woman on his agenda that was high class like Valentina. It wasn't about having Valentina as a show pony, it was about bringing her into his world. Tony wanted this since the day he had met her at Gallant's store. Now, the time was here. It was time to show Valentina that he was more than a bag boy.

Valentina picked up her Prada underwear off of the marble floor and put them in her sex kit bag. Then, she slipped into her dress and pulled out a thousand dollars out of it that she had put into the pocket of the dress the day before. She separated all ten-hundred-dollar bills, and then she laid them on the nightstand inside the suite. After looking at Diamond, whose real name was Pam Oliver, she made her way back to her suite.

Once inside her suite, she called her office back in Miami and found out that Mr. Castro had been murdered on the fourth of July. She couldn't believe what she was hearing from her assistant. Because before she had decided to take the trip to Vegas she had written Mr. Castro a check for a million dollars. This check was written on her business account and she had met with him briefly at his store to close the deal. Now that he was dead, she didn't know if the deal would go through.

Valentina booked the next plane back to Miami. Then, she took her a shower and packed up her luggage. After having breakfast and doing a little shopping, she took a cab to the airport. While at the airport, she thought about Tony. It had been a while since she had last seen him. Even though she hadn't saw Tony, that didn't stop her from having fantasies about him.

While on her plane ride back to Miami, Valentina decided that she would have a little fun by herself. She unbuckled her seatbelt and walked slowly to the restroom in the First-Class Section. Once in the bathroom, she closed the door behind herself. Then, she pulled out her rabbit as she pulled up her skirt. The small sex toy was small enough for her to carry inside of her skirt pocket.

It didn't take her long to get herself aroused after thinking about Tony. She needed this release. The sex episode with Pam in Vegas was okay, but it wasn't enough to calm her nerves. Knowing that Mr. Castro had been murdered, this put her in a state of doubt about the deal. The only way to calm her nerves was to get a quick release.

It didn't take Valentina long to get herself to climax. She closed her eyes and worked the rabbit around on her clit. She thought deeply about Tony as she did this. She pictured Tony licking in between her legs and thighs as he worked his way up to her breasts and her neck. Then, to her lips. They tongue wrestled while she helped him insert his penis inside of her. This picture was clear to her and it brought her over the edge when Tony pounded inside of her like he was trying to knock her back out of place. Valentina climaxed all over her manicured hands and looked at herself in the mirror after her sex act. She said to herself, "Wow. I know the real thing will be great!"

Valentina cleaned herself up and went back to her First Class seat. She relaxed as she put her headphones on and turned on Quincy Jones's Heaven's Girl. This was a 90's jazz feel hip hop joint. She enjoyed the song while thinking about Tony. In her mind, she could see herself with Tony. She had a change of heart after realizing that she had been dodging love. It was time for her to face reality. Tony was the man for her. But how would she convince him that she was serious about having a relationship with him after she had belittled him in front of his friend.

CHAPTER 39

Agent Tadeo pulled the H2 Hummer in the front area of Gallant's store. The store was still a crime scene. There were hundreds of people standing around watching the forensics team collect evidence. Agent Tadeo couldn't believe that Gallant was dead, because he had talked to him two days before his death. This was why he was shocked about Gallant's death, because Gallant didn't show any signs that he was in any trouble.

Agent Tadeo had heard about Gallant's murder on the police radio that he often listened to after his team was asleep. After hearing Gallant's name over the radio, he left his team a hand written note saying that he was doing some investigation, and he would be out for a while. While on his way to the murder scene, he thought back over the last conversation that he had had with Gallant. Gallant had told him about Tony Montana Jr. Was Tony the killer? This was what Agent Tadeo asked himself while trying to find a motive. Then, it hit him. Was Tony trying to get revenge for his father? Did Tony know about Gallant not paying the debt?

TONY MONTANA JR.

Agent Tadeo did his own investigation while on the scene. He noticed that several spots on the countertop had been wiped down, and that Gallant had imprints on his neck that looked like gloves. There were too many footprints inside the store to tell whether there was more than one killer, until he made his way to the back of the store. There were a set of shoe prints by the backdoor that looked like a size nine.

Agent Tadeo pulled out a pen and put it beside the shoe print. The pen fit inside the foot print twice. Agent Tadeo wrote down a few notes and then he went to the officer that was in charge of the case and advised him that there was only one killer. Then, he walked out of the back door of the store while following the foot prints. He noticed a homeless man lying behind a dumpster that catered to the stores on the block. Agent Tadeo walked slowly over to the man and shook him until the man looked up from under the newspapers that he had over him.

The homeless black man said, "Leave me alone."

Agent Tadeo asked, "How long have you been our here?"

"I haven't seen nothing or heard anything."

Agent Tadeo knew this routine. He spoke, "I'm not here to ask you if you've seen anything. I want to know if you had anything to eat?"

The man looked up with his big eyes. There was cold in between his eyelids. His clothes were old, secondhand and his hair was under an old Yankees cap. He smelled like the dumpster that he was sleeping beside.

"No, I haven't eaten in two days."

"Why?"

"I've got a drug problem that I've got to feed."

"Would you like something to eat?"

"Yes… give me the money."

"I can't do that."

There was someone shouting off in the distance that caught both of their attention before the homeless man said, "I don't fuck with cops."

'I'm not a cop at the moment."

"Get out of here."

"What's your name?"

"I don't have a name. I lost my name a long time ago."

"I know you have a name."

"If I tell you my name will you leave me alone?"

"Yes…"

"My name is crackhead."

"That's not your real name."

"Well, take me to jail. I can get something to eat there."

"I'm not going to take you to jail. I just want to know if you've seen anyone leave Mr. Castro's store since you've been here?"

"When, last night?"

"No, tonight."

"No…"

"So, did you see anyone last night?"

"I don't want to talk anymore."

Agent Tadeo watched as the homeless man turned over and put his head back up under the newspapers. He decided not to push on. He put one of his cards under the man's card board box that looked like it was being used for shelter, and then he walked back to the crime scene. After checking in with the lead officer, he left and went back to his headquarters. His team was still asleep. There was no need for the note, so he threw it in the trash. Now that Gallant was dead, Agent Tadeo was back to square one.

CHAPTER 40

Tony purchased a black Maybach, two Range Rovers and a black Ferrari. He decided to buy Valentina a white Maserati with pink interior and he put a set of a dozen roses on the front passenger seat. Then, he called Geno on his cell phone and said, "Come over to Import Car lot. I need you and Sam to help me surprise Valentina."

"What do you have in mind Tony?"

"I purchased her a Maserati."

"Tony you don't really know Valentina."

"I know enough."

Geno arrived fifteen minutes later with Sam and several hired hands. Sam handpicked these men and gave them jobs at Tony's estate. Tony didn't care that most of these men had been to prison, the only things he cared about with these men was that they were willing to kill for him.

Tony had two of the twelve men escort him over to Valentina's office. One of the wanna-be wise guys drove the tow truck with Valentina's Maserati on the back of it, while the other guy chauffeured Tony in the Maybach. While riding in the back seat of the Maybach, Tony pulled out Valentina's business card and dialed her number. A secretary came over the line.

"How may I help you?"

"I need to speak with Valentina Rivera."

"May I ask who is calling?"

"Yes. My name is Tony Montana Jr. I'm a friend."

"Hold on for one minute."

Tony could hear the sweet sounds of jazz on the line while he waited to be connected with Valentina. He couldn't help thinking about what all had transpired over the last six months. Things had really gotten out of control. First, Demiles was killed at Club Gambino, Big Paul was killed, and then Mr. Stein was taken out for his part in the plot of the assault against his grandmother. Then, he murdered Gallant. All throughout the course of meeting a connection and setting up a multi-million dollar drug operation, Tony had remained sane.

Valentina came over the line, "Ms. Rivera speaking. How may I help you?"

"Hello, lovely lady," Tony said.

"No time for games Mr. Montana. I have a business to run."

"No games today. I want to repay you for the damages that I caused to your car."

"As you might know, I have purchased another one."

"Please give me the chance to make good with you."

"You can't afford a two hundred thousand dollar Maserati so leave me alone," Valentina said, while playing hard to get.

"You don't know what I can afford."

"Never in a million years Tony, would I even consider giving you a chance to be my man. Like I told you before, we are in two different classes. It could never be you and I."

"Never say never."

"I don't have time to play."

"Step outside," Tony said. Tony looked at his Rolex as his driver pulled up in front of Valentina's office building. Once his driver stopped the Maybach, Tony stepped out on the pavement into the cool air. He was dressed in linen and a fine pair of gator low cut shoes. His hair was freshly cut and he smelled like a millionaire.

The tow truck pulled in the parking lot with the Maserati on the bed of the truck. There was a black cover over the car that had Valentina's name in pink letters on the cover. There was also a large pink ribbon wrapped around the Maserati. Tony shook his head in an approving manner. Then, he hit the send button on his phone and instructed Valentina's secretary to escort Valentina out of the door. They both came walking out of the building a minute later. Valentina was dressed in a black Fendi dress, heels and her face was flawless. Her hair was done-up in an African Bun. As the driver of the tow-truck pulled the cover off of the car, Tony said, "Here are the keys."

She spoke, "Is this some type of weird joke? Are you trying to punk me?"

"No… Just say I hit the lottery."

"Where are the cameras?"

"No cameras."

"Where did you get the money?"

"I hit the lottery."

"Seriously, Tony…"

"You told me if I hit the lottery that we could go out on a date."

"I was just being sarcastic."

"Your word is everything."

"You can't be serious."

"You don't want me putting word around town that you are running a bad business."

"You wouldn't."

"Only if I don't get my date."

"What do you have planned?"

"A trip to Costa Rica. Where we will hike rugged trails of Arenal Volcano National Park. Then, off to Rio de Janeiro's Copacabana beach, white sandy shores where it never drops below 75 degrees. Then to Napa Valley in San Francisco where we will shop and taste wines from exotic places."

A crowd was forming around Tony and Valentina. There were people coming out of their offices in the downtown business park like they were viewing a side show at the circus.

She spoke, "I don't know Tony."

"I have a private jet waiting."

An old woman with gray hair wearing glasses who was dressed modestly said, "Go on… give the guy a chance."

The crowd gave Valentina their approval by shouting out the same statement after the old lady.

"Do I need to pack some luggage?"

"No… I had Geno talk to Larry."

"My housekeeper?"

"Yes. He's sending your luggage to the airport."

"I guess, I'll take you up on your offer, Mr. Montana."

"Call me Tony."

When Tony reached her, the crowd responded by clapping and cheering. Tony and Valentina got into the Maserati and left the scene like they had just been married. They took a private plane to Napa Valley. Then, they tasted wine and did some shopping at several boutiques. They even took a hot air balloon ride, after they visited an antique store and galleries by the coast. They decided to go to Rio de Janeiro's Copacabana Beach second, where they enjoyed the white sandy shores with some of the greatest weather in the world.

A week together felt like two days. Time didn't exist. It was all about the moment to Tony and Valentina. This was why they both agreed to extend their date in which turned into a semi-vacation for the both of them. They decided to stay in Costa Rica for a week. They picked a beautiful bungalow from the brochure they found online at Gate 1 Travel.com. Then, they were off to their destination on a private jet. They arrived on the island of Costa Rica early in the morning as the sun was coming up. A limo was waiting for them at the airport. It took thirty minutes to reach their bungalow. Valentina faced Tony right before she stuck the key inside the door and said, "I think I'm falling for you."

They were tipsy from the high-priced champagne that they had consumed while on the jet. Tony responded, "I fell for you the first time I laid eyes on you at the store."

"That's funny… I felt something, but I blocked the feelings that day."

Tony reached his neck in and kissed Valentina. She had met his tongue right under the threshold of the front door. This was their first kiss. Their first week together on their extravagant excursion, they had only managed to hold hands and look each other in the eyes and lust. Nothing more. It wasn't that they were afraid. They both wanted the time to be right.

After their lustful tongue kiss, they made their way into the bungalow. Their driver brought their luggage inside the bungalow while they were looking around the place. There was a grand piano inside the front room area along with white carpet that was thick like grass. There was white furniture and large glass tables with small exotic lamps on top of them. The kitchen sat in the middle of the bungalow and the three large bedrooms surrounded it. There was antique furniture also and exotic paintings all over the bungalow. Valentina spoke as the driver carried the last bag to the master bedroom, "This is a lovely place."

"This is a great place," Tony responded. "I think I outdid myself."

"You've got class."

Tony asked, "Now you think so."

Tony watched as Valentina moved around the place touching different objects in the room. He pictured her in his arms making love to the sweet sounds of jazz.

She spoke, "I need to take a shower."

"I need one too."

"You can take one after me."

"I was thinking we could take one together."

"No, thank you."

Tony watched as Valentina disappeared into the master bedroom. He decided he would use the other shower that was located at the end of the hallway. While taking his shower, he thought about the kiss. He felt a spark in the kiss that he had never felt with another woman. After the shower, he returned to the living room area where Valentina was dressed in a white robe, Gucci slippers and a Gucci towel wrapped around her hair. She was staring off into space. Tony interrupted, "What are you thinking about?"

Valentina was startled. She looked at Tony and said, "The kiss."

"Between you and I?"

"Yes… silly."

Before Tony could get another word out of his mouth, she was all over him. They both let their robes fall open as they engulfed in the moment. They made love on the floor, couch, the kitchen table, and finished in the master bedroom. The next morning, they were awakened by their driver who was there to take them to the hiking post. After Valentina instructed the driver that they would be sleeping in, she returned to Tony who was sitting up in the large French style bed snorting cocaine.

Valentina asked, "What are you doing?"

"Just having breakfast."

"Is that cocaine?"

"Sure is."

"Get out."

"What's wrong with you?"

"Get out, Tony."

"I don't understand."

Valentina walked over to the side of the bed where Tony had the rest of the cocaine sitting. She picked up the cocaine, took it to the toilet and flushed it. Tony spoke, "You have lost your mind. What is wrong with you?"

"I don't like you doing drugs."

"You don't know me."

"I know enough, Tony."

"Maybe I should leave."

"Yes… Maybe you should."

Tony slipped into his linen suit and shoes. Then, he walked out of the front door and hopped into the limo. Valentina watched from the front window in the living room as the limo took off down the road. She couldn't believe that she had let her emotions get the best of her, but she couldn't get over the fact that Brad had been found dead with cocaine all over his nose. She knew about his drug usage before he was murdered, but she still didn't know who murdered him. Seeing Tony with the cocaine brought back the day that she had found Brad dead.

Agent Tadeo pulled the H2 Hummer into the parking lot closest to the Starbucks' entrance and shoved the vehicle into park. Rain pounded the hood of the vehicle and bounced off the asphalt as he turned off the engine. His gaze slid to the front of the strip mall and sought the green and white Starbucks sign next to the golden glare of the Hair Salon and Style sign. Light from within the semi-packed coffee shop poured out onto the wet sidewalk, while the rain drops slipped down the Hummer window and smeared vivid color and inky shadows like an abstract painting.

I hope this guy shows up, Agent Tadeo thought to himself as he turned and shoved the keys into his Army fatigue jacket. Going solo wasn't his choice but doing some private investigation was something he loved to do. After grabbing his umbrella from the back seat, he opened the Hummer door. Then, stepped out into the rain and strolled to the Starbucks with the umbrella over his head. He was here to inquire information about Gallant's case since the guy that called him said he could help. He hit the button on the umbrella with his thumb, and the black canopy closed up as he stood in front of the Starbucks front entrance.

Like all of the other interviews, it was about collecting information. Agent Tadeo had his pen pal in his right hand next to his cell phone and in the other hand he had his pen pal computer with his umbrella. He opened the front door of the Starbucks and moved in. The smell of the various rich, dark coffee filled his nostrils. The steady hum of voices echoed under the sound of coffee grinder and espresso machines filled his head. No matter what city he might travel to, Starbucks always looked and smelled the same. Grade A plus in his book of restaurant grades.

Agent Tadeo gazed over the crowd of patrons sitting at brown tables and hard wooden chairs. There was no man in a Miami fitted cap in the building. The informant was late.

Agent Tadeo shoved his umbrella in the stand by the door and moved to the counter. He ordered a dark coffee, no cream or sugar and took a seat at the round table in the far corner. He unbuttoned his Army fatigue jacket and touched his mother's necklaces that he received after her death. The Jesus' head had been his first wife's lucky charm that hung from the necklace. At the moment, he needed some luck.

Agent Tadeo ran a check on James Blackman's name after he received the call from James in which James informed him that he had information about Gallant's murder. During his check, Agent Tadeo found out that James was from the Pork n' Bean Projects in Miami. This was one of the deadliest projects in America. There were mostly black on black crimes that took place in this area of the city.

The front door swung open and a man with thinning blonde hair stepped inside. Agent Tadeo knew this wasn't James because the mug shot he had seen of James labeled him as an African American. Agent Tadeo shook off his paranoidness and took another drink of his coffee. Then, he pushed back his jacket sleeves and looked at his watch. Ten after seven. Ten minutes late, Agent Tadeo decided to give James another five minutes. While waiting, he took small sips of his coffee and looked over an old newspaper that was sitting on the table. After five minutes of reading, an African American dressed in dirty clothes and an old fitted Miami cap walked through the door.

Agent Tadeo looked up and saw the guy. Then he pulled the photo of James out of his pocket. It was James. The bill of his Miami cap was pulled low on his forehead and cast a shadow over his eyes and large nose. His brown skin had rain on it and the ends of his cornrows were curled up like fish hooks around the edge of the fitted cap. The rain soaked the shoulders of his old black nylon jacket. The zipper was laid open, and Agent Tadeo's gaze slid down a bright strip of white T-shirt to the worn waistband of sweatpants. As James stood there, his gaze moving from table to table, he shoved his fingers into the front pockets of his sweatpants.

Like his photo, he had owl looking eyes, cornrows and brown stained teeth. Agent Tadeo took notice as James gazed his way. He motioned James over and watched as James navigated over to him. Several coffee drinkers gave James an unwanted gaze. Once James reached Tadeo, he raised a hand and slowly pushed up the brim of his cap with one finger. Then he asked, "Are you Agent Tadeo?"

"Yes."

"I'm sorry I'm late. I'm James."

"I'm just glad you showed up."

"I have to tell you this, but you have to promise that I don't have to show up for court."

Agent Tadeo could see the nervousness in James' demeanor. He knew this weird behavior because he had seen it in so many witnesses on so many occasions.

"Have a seat."

James sat across from Agent Tadeo. His uneasy demeanor still didn't change. His eyes were red and looked like they needed rest. The scent in his clothes smelled musty. There was still a sense of shock in James' eyes.

"Do you want coffee?" Agent Tadeo asked.

"No, thank you," James responded.

"Now, what did you see the night Gallant was murdered?"

"I was in the back of the store when the murder took place."

"When you say you were in the back of the store, were you inside the store or outside?"

"Outside, but I could hear and see through the back window that was open."

Agent Tadeo hit the record button on the pen pal device. Then he asked, "What is your full name?"

"James Blackmon."

"Where were you on July 4th of 2007?"

"I was in front of Mr. Castro's store enjoying the fireworks show on South Beach."

"How did you hear about Mr. Castro's murder?"

"I was there the night he was murdered."

"What night was this?"

"July 4th, 2007."

"Do you know around what time it happened?"

"Around nine pm."

"Do you know who did it?"

"Yes."

"Who did it?"

"Tony."

"Who is Tony?"

"Tony is a young guy that worked for Mr. Castro."

"Would you know Tony if you saw him?"

"Yes."

"So you heard when Mr. Castro was murdered."

"Yes. And I saw Tony stick a knife through Mr. Castro's neck after he shot Mr. Castro."

"Where did you go after the murder?"

"I ran to the Homeless Shelter."

"Can you come to the station with me?"

"No."

"I need you to talk to a state prosecutor."

"No."

"Why?"

"I don't trust the system."

"Don't you want to help put Tony away for Mr. Castro's murder?"

"I don't know?"

"Then why did you come?"

"A friend of mine told me that you grabbed him up behind Mr. Castro's store after the murder."

"You're talking about the homeless guy that was asleep behind the dumpster?"

"Yes. He gave me your card."

"Was he there the night Mr. Castro was murdered?"

"No. He didn't see anything."

James stood up after his statement. Then he said, "I think I made a mistake."

Agent Tadeo didn't know if he should arrest James or try to talk to him some more about the murder. He decided it was best to let James go because he didn't want to become the bad cop on the case. He knew James was staying at the City Shelter and that James' arrest record prevented him from getting a job because he was a sex offender. James had been to prison for molesting a little boy inside the church that he had grown up attending while with his parents. There were even reports about James showing himself to several kids at the city park.

Agent Tadeo could only watch as James walked out the front door, back into the rain and disappear behind the strip mall. There was too much on his plate to try to convince a sex offender to come to his office and talk to a federal prosecutor. The time would come when Tony will have to face the music. Until then, José was still on Agent Tadeo's mind.

CHAPTER 41

Valentina stood by the French doors in the kitchen area of the bungalow, pondering on several issues. Issue number one, why was Tony using cocaine? She didn't want to date another man that used. She had gone through so much pain when Brad was found dead with cocaine on his nose. Issue number two, was with her grandfather. She didn't want her grandfather to judge Tony like he had done Brad. This wouldn't be fair to her or Tony, she thought.

Valentina pulled out a cigarette from the pack that she had sitting on the kitchen table. It had been years since she had smoked a cigarette. The last time was right before she had attended Brad's funeral. The fight with Tony had her nerves in a wreck. There was so much she was risking by even messing around with Tony. She knew her grandfather wouldn't approve of her relationship with Tony because Tony didn't have the means like her grandfather. Her grandfather held a high standard when it came to men that wanted to have a relationship with her. She knew this ever since she was a little girl.

Valentina lit up the cigarette and took a few pulls while staring out at the stars and the moonlight. She could hear the ocean waters slapping up against the rocks and smell the cool air filled with sand. Her mind returned to her grandfather after the nicotine took it's effect. She didn't want her grandfather to judge Tony like he did all the other men that had come into her life. His opinion mattered to her, but she wasn't in the spirit of getting disappointed because she really cared about Tony.

Valentina wasn't a regular smoker. She only smoked when she was nervous. At the moment, she was nervous about the fight that she had had with Tony, but she wasn't worried to the point that she didn't think Tony wouldn't come back. In fact, she knew that he was going to return because their love making had been off the charts.

When Valentina turned her attention to the beach, she was interrupted by a touch on her shoulder that startled her.

"Oh… my God."

Tony said, "I'm sorry to have startled you." Then he took a seat in one of the chairs at the kitchen table facing Valentina. She joined him after smashing the cigarette out against the wall and tossing it to the ground outside. Then she poured herself and Tony some herbal tea. Once they made eye contact, Tony spoke, "I'm sorry about what happened earlier."

"No Tony… I was out of line."

"No, you were not."

"I don't really know you Tony, but you make me feel good when I'm around you. I haven't felt this good in years."

"I haven't either. As a matter of fact, you are the only woman that I have opened my heart up to."

"So you feel like I feel?"

"I'm in love…"

"I love hard, Tony!"

"I do too!"

"There are a lot of things you don't know about me."

"Well tell. I'm all ears."

"This will have to be a process for the both of us."

"The process has already started. I take actions when I want something."

"You have a lot to learn about me, Tony Montana Jr."

"Teach me."

Valentina took a sip of her tea and after setting the cup down, she ran her index around the rim of the cup while staring in Tony's eyes. She was looking into his windows with eagerness that Tony had never seen before. She spoke, "My grandfather is José Rivera. He is one of the most powerful men in South America."

"I'm good with people."

"He's not. He's used to having his way."

"Maybe I can help change that."

"He's a hard nut to crack."

"We can crack him together."

"I don't know Tony."

"What does your grandfather do for a living?"

"You will never understand."

"Make me understand."

"My grandfather is one of the biggest drug dealers in the world."

"What kind of drugs does he sell?"

"Cocaine and H."

"I can't judge him. There is something I need to tell you about my father. He was a drug dealer. He left me thirty million dollars."

"So you didn't really hit the lottery."

"No…"

"Are there any other family?"

"Just Geno and Sam. My grandmother passed a few weeks ago."

"I'm sorry, Tony. If I may ask, how did she die?"

"She was attacked. She later died at the hospital."

"So you've been grieving two deaths?"

"No, just my grandmother."

"What about Mr. Castro?" Tony took a sip of his tea and stood up and walked over to the French doors. He looked back at Valentina and said, "He was my grandmother's attacker."

"You killed him Tony?"

"He killed himself."

"I'm sorry Tony."

"Don't be. I'm okay."

"What about your parents?"

"They're both dead."

"I'm sorry, Tony."

"Enough about me. Tell me about yourself."

Valentina watched as Tony rolled his sleeves up and then took a seat back at the table with her. She spoke, "My parents were murdered. I was just a kid when this happened. My grandfather had the men that murdered my parents hunted down and murdered."

"I could see the hurt in your eyes. I think that this is what we feel when we see each other. We both suffered a loss that touched our souls."

"There's more, Tony. When I saw you at the store, I knew you were the one for me."

"Are you telling me this because I'm thirty million dollars richer now?"

"No… I'm telling you this because I knew our paths would cross again. I knew you were more than just a bag boy at Mr. Castro's store. You just needed something to bring it out of you."

"What if we just change the subject?"

"I'm sorry that I keep bringing up Mr. Castro's name."

"Look… I want to know more about you. Tell me about yourself."

"I went to Yale College for International Business. I work for my grandfather now."

"Doing what?"

"Laundering his money."

"Why are you so free with this information?"

"Because I'm not the person that hides stuff from a man that I'm in love with. I want to put everything out in the open."

"Do you fall in love easily?"

"No. There was only one other man I was in love with and he's dead."

"What happened?"

"I don't want to talk about it."

Valentina stood up and grabbed both of the tea cups from the table and set them in the sink. The maid was coming in the morning, so there was no need to wash the cups. After giving Tony a serious lustful glare, she walked down the hallway to the master bedroom .Tony got up from the table and followed her to the room. She was lying on the bed naked when Tony walked inside it. She spoke, "I need you to know one more thing about me, Tony."

"What is that?"

"I'm a sex addict."

"How do you know?"

"Let me show you."

Tony stripped down naked. Then, he made his way over to the bed and made eye contact with Valentina. The dim light from the moon provided enough light for them to see each other. Tony asked, "What would your grandfather think about me being here with you?"

"He would probably be upset, but I don't care what he thinks right now. I want to enjoy this moment."

"Maybe you can take me to meet him?"

"I can arrange that, but first you have to remind me why we came here."

The sex took off like a rocket. Long, hard and up close. The fire in both of them could have heated the earth for years. The World was satisfaction for the both of them. After their mayhem of sex, they both sat up in bed looking at each other breathing hard. As Valentina inhaled the sexual aroma and covered herself, she said, "You were great."

Tony smiled and said, "You weren't bad yourself."

Tony's cell phone interrupted their moment. He slipped into his T-shirt and shorts. Then, he walked out on the patio. It was Geno.

"Tony… there's trouble."

"What is it Geno?"

"The Mob sent a message, Tony."

"What did they say?"

"They want Sam."

"Where is he?"

"He's here at the Estate with me, Tony."

"Make sure you protect him with your life, Geno. I'm coming back to the States in a couple of days."

"How is Valentina?"

"She's okay."

"One last thing, Tony."

'What is it?"

"El Chapo wants to see you. He has the product."

"Let him know when I get back, we will do business."

"Okay Tony."

Valentina was wrapped in her robe standing right behind him with her arms folded over her chest. She asked, "Trouble?"

"Not really. Business."

"Do you have to go? Because if you do, I'll understand."

"Business can wait."

Valentina and Tony returned to the master bedroom. Then they made love until the sun came up. They were served breakfast in bed and after their gourmet made meal, they took a hot shower together. Then, they dressed in their hiking gear. They hiked the rugged trails of Arenal Volcano, National Park and went to several bars for drinks. This was the life of the rich.

Tony couldn't stop thinking about how great he felt while he was with Valentina. This really was the first woman that he had cared about besides his grandmother. He was even leaning towards love. He let his guard down after the first night with Valentina. The rich Napa Valley wine helped a little, but it was her gentle demeanor that cracked Tony's hard shell.

On the final day on their trip, Tony and Valentina visited an antique shop around the corner from their bungalow. They both were dressed in shorts and T-shirts. Their outfits made them look like true tourists. This was Valentina's first time in a long time not dressing in her high fashion while on an excursion. While walking on the trail to the shop Tony said, "You still look beautiful in anything."

"Thanks. I'm just trying to reinvent myself a little."

"I hope I'm not rubbing off on you."

"Trust me, I love being high maintenance. I won't change that for the world."

"Not even for me?"

"You have a big ego, Mr. Montana."

"I like the way you say my last name."

"Montana…"

"Sexy."

"You are very humorous."

Valentina took off her Gucci sunglasses and her straw hat when they reached the front door of the antique shop. There weren't many people on the walkway of the shopping strip area. The sound of a live band was playing island music in the distance. The smell of fresh bread and different kinds of Costa Rica's food lingered in the air. This moment reminded Valentina of her home in Brazil where she had grown up at as a child. This very moment had her feeling nostalgic. Exploring the island was like exploring the jungle in her childhood country. There was nothing like walking through town enjoying the culture of the native land.

The things Valentina missed most about where she had grown up as a child, were spending time with her grandfather in the jungle. Her grandfather was always giving her life lessons about the jungle.

There were steel bars around the windows of the antique shop that made the shop look more like a prison than a shop. There was enough space in between the bars to see inside the shop. There were paintings, chairs, tables, and other items that caught Tony's and Valentina's eyes as they walked through the door. Tony took notice of several large genre paintings. There was one that had the theme of a Victorian scene of a family in a large frame that took up almost one side of the wall inside the front area of the box-shaped shop. There was a work, La Question Embarrassante that was also on the wall.

Tony stood there staring at this picture for a full minute before he was interrupted by the dealer. "Excuse me, Sir. Do you know what you're looking at?"

Tony turned in the direction of the tanned face man with the apple size jaws, teeth like an old tiger, lips made for cooling soup, eyes like an owl and a body that looked like it holds fat for the winter.

He responded, "Yes. Fine art."

"Do you know what the art is saying?"

The man's accent was something that caught Tony's attention. He didn't understand how a New Yorker was selling paintings on an island. He responded by looking deeply at the nasty reddish color picture with exact interest. He was trying to make out the message inside the art. His sixth sense told him that the dealer had another agenda inside of the store instead of selling him art. Tony was really interested in the art. He wanted to purchase a couple of pieces for his new home. The art he had seen in the galleries in San Francisco weren't the type of art he was looking for.

The canvas depicted three people: a catholic priest, a man and a woman, all in the priest's study. The men appeared to be waiting for a response from the woman in a state of profound contemplation. Tony pondered it for a while in silence. Valentina came over and interrupted, "I know the meaning." Tony and the dealer looked at Valentina. She said, "The man and the woman have come to the priest to arrange their marriage, and the priest has just asked him whether she has been married before. She has. For all three of them, the priest has just asked la question embarrassante. Tony was impressed by Valentina's answer. He spoke, "You are very smart."

She responded, "Yale did me some good. The life of the rich."

Tony asked the dealer how much for the picture. The dealer responded, "two hundred fifty thousand dollars."

"I now see why you have the bars on the windows."

"Do you want it?"

"Wrap it up."

"You're going to need some insurance."

"I'll take care of that."

Tony watched as the dealer called a woman that looked around the dealer's age and two men that looked like they could be the dealer's sons. The woman had a fat rock on her finger that looked like a onion ring. This gave Tony the assumption that this was the dealer's wife. After the dealer introduced Maria as his wife and Jerry and Berry as his sons, Tony watched as the family wrapped the picture up.

Tony knew Valentina was impressed from the purchase because when he pulled out his black card, she kissed him on the cheek. As they returned to the bungalow after Tony gave the dealer all the information as to where the art was going to be delivered, they got lost in a deep conversation. Valentina spoke, "Tony... You really impressed me today."

"I wasn't trying to. I purchased the picture because I liked it. I'm going to put it in my new house."

"You purchased a house too?"

"Yes. My father's old estate. The house that he was murdered in."

"How much did you pay for it? If you don't mind me asking?"

"Ten million."

"That's a lot of money."

"Money doesn't matter when I'm searching for closeness to my parents."

CHAPTER 42

Agent Tadeo put his weekly report in to his superior. In the report, he told his boss that Tony Montana Jr. could be the suspect of the Mob bosses' murders and a possible link to Mr. Stein and Mr. Castro's murders. He didn't want to make Tony look like a serial killer, but he couldn't sugarcoat what he found out about the murders. When his boss contacted him and told him to turn the files over to the locals since the murders were in their jurisdiction, Agent Tadeo was relieved. Especially, when his boss gave him and his team permission to return to Brazil to continue their investigation on José.

When they returned to Brazil, the other team had filled them in on the new information that they had collected. There were no hard feelings between the two teams, and this was what made the investigation, continue to go smoothly because both teams knew the main objective was to catch José at any cost.

Their new post was to set up a hundred yards from the side of José's Compound, and it was easier to see all entrances of the Compound now. The fly spy device had been used while Agent Tadeo and his team were away. The device made it easier for them to get access to the Compound. After flying the device around in the dark, Agent Tadeo decided that it was time to do a real run inside the Compound. He and his team could see through the small screen on the front of the device, and they were watching as the device was providing images of the Compound as the device was being controlled by Dean.

Josh spoke, "This fly spy is the best piece of equipment I have ever seen."

Dean spoke, "Watch this." He pushed a button on the device and audio was provided for the team. There were two guards patrolling the ground and they were talking. Dean flew the fly spy right above their heads. Everyone watched as the fly spy came within inches of the men's heads. The two men were speaking in Spanish dialect in which Agent Tadeo made out the conversation the men were having.

He spoke, "They're just having a general conversation about the weather."

The night was hot and the moonlight wasn't helping with the heat. The image on the handheld computer was large enough for all the men to see it.

Dean spoke, "I'm going to fly it inside of José's bedroom."

The team watched as Dean flew the device in José's room. The lights from the towers gave Dean enough light to land the fly spy right beside José's bed on the nightstand. They could see José was talking on the GPX-4000. When the audio button was pushed once again, José's voice came alive. He was having a conversation with his granddaughter, Valentina.

Agent Tadeo spoke, "I think his granddaughter wants to come visit. She said something about she has a surprise for him."

John said, "This can be our chance to get him. All of his attention is going to be focused on her."

Josh responded, "John might be on to something."

Dean said, "I agree."

Agent Tadeo said, "We must plan. Plus, we call in the other team along with extra help."

Valentina hung up the phone after talking to her grandfather. She had informed him that Mr. Castro's death didn't stop the deal from going through. She also informed him that construction had already begun on the hotel. Plus, she informed him about her new friend that she wanted him to meet. She didn't tell him Tony's name or his gender, because she wanted to surprise him.

Valentina was excited by her grandfather's decision to meet Tony. Usually, he didn't' want Valentina to be involved with anyone while she was working on something that was so important. Especially, when it was connected to his business. He grandfather's opinion meant a lot to her when it came to life. This was why she asked if she could come and visit him.

CHAPTER 43

When Tony arrive home, Geno and Sam were waiting at the airport for him. Geno drove the Maybach while Sam rode on the passenger side. Tony took to the back seat and played with the computer that came with the car. He wanted information on both Mafia guys that he had killed. He typed Big Paul's name in first and received some important information about him.

Tony was scrolling the Criminal International page while Sam was talking.

Sam spoke, "Tony... I think Big Paul's nephew Jimmy is going to come after me. He's been sending threats around the city about me. I thinks he's got like a half mill on my head. He also has money on your head, Tony."

"How much is it?"

"Half a million."

"I'm worth more alive."

"This is serious, Tony."

"I know, that's why I'm going to put money on his head."

"What about Demiles' people?"

"I'll take care of that problem too."

Tony typed in Toby Redfirm's name. He decided to focus on Toby, because Toby was next on the hit list. Toby's nickname: Sickness, was given to him by the Aryan Brothers. Toby had done a bid in the 90's for robbing a bank. There were other meaningless charges on Toby's record on the database that didn't carry prison or jail time under Toby's name. When Tony came across Toby's mug shot after looking over several cases of Toby's, he knew Toby was the right man because he was around the same age as his father. He scrolled down to Toby's background and found out that Toby had become a member of the Aryan Brotherhood in 1972 at the age of 17. He was currently living in Texas. His weight was 250, and his height was six foot even. Hair color: Brown-blackish and different tattoos were all over his body. This was enough information to form a plan.

Tony logged off of the computer and then said, "Geno, I need you to arrange a trip to Austin, Texas."

Geno responded, "No problem, Tony."

Tony continued, "Sam I need you to get El Chapo on the phone. Let him know I'm back in the city, and I'm ready to do business."

Sam responded, "No problem, Tony."

Tony turn on Rick Ross's song: "Push it to the Limit" from the album version: Port of Miami. Then, he laid back in the seat and thought about how he was going to move the thousand kilos and kill Toby. First, he was going to get the kilos from El Chapo and sell each of them for twenty thousand a kilo since the city was still in a drought. But first, he had to rent more space to store the cocaine.

When Tony arrived at home, he went to his home office and placed a call to the pool hall that Toby owned in Austin. No one answered the phone. This didn't stop Tony from investigating Toby even more. Tony pulled Toby back up on the International page. This time, Tony came across more helpful information on Toby. There was information about Toby that Toby had his hands in extortion. This took place while Toby was serving time at a federal prison called: Marion. Jason Gotti, a mafia boss had been the victim.

Toby had a right hand man while he was at Mario named Mark Gasponder. AKA: COWBOY. They both had been into meth and the porn business before catching their federal sentences. Tony read more of the profile and then decided that he would use Cowboy's name to get close to Toby. He decided this would be the best route since Cowboy was now serving time at ADX Federal Prison in Colorado. There was no way that Toby could reach Cowboy from ADX, unless he had a cell phone and this was impossible since ADX was the most Secured Max Security Prison in the United States.

Geno and Sam interrupted Tony's investigation when they entered his office. Geno spoke, "I booked the trip to Austin like you asked me to do."

Sam interrupted, "El Chapo is in the city. He wants to know where you want the kilos delivered to."

Tony responded, "Call him back and let him know I'm going to need two days to get the meeting place."

"I will do that, Tony."

"Then find me another warehouse."

"I got you, Tony."

"Geno, what time does the plane leave to Houston?"

"Tonight at 7:00pm."

"That's great, because Toby will be dead by midnight."

"What are we going to do about weapons?"

"Money talks. We can get weapons."

Tony took a shower, and then he got dressed in some linen. He put on some Armani gator shoes that were green and black. Then, he placed a call to Valentina inside his office. Her voice mail came on. Tony hadn't talked to Valentina since they had arrived back in Miami. He wasn't worried about her. He just wanted to know if she was feeling the way he was feeling about their relationship.

After Tony made several more phone calls, he and Geno were escorted to the airport where they hopped on a first class flight to Austin. Once they landed several hours later they rented a Lincoln from the rental car place at the airport. Then, they made their way over to where Toby's pool hall was located. Sixth Street was packed with college kids because there was a big in state football game. Cars were lined up and down the street, bumper to bumper. This was the busiest street in the entertainment district of Austin. On Friday nights in the District, there was everything from college girls, drugs to cheap liquor. Tony had run a copy of Toby's profile from the International Crime Page so he could study a few things about Toby. This had been done before Tony and Geno had gotten on the plane. After Geno found parking space on the back side of the pool hall, he turned the car off and asked, "What's the plan?"

Tony responded in a serious tone, "We mingle until we find Toby."

"I don't think this is a good idea, Tony."

"Trust me, Geno."

"You couldn't just pay someone to do him, Tony."

"Then it wouldn't be revenge, Geno."

"So, this is what this is about? Revenge?"

"It's about respect Geno, and loyalty."

Tony opened the door to the rental car and stepped into the warm night air. It wasn't too hot or cold. The weather was just right according to Tony's senses. The cameras on the building were broken and there weren't any police in the area. Tony entered the side door of the pool hall after he looked back at Geno. The pool hall was crowded with college kids, and they were enjoying the sounds of Kid Rock. Tony made his way through a bunch of kids that were drinking from a funnel and pulling different color pills from a large white plate. They were popping them in their mouths. After Tony made it to the bar he looked back and noticed Geno at the door that he had walked inside the building. Tony watched as Geno mingled in the crowd. This crowd was what Geno was used to. Tony didn't like to be around a lot of people.

Tony ordered a shot of white liquor and then he looked over the room for Toby. He pulled out a picture of Toby. The internet was a powerful source for information. It was like having an authorization to do anything or find anyone. Tony noticed a man pointing at the ceiling of the bar. The man was dressed in cowboy boots, jeans, and a T-shirt that had 'Life is a Bitch' on the front of it. Tony looked over the crowd and noticed Toby at the bat with a woman. He looked at the picture again. It was Toby. Tony watched as Toby dismissed the woman. Then, he noticed how Toby's fat belly over lapped his pants and how his blonde hair was short. Then, Tony looked towards a door behind the large octagon shaped bar area. Right by the door were glasses hanging from the ceiling. The upper interior surface of the room was made up of marble and wood and had Toby's whole name carved perfectly in it, in English black letters. This upset Tony, because the word loyal was underneath Toby's name. This was what they had been looking at, Tony thought as he looked over at Geno. Then Tony took down the shot of liquor like a cowboy. As he raised his glass to order another drink, he shouted, "Hello, Sickness." Tony watched as Toby turned in his direction, which they made eye contact with one another. Toby walked over to the front of the bar where Tony was sitting at and asked, "How do you know me?"

"Sorry… I'm Donald."

"How do you know me?"

Tony smiled and said, "Cowboy told me all about you."

"How do you know him?"

"Sorry… I'm rude."

"How did you meet Cowboy?"

"I met him while we were serving time."

"You look too young to have served a bid."

"Don't let the baby face fool you."

Geno walked up and interrupted the conversation.

"Hi. I'm Richard. I know cowboy too."

"What brings you two to my neck of the woods?"

"We are trying to get into the Meth-Porn Business."

Tony had read about the case Cowboy caught to land him in the Federal prison.

"How do I know you two aren't working with the police?"

"Tony responded, "Do we look like cops?"

"No… But I was tricked once. I'm not trying to go back down that road."

"I'm Donald. This is my partner, Richard."

Tony pulled a stack of bills out of his pocket, so he could pay for his drink. Then he watched as Toby looked at the knot of bills. Before Tony could get a word out of his mouth, Toby said, "Your money is no good here."

Geno interrupted, "Why not?"

"I have a policy that I go by," Toby responded.

Tony asked, "What's that?"

"Any friend of Cowboy's is a friend of mine. Therefore, all drinks are on the house," Toby said.

Both Tony and Geno gave Toby a smile.

Toby continued, "Now, can we get down to business. We can discuss business in my office upstairs gentlemen."

Tony looked at his Rolex. It was 11:46pm. He tapped the front of the watch while he was looking at Geno. This was done while Toby made his way from around the bar. Geno and Tony followed Toby to his office after Toby dismissed the two men that had been watching from the corners of the bar. He did this with a head nod.

Once at the large steel door of Toby's office on the second level of the pool hall, Tony and Geno was patted down by a guard at the door. This guard was seven foot tall with light pole sized legs and cannon ball muscles in his arms. His long blonde hair was wrapped in a long ponytail and the tight leather pants that he was wearing looked like they were about to bust at any minute.

Tony sized up the situation while the guard check him. When the guard ran the metal detector over Geno, Tony noticed a gun sticking out of the back of the man's black leather pants. He nodded to Geno to let him know about the gun. The only weapon

Tony managed to conceal on himself was a knife that he had in a pocket in the heel of his shoe. He had these shoes specially made for times like this one. Just a push of a button on the side of the shoe and the knife would pop out.

Tony watched as Toby took a seat in the office chair behind the wooden and marble desk. All of the furniture inside the office looked exotic, and there were bear heads and deer heads hanging from the walls. There was a fireplace in the corner of the box shaped room. There was even a glass window that could be used to look out over the bar.

Toby lit up a cigar after he pulled it from the desk drawer. Tony watched as Toby took a pull and sat the cigar in a glass ash tray that was sitting on the desk. Then Toby spoke, "Donald and Richard. That's you two names right?"

Tony answered, "Yes."

"Now… I usually just don't do business with anyone, but since you two know Cowboy, I'm only going to do this with you because of him."

Tony could feel the greedy energy coming from Toby. There was no trust or loyalty in Toby's vibe. Tony looked over at the bodyguard that was standing by the door before he turned and said, "I have two hundred thousand dollars. I want to invest it in the businesses that you have set up."

"No problem. I can arrange that. Now, where is the money?"

"I have it close by."

"How close?"

"In the car."

"It's not safe in these parts, Donald."

"Richard can get the money."

Tony nodded at Geno. Then watched as Geno walked over to the door and walked out. The sound of pool balls being smashed with pool sticks and rock and roll blasting throughout the large speakers inside the bar could be heard right before the body guard closed the door back. Tony and Toby were alone now.

Toby spoke, "Now, where were we?"

Tony responded, "I want in on the meth and porn business."

"I can do that Donald, but I have to tell you that you have to trust me."

Tony watched as Toby pulled out a handheld computer from underneath his desk. Toby asked, "What is your government name?"

"I told you I'm not the police."

"I need your name to see if you've been in."

Tony didn't know anyone that he knew that had been to prison but Sam. Sam had done a three year bid in Federal prison for tax fraud. The only problem with Sam's name was that Sam was thirty years older than him.

"I'd rather not give you my name."

"Do you have anything to hide?"

"No…"

"Well, give me your name."

Tony hit the button on his shoe against the desk and the knife popped out. The smell of the cigar was in the air and the smell of sweat was also in the atmosphere. This didn't stop Tony from reaching down for the knife that was on the floor. Then, he slowly said, "Sam Walton." Tony watched as Toby typed in the name. He knew he wouldn't have much time after Toby typed in the name so he asked, "Do you remember a man by the name of Tony Montana?"

Toby looked up with a perplexed facial expression from the computer and said, "I don't recall."

Tony slowly gripped the knife in his hand while saying, "Well, let me refresh your memory. He was my father. You owe him a half-million dollars."

"Are you kidding me?"

"No… I'm here to collect."

"Your fathers been dead for twenty-one years."

"I know. And I also know about the money you owe him."

Tony made sure Toby couldn't see the knife in his hand as he placed his hands on Toby's desk. Toby spoke, "The debt was dead when your father was put in the ground."

"So you're not going to honor your word?"

"My word hasn't ever been shit, boy."

Tony stood up slowly while saying, "I knew you were going to disrespect my father."

"Damn, your father! Now, what are you going to do about it?"

Tony briskly moved over the desk and pushed the knife through Toby's chest while looking into his blue eyes. As he twisted the knife, Tony said, "This is for my father." Tony watched as the life slowly left out of Toby's fat body. A sense of closure took over Tony when he smelled the urine dripping from Toby's pants. Revenge was like having great sex. The deed was done… It was time to go. This was what Tony was thinking as he put Toby's body straight up in the chair and turned the chair towards the wall so only the top of Toby's head could be seen. Then, Tony made his way over to the security system door and opened it. Inside the small room, Tony removed all of the small discs that were recording in the machine. Then he stuffed these discs in his pocket and then destroyed the cameras in the room. He wiped the knife off and put it back inside of his heel. Then, he made his way out of the office. There was no need for Tony to panic, because the deed was done. This was why he nodded at the body guard after he closed the door back to the office. As he walked slowly down the stairs, he noticed Geno was walking back inside the back entrance of the pool hall.

Tony noticed the bag in Geno's hand, and that he knew Geno had put two small bottles of gas in it too. Tony had planned to burn Toby alive, but he had to change the plan when Toby asked for his name. When Tony reached Geno in the middle of the pool hall, he noticed several men standing by the entrance. The music was so loud in the club that Tony couldn't tell Geno that he had killed Toby. Instead he said, "Open the bag." Geno opened the bag and pulled out the two bottles of gas that were made into two small bombs. Tony spoke, "Light them up."

The crowd was so large that the crowd couldn't make out what Tony and Geno were doing in the middle of the pool hall. There were over three hundred people that were dancing to 50 Cent's In Da Club song. Once Tony got the two gas bombs lit, he handed one to Geno. Then he and Geno made their way towards Toby's men. They both raised the bombs up at the same time when they were about twenty feet from the men. They threw them at the same time at the men.

The bombs exploded at the same time. This caused mayhem inside the club, and all five of the men that were coming towards Tony and Geno were killed instantly. There were innocent people injured in the blast, but this didn't effect Tony. He just wanted to get out of the building. His deed was done.

CHAPTER 44

Sam was waiting at the warehouse that he had just purchased like Tony had asked him to do before Tony had left town. This warehouse was in downtown Miami. There were other businesses in the area that were located on the same busy strip, but these businesses weren't going to affect what Sam and Tony were planning to do here.

After looking over the building and changing the locks, Sam noticed a black Crown Vic sitting outside of the building. He didn't know the car, but there was something strange about the driver. He was dressed in all black. There was a guy in the back-seat that Sam couldn't make out because it was dark out and there wasn't much light out in front of the building. The street lights were the only lights on. Sam decided to get his gun out of the briefcase that was on the floor of Tony's new office. Then, he walked slowly to the front door where he could see the car that was located about twenty feet away. As he opened the sliding steel door, he was hit in the face with a baseball bat. The nine mill that he had in his hand fell to the floor. Sam shouted out in pain."

"Ohh... God!"

"God can't help you." The voice said. It was deep and harsh. The guy hit Sam with the steel bat again. Then, he hit Sam with the steel bat again. This time, he hit Sam across his arm. The sound was so loud, it had sounded like Barry Bonds had hit a homerun. Sam screamed out again.

"Please, God!"

"I'm God!" The dark figure shouted.

The guy hit him again. This time, the guy hit him in the other arm. The bat made the same sound. As Sam tried to crawl away, he could hear the sound of some hard bottom shoes slapping against the hot pavement.

"That's enough for now," a voice said.

Sam turned and looked up to see that Big Paul's nephew Johnny was standing over him. Johnny spoke, "You thought I wasn't going to find you?"

"Let me explain, Johnny."

"There is no explaining, Sam. My uncle is dead and I'm the laughing stock of the underworld."

"Just give me a chance," Sam said.

"You only have one chance. Where is Tony Montana Jr.?"

"I don't know."

Sam was watched as Johnny raised the gun up that he pulled from out of his waistline. In Sam's mind, he knew his time had come and gone. The streets were no longer his home. Times had changed. Before Sam could speak again, Johnny pulled the trigger. The bullet hit Sam in the head. Sam thought he was dead until he heard Johnny say, "Let's get out of here. Let this be a message to Tony Montana Jr."

Sam played dead until Johnny and his crew pulled off in the Crown Vic. Then, he crawled inside the building and tried to crawl up the stairs where he had left his cell phone. The only thing that was running through his head was the Johnny and his men were going to come back. When he heard several Mexican voices talking outside the building when he made it to the top of the stairway, he knew it was El Chapo and his men. This cheered Sam up, because he knew he had dodged death. When he grabbed his cell phone from Tony's office table, the phone started ringing. Sam hit the send button. El Chapo came over the line in Spanish. "Que paso, Sam?"

Sam spoke back to El Chapo in Spanish. He let El Chapo know that he was upstairs in the building and that he had been shot. While Sam waiting on El Chapo and his men to come to his rescue, he hit a button on his phone and the 50 Cent song "Many Men" came blasting from his phone.

CHAPTER 45

José sat reminiscing about all of the dangerous men he had come in contact with over the years. All of these men had worked for him. His visuals of these men were unequivocal. He could see Omar Abdel Rahman AKA: The Conspirator. This was the name he had given Omar after the 1993 bombing of the world Trade Center.

Omar had been the leader of an Islamist group and while he was the leader, José had hired him for a couple jobs. Their relationship turned sour when Omar tried to send a message to José while he was in jail. This was a No-No in José's book of crime. José's number one rule was "Never Become An Informant." Even though Omar didn't become an informant, he violated another rule of José's. That rule was never give anyone José's number. Omar did just that. José disconnected the number and never contacted Omar again.

While basking in memories of Omar an unequivocal flashback, Wadih el-Hage appeared in José's mind. The former Al-Queda member who participated in the 1998 U.S. Embassy bombing in Africa had been on José's payroll throughout the 90's. José had gotten Wadih to do several jobs in Africa. These jobs had been successful until the 1998 U.S. Embassy bombing in Africa. José cut ties after that bombing.

Another key figure in José's army of hitmen was Zacarias Moussaoui AKA: 9/11 co-conspirator. Zacarias helped plan out the 9/11 attacks on the United States. Even though José didn't have his hand in the attack, he clapped as the buildings were crashing down. He did this while sitting at his Compound in Africa.

Zacarias had done a couple of hits for José. These hits were orchestrated by José, but one hit fell, that's why José dismissed Zacarias. It wasn't personal, it was all business to José. Zacarias got lucky when he got locked up by the Feds, because José had put a hit on Zacarias head. José had sent Richard Covin Reid to eliminate Zacarias, but Zacarias was always a step in front of Richard. José even tried to get rid of Zacarias with his assassin Eric Robert Rudolph.

Eric was an American, and this was the reason José hired him to eliminate Richard and Zacarias. José didn't like Americans because he thought that they were greedy, and unintelligent and had no morals, values and bullied people who didn't have the resources to fight them back. Even though José operated like a terrorist, he felt like he was morally doing the right thing to exist.

All of the hitmen that José had hired had come and gone. The only hitman that José knew he could count on was unknown to the FBI and the International Police. This same hitman had took out Tony Montana Sr. when José asked him to, but now at the age of sixty he was no longer taking contact. But there was hope for José, because this hitman had a son that was just as deadly to him. José knew this because he had met the young man right before he instructed Eric to kill Richard and Zacarias.

José snapped back to reality when the sound of the Blackhawk's engine hit his ears that was off in the distance. He wasn't looking forward to meeting anyone or wasn't expecting a visit from anyone. This was why he was perplexed from the Blackhawk that was approaching off in the distance.

Agent Tadeo turned his binoculars towards the sound of the Blackhawk as it was approaching from the east side of the Compound. According to his chart on his handheld computer, the Blackhawk wasn't due on the Compound until another week. This was why he was confused about the whole scene. He turned to his crew and informed them that the Blackhawk was coming in.

He spoke, "I don't know why this Blackhawk is here, but there might be a special shipment on this Blackhawk."

Dean asked, "What should we do?"

"Just take all of the pictures you can take."

The crew did as Agent Tadeo instructed them to do.

CHAPTER 46

Tony and Geno arrived back in Miami after their trip to Dallas. Tony's new driver Reno was waiting at the airport when they landed. Tony instructed Reno to take him home after they had visited Tony's warehouses. On his way home, Tony received a call from El Chapo's people. They informed him that Sam had been checked into the local hospital after he was beaten by some men they didn't know. Tony sent a text to some of his men to go to the hospital and stand guard over Sam's door. After he informed his men about Sam, he called Valentina. She came over the line, "Como esta, Tony?"

Tony responded, "Hello, my love."

She asked, "Why haven't you been answering me?"

He responded, "I've been out of town on business."

"No, you haven't Tony... You've been dodging me. You American men are all the same. You only want one thing and you all are selfish." Tony could hear the seriousness in Valentina's voice.

He protested, "No... Listen Valentina. I love you too much to play games with you." After Tony made this statement, he motioned Geno to open his gold case where he had a mountain of cocaine stashed. Tony took a nose full before he continued, "I want to see you now. Please come to my home."

"Why should I come, Tony? You don't love me like you say you do."

"This is why I called you, Valentina. I miss you and I want you to see my home. Maybe one day it will be your home."

"I told you Tony Montana Jr., you cannot afford me."

"I'm not trying to buy you."

"What do you call, what you are doing?"

"I call it showing a woman that I love her."

"If I come, I need you to do something for me."

"What is it? Anything for you my love."

"My grandfather's birthday is coming up. He will be seventy-seven years old. Can you visit him with me?"

Tony interrupted, "It will be my pleasure…"

"There will be a jet waiting this weekend for us at the airport."

"I'm in."

"Well, I want you to know that you can't bring anyone."

"Geno is my right hand man."

"Just us, Tony."

"Will I be safe?"

"You have to ask yourself that."

"Can you come over tonight? Dinner is on the agenda."

"Maybe. I have business I have to take care of first."

The phone went dead in Tony's ear. He knew Valentina was playing chess with him. This chess match with her wasn't something Tony liked to do, but he knew he had to play along to get her to be his wife.

Tony dismissed his thoughts about Valentina after thinking that he should have told her about Sam's condition. He knew that Valentina had developed a bond with him and his crew, the night he killed the Mafia Boss. Even before that night, Tony's bond with Sam had run deep but after that night, he looked at Sam more in the sense as a father figure. This was why he had ordered his driver to take him and Geno to the hospital where Sam was at.

Once in the parking lot of the hospital, Tony searched the lot for his men. Two of his body guards were waiting by the front entrance for him. After exiting the car, Tony looked around to see if he was being followed. There was no indication that he had been followed, so he proceeded into the lobby of the waiting room. He asked the nurse at the front desk what room Sam was in. After getting the room number, he made his way over to the elevator.

Sam was laying back on his hospital bed when Tony and Geno walked inside the room. There was an IV in Sam's right arm and bandages on his head, but in Tony's eyes he could see that Sam was going to be okay. Tony asked in a whisper, "Are you okay Sam?" The soft whisper that Tony used was new to Sam. He knew Tony cared about him, but he had never seen this type of tenderness from Tony. Sam responded, "I'm okay. Just a flesh wound and some broken ribs. Nothing I can't come back from."

Tony asked, "Who did this?"

Sam hesitated and said, "Don't go worrying yourself about me, Tony."

Geno noticed a basket of black roses sitting on the night-stand. He walked over and grabbed the card that was sticking out of the roses. He interceded, "I think it's the Mob, Tony." Tony watched as Sam pushed himself up on the bed with his elbows. Then he said, "It was Johnny. Big Paul's nephew." Tony put his index finger to his chin. Then fell right into deep thought. In his mind, he knew he should have killed Johnny too."

Sam spoke, "He wanted revenge, Tony. He wants you dead."

Tony turned back in the direction of Sam and then spoke, "People in hell want ice water, but they can't get it."

Sam responded, "I'm serious Tony. He's going to come after you. He feels like he has to kill you, because you killed his uncle."

Geno interrupted, "El Chapo is ready to meet, Tony. He just sent me a text letting me know the trucks are in route."

Tony responded, "Let the man know to meet us at the ware-house. We will discuss this later, Sam. Until then, get some rest."

Tony and Geno walked out the door where two body guards were sitting by Sam's door. Tony said, "Guard this door with your lives. I don't want to hear that Sam was killed on you two's watch."

Three days later....

Valentina pulled up in front of Tony's mansion in the Maserati that Tony purchased for her. She noticed the four armed men that were dressed in black suits standing on the lawn of the property. She sent a text to Tony as she was opening the door to her vehicle. The text said: "I'm out front."

A minute later, the front door to Tony's mansion opened and an armed man walked out the door. Tony walked out after the man and said, "I've been waiting on you. Come, dinner is waiting." Tony grabbed Valentina by the arm after he laid a small kiss on her lips that had strawberry lip gloss on them. The moment was intense because they hadn't seen each other since Tony had gone on his trip to Austin.

Tony and Valentina enjoyed a beautiful seafood dinner that was made up of the highest priced seafood that was purchased in the South Beach area. Tony knew Valentina was a seafood lover from the way she ate so much of it on their trip. Dinner ended as fast as it began. Tony gave Valentina a tour of the house after dinner. He showed her the whole Estate in less than an hour. When he reached his office on the top level of the house he said, "This used to be my father's office. Him and my mother used to spend their time here." This was the first time that Tony had brought a woman into his home. Valentina responded, "It's lovely. I can see why your father and your mother spent a lot of time here."

The floors and the walls were made out of marble. Everything was upgraded, but looked exactly like his father would have wanted it. Tony knew this because he took the picture of the old house that was in the box of stuff that his grandmother told him about before her death and asked Sam if it was his father's house.

This was one of the reasons that he purchased the house. After the tour, Tony and Valentina made their way to the master bedroom. Valentina was impressed by the room. She couldn't believe such a common man like Tony could have so much good taste. She was even surprised to see that Tony had put the artwork that he purchased while on their trip on the wall. She spoke, "You've really out done yourself in this room, Tony."

Tony responded, "These are all my mother's ideas."

"Your mother has great taste."

"I have to agree."

Before Tony could say another word, Valentina planted a kiss on his lips. Their tongues met in unison and they fell into a passionate wave. All of the lust and love came out of both of their bodies as they fell back onto the bed. They made sweet love until the clock reached twelve. Then, they both went to sleep.

Valentina woke up to the sound of her phone an hour later. She didn't understand why her grandfather was calling her so late. Then she thought to herself, that the time zone he's in was different from the time zone she's in. She knew she had to take the call. This was why she hopped out of bed, got dressed and pulled her hair into a pony-tail. This was after she looked at the text that she had received from her grandfather. The text didn't seem true to her, because she didn't think that anyone had the guts to rob her grandfather.

The thousand kilos that her grandfather sent to America was supposed to arrive two days ago, but never did. Now, seeing the text again told Valentina that the shipment had been picked off by someone. But who? Who would dare rob someone as powerful as her grandfather? Who would take the chance of going against the most powerful man in South America? Then it hit her. "El Chapo."

Valentina decided it was time to call her grandfather back after she had arrived at her warehouse. After walking in to the empty building, she had placed the call to her grandfather. He came over the line in a foul mood. He said, "I've been trying to reach you. Why haven't you been answering my calls?"

Valentina responded in a concerned voice, "I've been busy, Papi."

"Well, there is a problem."

"What is it?"

"The shipment was taken."

"Do you know who took it, Papi?"

"I believe some of El Chapo's men took it."

Valentina knew about all five of the Mexican Cartels. She knew they were at war with one another, and she knew her grandfather was supplying most of the East Coast in America. This was why she didn't understand why El Chapo would risk an all our war between the cartels now. Valentina asked, "What are you going to do?"

"I'm going to send some men to American to hunt for the product. I need you to assist with the hunt and when they find the product, put it in the warehouse there."

"Okay, Papi. I won't let you down."

"Remember Valentina, El Chapo is a powerful man like myself, so be careful."

"I will find the product."

Johnny knew he had had to round-up the best men money could buy. The job he had pulled took more than heart. It took skills and wits. Robbing a bank or a store was one thing, but robbing a warehouse for a load of pure South American cocaine had been a big task for Johnny and his men. Johnny knew this was the biggest robbery that he had ever pulled, and he had gotten away with it.

He knew if his uncle Paul was living that Paul wouldn't have even thought about doing such of an act. But Paul was dead and the streets were clowning Johnny like a circus clown. This was why Johnny had decided to take Tony's shipment.

Johnny knew that Tony had kilos coming from a Mexican plug because he had planted listening devices in Tony's warehouse. He did this after he had found out that Sam was in the hospital. He had planted the devices in the warehouse because he was planning on killing Tony but when he heard about the truck loads of product, this was a plus. When the trucks had shown up with Mexican drivers behind the wheel of all three eighteen wheelers, Johnny had ordered his men to seize the drivers. The men at the warehouse had already been handcuffed by Johnny's men.

The Mexican drivers were ordered to the ground by Johnny's men and they had responded, "No English..." Johnny had walked over to the three drivers and shot one of them in the head. Then he had asked, "Do you two understand English now?" Johnny and his men had taken the three truck loads and ten million dollars of Tony's. This still didn't satisfy Johnny, because Tony wasn't dead.

After answering the beep from his phone, Tony picked up his cell phone off of the nightstand. He did this after he felt under the colorful blanket for Valentina's body. To his surprise, she was gone. Tony asked, "Who is this?" Then, he looked over at the nightstand where the gold clock reads: 3:00am. The called was Geno. Geno said, "Tony... There is trouble at the warehouse." Tony sat up in bed after hitting the switch to the lamp. Then he asked, "Where is the money?" Geno hesitated before he responded, "The money is gone. All ten million." Tony was on his stealth non-trackable phone. He knew the Feds couldn't track his phone or Geno's phone if they wanted to. He spoke, "I'm on my way over, Geno." He hit the end button and ended the call with Geno. Then, he hopped out of his king sized bed and walked over to the huge window. Then, he looked out over his front lawn to see if he could see Valentina or her vehicle. She was not in sight. Not a sign of her. Tony placed his index finger on his chin, while he fell into deep thought. He didn't know why Valentina had left without notifying him. He decided he would call her after he took care of his business at the warehouse.

✦ 268 ✦

Tony dressed quickly in one of his black Armani suits and matching gators. After putting on his gold cufflinks, he strolled downstairs where two of his bodyguards were waiting on him. They escorted him to his Maybach after they armed themselves with Tommy guns.

Once in the car, Tony's thoughts went to Valentina. He couldn't stop thinking about why she had left so sudden. The thought of her having something to do with his warehouse came to mind, but he quickly dismissed the thought after he thought about Valentina's statement about how rich her grandfather was. Then, Tony's mind switched to overdrive. Who would have the balls to rob him? He couldn't think of anyone but Johnny. Thirty minutes passed so quickly that Tony thought he had fell asleep in the back of the Maybach. He was so lost in his thoughts that he almost forgot where he was headed. This was due to all of the cocaine he had been pumping up his nose. Tony asked, "Are we almost there?" Tony's new driver Reno responded, "Yes, boss. We are five minutes away." The sound of Rick Ross's "Push It…" was ringing inside the surround sound system in the car. Due to Tony being a hip hop head, he liked Rick Ross's music.

The parking lot of the warehouse was filled with different kinds of vehicles. This was normal to Tony. But he could feel the tension in the air after he stepped out into the night air. His new bodyguard escorted him inside the warehouse after his driver closed the door to the Maybach. Once inside the warehouse, Tony looked at the twelve men that had been robbed by Johnny and his men. He didn't know all of the guys' names, but he knew that they would have put their lives on the line for him. After nodding his head at each man, Tony made his way over to his office where Geno were waiting. Once inside the office, Tony said, "Now, what is the problem?" Geno responded, "Someone stole the shipment." Tony looked at Geno in his brown-greenish eyes and then Tony said, "Is this some type of cruel joke? You get me out of my cool warm bed to tell me someone took a thousand kilos of my cocaine? I know this is a joke, right?"

Geno responded, "This isn't a joke, Tony. They took the money too."

"This has got to be the best joke ever. I have to give you and Sam a hand for this." Tony claps his hands together in a playful manner. Geno said, "It was Johnny. It was that stupid, dumb moron." Sam told me.

Tony responded, "I'll kill that cockroach myself. I should have killed him when I killed his uncle." Geno interrupted, "There is another problem Tony. El Chapo wants his money."

"How do we know that El Chapo didn't do this?"

Geno said, "Johnny did it, Tony. Word is already on the streets."

"It's only been one day."

"Word travels fast." Tony pulled out his gold case and took a few snorts before he shouted, "So, El Chapo wants his money?" Geno responded, "I think I can buy us some time to pay El Chapo."

"You do that Geno."

Geno said, "What now Tony?"

Tony responded, "Go tell the guards to stand in a straight line next to each other." After Geno ordered the guards to stand in a straight line, Tony came strolling out of his office with a forty cal in his hand.

In Tony's mind, he didn't believe that twelve armed men would allow someone to take a thousand kilos and ten million dollars. Tony ordered all of the men to drop their weapons. Then, he said, "Geno put all of their weapons in my office. While Geno was doing this task, Tony said, "Now, you guys were here when my warehouse was robbed. Now, I want some answers and I want them now. Who took my Ya-Yo?" Silence took over the room. It was so quiet that you could have heard a mouse piss on cotton. All of the men just stared at Tony. This was after he put the clip into the Forty cal. Tony continued. "This is you alls' last chance. Who took my Ya-Yo and Money?"

Tony didn't have any understanding at the moment. He didn't know that the twelve men really didn't know who took the money because Johnny and his men had on black masks and black clothes. Geno returned to Tony's side after putting the guns away. He spoke, "The guns are in the office, Tony."

Tony looked at Geno and Geno asked, "Now what?" Tony turned the gun on the men and said, "Now this." Geno watched as Tony went down the line and shot each man in the head. Four of the men took off running, but Tony caught up to them and shot them in the head too. Reno walked out of the office after the killings were over. Tony said, "Now, clean this mess up. We have to go find Johnny."

Valentina couldn't believe that El Chapo had ordered his men to rob her grandfather. She was perplexed about El Chapo's decision since she knew that her grandfather and El Chapo used to be business partners. Her grandfather had taught her about loyalty, integrity and betrayal. In her eyes, she felt like El Chapo had betrayed her grandfather by instructing his men to take the money and kilos'.

Valentina couldn't stop thinking about how she was going to tell Tony about how El Chapo betrayed her grandfather's trust. At the moment, she felt like she could trust Tony with this information and confide in him on what to do. Time with Tony had shown her that he was loyal and trustworthy. But, could he stomach a war with a drug lord like El Chapo? This was the question that Valentina had asked herself as she pulled up at the warehouse where her grandfather's men were waiting on her.

They were all dressed in suits and they were carrying heavy artillery. The sight of all of the men standing with their guns in hand enticed her juices to flow in her body. She knew she had to perform her duty to her grandfather of finding El Chapo and the shipment. She also knew that it would take money to do so. But first, she had to get Tony's opinion about the matter.

Valentina called Tony on her cell phone. He showed up on the scene after he had hit the chat button on his phone. She spoke,

"I need to meet with you for lunch. Are you available?" Tony responded, "I'm about to go see Sam at the hospital." Valentina made a facial expression that she wanted to see Sam too. Then she asked, "Is he going to be okay?" Tony hesitated and said, "I think so. I'm going over to check on him and get some advice."

"Can I join you?"

"Yes... Meet me at the hospital."

It didn't take Valentina long to reach the hospital. She drove over to the hospital after she had advised her grandfather's men to go hunting for the product and call her if they found anything. She advised them to check: strip clubs, drinking bars, night clubs and restaurants in the downtown Miami area. She also told them to look for big spenders.

Tony and Geno were waiting in the lobby area of the hospital when Valentina walked in the lobby. She kissed Tony on the cheek after giving Geno a light hug. Then she said, "I need to speak to you alone, Tony." Valentina watched as Tony dismissed Geno with a head nod. Then she continued, "I have a big problem, Tony. I think I need your help with it." Tony asked, "First, let me ask you why didn't you let me know you were leaving the other night?" In Valentina's eyes, she could see that Tony had something on his mind. Even though he was dressed in a black Armani suit and his hair was cut in a neat style, his eyes were red. This told Valentina that he hadn't had any sleep. She responded, "El Chapo is an associate of my grandfather."

Tony interrupted rudely, "Answer my question first."

"Well, I left because my grandfather called. One of his shipments was taken. He believes that El Chapo had something to do with it". Valentina watched as Tony put his index on his chin. She knew that he was thinking from spending time with Tony when they went on their trip, and she could see that he was deep in thought. She continued, " I need your help with finding the shipment and EL-Chapo." The shocked facial expression on Tony's face took over the atmosphere. She asked, "Why didn't you tell me?"

"I didn't think, it was important."

"You know he is one of America's Most Wanted?"

"Yes." Valentina turned and looked over at the snack machine. She noticed Geno eating a bag of chips. Tony spoke, "My warehouse was robbed the night you left me in bed alone. Are you sure you didn't have anything to do with it?"

Valentina gave Tony a shocked facial expression. She knew that she didn't have anything to do with Tony's ware house being robbed. She only made this expression, because she was shocked that Tony would even think she would participate in a wrong doing against him. In fact, she felt at the moment that she was in love with him. She responded, "I cannot grasp the fact that you would make an assumption like this."

"I have a question everyone, because a thousand kilos are missing from my warehouse." Valentina interjected, "I didn't have anything to do with it. I need to find them the men that robbed my grandfather. Tony said, "Well, I think the man your grandfather is looking for would be a mob-guy by the name of Johnny. He is the guy that robbed my warehouse and if you are right about El-Chapo taking your grandfathers shipment, then maybe Johnny is sitting on the kilos?" I don't want Johnny. I want El-Chapo. Can you deliver him to me?"

"Are you asking me to be disloyal?"

"No, I'm not asking you to be disloyal, I'm asking you to help fix a problem." Tony couldn't believe that Valentina would put his loyalty to the test. He responded, "I can never betray someone that's been feeding me."

"My grandfather can give you a whole new meaning to life, Tony. All you have to do is help him."

"I cannot do it, Valentina."

"Now I know where your loyalty lies."

'I love you Valentina, but Tony Montana Jr. cannot be bought."

Valentina hesitated and said, "I can help you find this Johnny guy."

"Do you know where he is?"

"Not yet. But I can put my team on it."

"I appreciate your offer, but I cannot betray El Chapo."

Tony watched as Valentina walked out of the lobby of the hospital. He couldn't believe how cold she had turned after he didn't agree with her terms. The coldness in Valentina's eyes told Tony that she would kill him if he ever got in her way. This was why Tony decided it was time to call El Chapo and warn him about Valentina.

Chapter 47

Johnny ran his fingers through his black hair and sighed tiredly. Everything was so damned complicated at the moment, he thought to himself. It appeared that every decision that Johnny had to make had to get approved by the commission. This was something he didn't like at the moment, but he knew in order to go through with his revenge plot that he had to go by the rules.

Being the nephew of a mafia boss was a task in itself. Especially, since his uncle was murdered by a non-member. Getting revenge was a must, but first it had to be approved by the commission, in which Johnny knew it would get approved fast because Tony wasn't a member of one of the Families. The problem that was standing in Johnny's way was hiding the thousand kilos from the commission. Word on the streets had spread like a wild fire about the missing kilos. The Commission was asking Johnny's crew about the kilos and money, because they wanted to know who was responsible.

Johnny knew there was only a matter of time before the commission would find out about the robbery. That's why he decided to call a meeting with the commission to disclose that he had taken the kilos and the ten million dollars. But first, he had to eliminate Tony. This was why he put a million dollars on Tony's head. Johnny had decided this before he had decided to tell the commission about his plan.

When Johnny arrived at the front entrance of "PaperDolls" to celebrate his new fortune, he didn't know that he was being stalked by two different crews. He was too busy shaking hands with his crew members and his uncle's old crew members. They were all dressed in high priced suits and gator shoes. All of the men were armed with the best weapons money could buy.

After walking into the club, Johnny and his crew headed to the VIP section where there was a circle of nude women surrounded by trays of appetizers and bottles of extravagant champagne. Johnny grabbed the first slim built stripper that he saw when he had walked in the section. He pulled her into a corner after whispering something in his body guard's ear. He was too busy to notice that a spotter was in the club. A spotter that wanted his blood.

Tony was sitting calmly in the front passenger seat of a beat up Chevy Caprice as a stinging of rain was pelting him through the half opened window. He was watching Johnny's crew as they were entering the club. Now on Tony's driver's side was Geno, who was holding a Newport Cigarette in his hand. Behind the two of them, were Tony's two bodyguards, Tim and Jim armed with machine guns. They both were dressed in black like Tony and Geno, and they had on their killer demeanors too.

Tony was wondering if Johnny had really shown up to the strip joint. He had been told by a street source about the party. As Tony wiped the rain off his black leather jacket with a napkin, he noticed three men dressed in colorful suits walking inside the club after they had gotten out of a limo. Tony couldn't make out the three men, but he was going to find out who they were when he entered the club.

Tony knew that Johnny was the only insane person that would even think about robbing him for the thousand kilos, after he had narrowed down his list of enemies. Tony had put two and two together after he had looked at his black book of names. Everyone whose name was in the book was dead, except The Source and he didn't even know that Tony was hunting him. This had left the untied string to Johnny.

Tony and his men had been sitting in the Chevy for over an hour while they were watching the front entrance of the club. The rain was helping with concealing Tony and his men. Tony stared out into the rain. He fell into deep thought about how he was going to make Johnny tell him where the money and the shipment were stashed at. First, he wanted Johnny to suffer just for the fact of taking the money and the shipment. Secondly, he wanted to send a message to the Mafia by sending pieces of Johnny's body to them for Johnny's transgressions against him. The sound of the front door of the club closing interrupted Tony's train of thought. He spoke, "It's time to go kill the cockroach." As Tony and his men stepped out into the night, they noticed a black caravan pulling up to the side of the building. Tony watched as a short, slim man hopped out of the back of it. Then, the man behind it entered the side door of the club.

Tony watched as Geno placed two hundred dollar bills into the doorman's hand. This prevented the two huge bouncers from searching them. Once in the club, Tony looked around for Johnny. The music in the club was classic, and the vibe spelled out that it was a money joint. The smell of sweet perfume, liquor, cigar smoke, and the mix of sweat was in the air. This didn't stop Tony and his men from scouting the room for Johnny. The club was made up of three sections. There was an area where several pool tables and a large bar were located. The second area was where the main strip poles were located, along with several restrooms and a large bar. The third area was located in the back of the club. This area was made up of the VIP section and a large bar with colorful glasses sitting on the shelves of the wall. There were strippers nursing drinks at the bar in this area and a set of bouncers in front of the entrance way. Tony could see the marble walls and glass floors as he entered the VIP section after this short, slim man dressed in a black suit had entered in front of him. He knew the man in the black suit was looking for someone. But who? Was this man after Johnny too? Tony touched Geno on the shoulder and pointed to the man and said, "He's a spotter. He's looking for someone." Tony ordered a shot after Geno and him took a seat at the VIP bar.

Tony knew he had to be careful in this upscale place, because he didn't want to injure anyone on the account of Johnny. He wouldn't have hesitated if the place was run down, and Johnny didn't have his drugs and money. But due to these factors, Tony knew he had to keep calm. The cocaine in his system had him on edge. This wasn't new to him. Tony was used to getting high now. This was how he coped with everything. At the moment, he wanted another hit. Without a saying a word, Tony pulled out his gold case and took a hit of cocaine. The pure substance gave him an instant rush and this was what Tony was looking for to relieve the stress. After taking another one-on-one, Tony looked around the room for Johnny. While doing this, he was interrupted by a blonde headed stripper. She spoke, "How about you give me a hit of that nose candy?" Tony was caught off guard by the stripper's bluntness. He responded, "Get out of my face." Geno noticed what was going on between Tony and the stripper and interrupted, "Excuse me... Does anyone care for a drink?"

Johnny didn't know the short, slim man in the black suit was inside the room looking for him. He found this out after the man made his way over to him and pulled out his weapon. The weapon was a small hand gun that had been concealed by the man's jacket. Johnny was being entertained by the same stripper that he had grabbed when he first entered the VIP section. He was lying back on the soft white leather couch when the short, slim man whispered in his ear. "Don't make a scene, Johnny. I don't want to kill you right where you are sitting." Johnny didn't recognize the man's voice, but he knew the man was serious after he opened his eyes. Johnny excused the stripped with a nod. Then he asked, "Who sent you?" Johnny's men were too busy with the other strippers in the room to notice that their boss was being held at gun point. The music that was coming from the sound system was a song called: "Bottom of the Map" By Young Jeezy. The man said, "There is a pretty young lady that wants your head." Johnny responded, "Whatever she is paying you, I will pay double."

"I could never betray this woman. She would hunt me and you down."

"What is this woman's name?"

"You will find out soon enough. Now, let's get out of here."

"So you are not here for Tony Montana?"

"I don't even know him. I'm here for the thousand kilos you took."

"So you are here for Tony?"

"Like I said, I'm here for the kilos."

Johnny's men were still too busy taking shots and dancing with strippers, and they still didn't know their boss was in trouble. Johnny spoke, "What do you want? Name your price."

The 50ish middle aged man responded, "I want you to get up out of your seat and come with me."

"I can't."

"Why not?"

"My men will know something is wrong. Then, there will be hell to pay. Now we don't want anyone getting hurt in here do we?"

Johnny started laughing after his statement. His high pitched laugh got under the man's skin. The man responded, "Shut your mouth." Johnny continued to laugh. The man grabbed Johnny by his arm and was met with a blow to his head. The man stumbled to the floor. Johnny stood up and began kicking the man while shouting, "You are a dead man. Do you know who I am?" The man had been hit in the head by one of Johnny's body guards after the guard had returned from the restroom.

Tony couldn't believe his eyes when he walked into the back area of the VIP section. This area was filled with smoke, men and strippers looking at Johnny stomping a man out. Tony didn't want to make a scene, but a thousand kilos and ten million dollars were at stake. This was why Tony didn't hesitate to interrupt Johnny's little stomping session.

Tony and his men pushed past Johnny's men. Several of Johnny's men pulled out their weapons and all hell broke loose. Tony pulled out a Tech-nine that he had under his jacket and shouted, "Say hello to my little friend, gentlemen." Johnny rushed to the back door in the corner of the room behind the bar. He ran out after Tony fired the first shot. Gun shots took over the room and bullets were flying all over the place. People were running to get out of the club. It was total mayhem. Geno and Tony sprayed down several of Johnny's men as Johnny had escaped out of the back door. Tony raced over to the back door after the room had cleared. When he opened the door, he noticed two men dressed in black pulling Johnny into the back of a black caravan. Johnny was fighting the men, but they overpowered him and tossed him into the van. The van disappeared into the night as Tony watched from the club door. Geno rushed over to the door and shouted, "We've got to go Tony. We've got to get out of here before the cops come." Tony's other two men had been gunned down along with several of Johnny's men. They were all lying dead on the floor. Blood was on the walls, floor and the bar area. The place looked like a tornado had hit it. Tony quickly looked over the scene before Geno and him had disappeared into the night.

Geno and Tony couldn't believe that Johnny had escaped their trap at the strip club. They had spent a full day planning the death of Johnny, but their plan had deteriorated, when Johnny had escaped out the back door. When Tony and Geno noticed that the men in the van had been Johnny's men it was too late. The rain had made it impossible to see the tag on the van. After Geno and Tony got back to Tony's mansion Tony spoke, "We have to find out who took Johnny. Call and get some men on it, Geno."

Two days later….

Tony was sitting in his office going over some numbers when he received a call from an anonymous person. The number was blocked, and the voice of the person was some type of machine device that disguised the caller's voice. The caller instructed Tony to come to a warehouse on the west end of downtown Miami. Tony knew the address that the caller had given him, because it was close to Valentina's work place.

It didn't take Tony and his men long to get to the warehouse. Once they arrived, they noticed on the backdoor of the entrance way of the building, two signs that said, "Export and Import." The area was dimly lit because of the light poles that were sta-tioned on the side street. The backdoor had a white man standing at the door with an AK-47 weapon in his arms. He was dressed in a black suit and his head was bald. This didn't stop Tony and his men from approaching the man. The man was standing right in front of the steel door where the address to the building was located. The only sounds that could be heard in the night were Tony and his men's hard bottom shoes.

Tony stepped to the man in front of the door and asked, "Is this 3232 Leaf Street?" The man nodded his head and tapped on the steel door with his gun. A taller man answered the door. He was also dressed in black and had an AK-47 in his arms. The man looked like he was in his mid-twenties to Tony. His nonchalant facial expression told Tony that he would kill at the blink of an eye. When the man said, "Come in," Tony did as he instructed. This was after the man waved Tony's men away. Tony looked back at his men and said, "I'll be okay. Then he looked at the man and said, "I'm Tony Montana Jr. I'm here to see your boss." The man instructed Tony to follow him. This was after he closed the steel door in Tony's men's faces. As they walked down a large hallway, the man asked, "Do you have any weapons on you?" Tony responded, "Yes. This nine mill." The man stopped in his tracks and turned around to Tony. He stuck his hand out and Tony dug into his jacket pocket and placed the nine mill in the man's hand. Before Tony could say another word, two men appeared out of the darkness. They searched Tony thoroughly before they started escorting him to a room on the end of the hallway. As Tony strolled down the hallway with the men, he took in the smell of fresh fish and motor oil. There were no signs of life in the hallway. There was not a single picture or any type of art to bring the place out. The door to the room on the end of the hallways opened when Tony reached it. Inside the room was a woman talking in Spanish on the phone. The voice sounded familiar to Tony. The room was cold and the smell of fresh fish was still in the air. The woman was sitting in a leather chair behind a large wooden desk. These were the only items in the room. There was a closet in the corner of the room. The woman in the chair had long black hair that hung down her back and the dress she was wearing looked extravagant to Tony. It was something about the woman's demeanor that told Tony that he knew her. He watched as the woman ended her call and turned in his direction.

Tony couldn't believe his eyes when he made eye contact with Valentina. She asked, "Are you surprised, Tony?"

Tony responded," Yes. Now, tell me what's this all about?"

"You know Tony... Carlos!" After Valentina's statement, her men removed Carlos from the closet. Tony watched as a handcuffed Carlos fought with Valentina's men. Carlos had a black bag over his head and it was tied tight with a shoe string. Tony turned his attention back to Valentina after her men had placed Carlos in a chair in front of her. This was after they had pulled the chair from the closet too.

Tony watched as Valentina grabbed the gun out of her desk drawer and pointed it at Carlos. Then one of her men ripped the bag off of Carlos's face. Tony knew Carlos was one of Johnny's men. He knew this from the day they kidnapped Johnny's other Do-Boy. Valentina asked, "Where are the kilos of cocaine, Carlos?" Carlos didn't say a word. Tony watched as Valentina stood up, walked around the desk and slapped Carlos with the handgun. She shouted, "Why would you be so foolish to work for someone like Johnny?" Carlos didn't say a word. When Valentina's men brought Johnny in, Tony couldn't believe his eyes. He charged at Johnny and started choking him. Valentina said, "Enough, Tony. You will have time for that later." Johnny started spitting in Valentina's direction

Tony took Johnny's blood spitting as disrespect and intervened. "Kill this cocksucker. But first, get him to tell me where the Ya-Yo is." Tony watched as Valentina's men worked on Johnny's face. They beat him senseless. Carlos finally shouted, "I'll tell you where the money and the kilos are at if you stop." Tony grabbed the gun from Valentina's hand and rushed over to Carlos, slapped him with the gun several times, until he told Tony where the kilos and money were located. Then, Tony put two bullets in Johnny's head. Then, he turned to Carlos and said "Now if you are lying Carlos, you will face the same."

Valentina ordered her men to clean up the place, after she placed the weapon Tony had murdered Johnny with into a bag. Then she said, "My grandfather is going to be happy. But, he won't like the fact that we didn't get El Chapo." Valentina hesitated and continued, "A jet will be waiting Friday at the airport. Remember Tony, you will have to pick a side. Now, we must go get your money and my grandfather's kilos." Tony couldn't believe that Valentina had put him in between a drug war. He didn't' want to betray El Chapo, but he didn't' want to lose Valentina. This was why he said, "Let me think on it. Maybe after the trip I will make my decision."

CHAPTER 48

Agent Tadeo noticed the second Blackhawk in two days flying off into the distance. He heard the blades of the machine before he noticed the Blackhawk in the sky. Him and his crew were now used to these Blackhawks going in and out of the area in different times of the night. Usually, the machines would land on a landing pad close to the Compound and the men on the machine would unload whatever was on the machine. But, this Blackhawk mission was different. Agent Tadeo came to this conclusion, after he had noticed a beautiful black haired woman step off the machine.

Agent Tadeo noticed that the woman's hair was in a long pony tail that reached to her back. There was something in the woman's demeanor that told Agent Tadeo that he knew her. The bounce in her step and the way she demanded respect as she instructed the men that help her and her companion off of the Blackhawk told it all. This woman was dressed in a colorful exotic, extravagant short cut dress that showed off her beautiful attributes. When the unknown male had stepped off of the Blackhawk, there was something in his demeanor that told Agent Tadeo that he was trouble. This unknown male was dressed in a linen suit with matching light brown shoes. The night vision that Agent Tadeo and his crew were wearing was providing the light to see in the darkness. As the unknown woman and man walked towards the Compound, Agent Tadeo got lost in his thoughts. There were so many questions that were running through his head about these two unknown people, that his head began to hurt. Agent Dean interrupted, "Who's the girl, Terry?"

Agent Tadeo answered, "I'm not sure."

John interrupted, "We need to find out who these two people are before we go busting up in there.

Agent Tadeo reached around and turned on the fly spy speaker. He guided the fly spy over towards the woman and the man while they walked towards the Compound. Agent Tadeo listened as the woman talked in a Spanish tongue to the men that were carrying her luggage. He knew a little Spanish from dealing with so many Spanish people throughout the years. This is why he understood when the female asked, "Where is my grandfather?" in Spanish. Instantly, Agent Tadeo knew this was José's granddaughter. This was Valentina. It had been years since Agent Tadeo had seen Valentina. The last time he saw her was when her boyfriend Brad was murdered. That had been over five years ago. Agent Tadeo spoke, "I know who the woman is."

Josh asked, "Who is she?"

"That's Valentina. She's José's granddaughter."

Dean interrupted, "I never got the full report on this factor."

John interjected, "She is still beautiful."

Agent Tadeo responded, "And a killer." The next statement from Valentina's mouth surprised Agent Tadeo. She said, "Hurry up Tony Montana Jr… My grandfather is waiting."

John asked, "Who is the guy?"

Agent Tadeo answered, "Someone that's been flying below the radar?"

Josh asked, "Do you want me to call the other team?"

Agent Tadeo put down his eye wear and said, "It's time to kill two birds with one stone. Call in the other team."

José couldn't believe his eyes when he noticed his grand-daughter and a young man walking into the common area of the Compound. He watched from the balcony as they entered the common area. It was something about Tony's demeanor that was familiar to José. When Tony spoke to Valentina, it hit him. This voice and the cockiness gave José the assumption, that this guy was the son of Tony Montana. This disturbed him because he didn't know if Tony Jr. knew that he had had Tony Sr. murdered. This was what José was thinking as he made his way down the stairs to greet Tony and Valentina. When José had reached the common area, he had noticed that Tony was admiring his palace. There were so many exotic and extravagant items in the room that it reminded José of King Solomon's palace. José raised his hand to greet Tony as he asked, "Who is this guy, Valentina?" Valentina responded, "This is Tony Montana Junior, Papi!"

José responded, "Why didn't you tell me that you were bring a man?"

"Because I knew you wouldn't approve."

"You know this place is off limits to strangers."

"Tony isn't a stranger. He's my boyfriend. He helped me get the thousand kilos back."

"He did?"

Tony interjected, "Yes…"

José crossed his arms across his chest and said, "I'd like to formally introduce myself. I'm Valentina's grandfather. Call me José."

José watched as Tony looked over at Valentina. José couldn't tell if Tony was at his Compound to kill him. It was too early to read. José continued, "My granddaughter must think highly of you to bring you here. Since she thinks you're worthy of being here, then I welcome you. Now, I have rules here. My first rule is never tell anyone about this place. Rule two: Don't tell anyone about this place."

Tony responded, "I understand."

After José gave Valentina and Tony a tour of the place, he ordered the maid to show them to their living quarters. The next morning after a shower and breakfast, Valentina sat down in the patio area for a conversation with her grandfather. He was sipping on a cup of freshly brewed coffee when she took a seat right in front of him. The birds and the bees were singing and the weather was perfect. It was still cool from a light morning rain. The smell of fresh flowers were in the air along with coffee.

Valentina was dressed in a Prada dress and sandals. She slipped out of her sandals to let her feet breathe a little. She spoke, "Such a beautiful day."

José responded, "Yes… One of the most beautiful days of the year."

"I wish I could live here forever. It's so peaceful here."

"Yes, it is."

José watched as Valentina looked into the jungle and off in the distance was a black panther. The maid entered into the patio area to refill José's cup. He waved her away and said, "Now, I need to speak to you about this Tony Montana guy."

"That's why you asked to see me?"

"Yes."

"He's the greatest guy I've ever met."

"Those are some strong words."

"I'm in love, grandfather."

"You don't know what love is."

"I know what love is. I'm not a little girl anymore."

"You said you were in love with Brad."

"I was."

"Look what happened to him."

"Brad has nothing to do with Tony."

"Well, I have an offer for Tony. You think he will take me up on it?"

"You can ask him yourself."

"I don't think a man like Tony will work for me if he really knew me like you do. That's why I need you to convince him." José didn't know how he was going to tell Valentina that he had

had Tony's father murdered. At the moment, he was thinking of a way to ease this revelation into the conversation. When she asked, "Is there a conflict of interest with you and Tony?"

"As a matter of fact, there is."

Tony was walking down the hallway on the main floor of the Compound when he heard Valentina and her grandfather talking out on the patio. He turned his attention to their conversation when he heard his name. He slowly walked over to the open glass door and made sure that they couldn't see him as he stood behind a large curtain by a window.

José spoke, "Tony has potential to be in our family. I'm willing to give him a chance only if you agree to end the lover relationship and make it only business." Tony couldn't believe what he was hearing. He didn't think José would ever let him marry Valentina. He knew this from the moment he had met José.

Valentina responded, "Papi… Tony has as good business back in the states."

"I know. I had my people in the states do a background check on him."

"You did!"

"Yes. That's why I asked you here today. I really want Tony on my team."

"No problem, Papi. I'll get Tony to agree, but I don't know about him just giving me up."

"He doesn't have ae choice."

"There is one problem, Papi."

"And what is that?"

Valentina stood up and walked over to the patio door. She looked back at her grandfather. Tony was standing behind the door, but she couldn't see him. She spoke, "I think I'm having a baby by Tony."

"A baby. You can't."

"Why?"

José hesitated before he said, "Because I had Tony's father killed."

"What! What are you talking about?" Valentina was in shock from the new revelation. She couldn't believe what she was hearing. But, she listened as her grandfather told her the story about how he had Tony's father murdered.

CHAPTER 49

Agent Tadeo and both teams were ready to hit José's Compound. They had all the gear and artillery they needed to start a small war. They all had their night vision on their eyes, and their black army fatigue gear on. As they made their way to the Compound, they loaded up their weapons. They knew that they were going to his the Compound at night fall. This gave them amp time to plant bombs and use the fly spies to get a better view of the place. They didn't want José to slip out of their grips before the raid could even take place.

Agent Tadeo knew that José had secret tunnels all over the Compound. He had found out this information from one of the informants that had been inside the tunnels. The sun was setting as Agent Tadeo and his team crossed the mountain to reach the Compound. They knew it would be totally dark when they would reach the Compound. They decided it was best to go over their plan before they reached the embankment to the Compound.

Dean spoke, "There are over thirty men on the Compound. Five at the check points, and the other twenty five are stationed all over the Compound."

Agent Tadeo responded, "That's to our advantage. Everyone knows their positions when we get there, right?"

John interrupted, "What about the women and kids?"

"If they get in the way of capturing José, kill them too."

CHAPTER 50

José checked his watch as he looked into the dining room area. He was perplexed about why Valentina wasn't at the dinner table. Dinner was due to be served at any minute.

José took a seat at the table after he walked into the room. Then, he called out to his maid. She come like a mother racing to pick up her crying child. She asked, "What may I do for you, sir?" Her Spanish tone was soft and sweet. But José could see the concern in her eyes. He asked, "Where is my granddaughter?" the maid answered, "She's not feeling too good. She and her companion decided to skip dinner."

"When were you going to tell me?"

"I'm sorry sir. I was busy assisting her in her room."

"Is Tony okay?"

"He's fine. He wishes to take his meal in his room."

José decided after the conversation that he would go to his living quarters and catch a nap. On his way to his room, he had heard Valentina and Tony in a heated conversation. He walked quietly and slowly over to their bedroom door. He peeped inside the room and saw that Tony was in a rage. In Tony's hand was a gold case and in the case was white powder that José was familiar with. José could see that Tony had residue on his nose. Valentina spoke, "My grandfather is only trying to help you, Tony. He didn't mean anything and towards you. He doesn't know you like I do."

Tony responded, "I have murdered people for less."

"No need of throwing threats, Tony."

"You don't understand Valentina. Your grandfather and I will never be able to do business together."

"Why Tony?"

"I heard what your grandfather said about my father."

"You were eavesdropping on us?"

José couldn't believe his ears. He didn't know that Tony had heard him and Valentina talking out on the patio. Usually he was a private person when he was conversing with someone, but he let his guard down because it was Valentina. Tony responded, "I heard everything. I know who murdered my father now. My hunt is over." José didn't know that Tony was hunting for the person that murdered his father. This was new information to him.

When Tony came rushing out of the room, José ducked behind the door so Tony couldn't see him. José watched as Tony strolled down the hallway in a mad mood. There was something in Tony's demeanor that told José that he had to watch his back. This still didn't stop José from going to his room to catch a nap. But this was after he put two armed guards in front of his door. After lying in bed for an hour, José finally fell asleep. He dreamt about the day that he had sent his best hitman to kill Tony Sr. He knew he had no choice when it came to ordering the murder of Tony Sr. At that time, he had too much to lose. This was why he had ordered the hit.

The slapping sound of José's maid's shoes interrupted his peaceful rest. This wasn't the first time his rest had been interrupted by his maids hard bottom shoes. He decided to get out of bed and go for a walk. This was after he had scolded his maid about her shoes. The moon was glowing along with the stars. The sound of night creatures could be heard as José walked over to the window and looked out. He didn't know that there were two teams of Special Forces outside the Compound lurking in the dark.

José turned his attention to the hallway of his Compound. His two armed guards were missing from the doorway. That was odd. He strolled passed Valentina's room as he made his way to his gun room. Once in the gun room, José walked over to his gun case. He wasn't expecting to find his gun case cabinet door open. And to top this off, one of his two gold nine mills were missing from it. José walked quietly over to the cabinet and closed it. This was done after he had done another check to see if anything else was missing from the room.

José was perplexed by the missing weapon. He didn't have a clue who would take the gun without his permission. While looking over at the missing spot of the gun, the sound of hard bottom shoes interrupted José. He shouted, "Didn't I tell you to change those shoes, Mary?" José turned in Tony's direction to find Tony with the missing nine mill in his hand. Tony was pointing the gun at José's mid-section. José asked, "So, you are the one that took my gun?"

Tony responded, "Yes. I took it from the case for protection."

"There are no threats here, Tony. There is no need for a gun."

"So you say."

The sounds of the sensor alert interrupted them. "I think we've got company, Tony," José said. Then he slowly removed his hand from his pocket revealing a cigar. Tony shouted, "Don't make my day."

José said, "I just need a cigar, Tony."

Tony watched as José lit the cigar. He was wondering where José's bodyguards were at. After José lit up the cigar, he took a few pulls and then said, "Now where were we?"

Tony spoke, "My father. Why did you kill him?"

"I know you know why, Tony."

"I want to hear it from your mouth."

José busted out laughing. This hit a nerve in Tony. Tony took José's gesture as if he was taunting him. He pointed the gun at

José's head. Then, he listened as José said, "It's all in the past, Tony. Your father was a good man, but he didn't listen when I told him that the guy couldn't deliver that speech. Now, let's talk this out. I can make you a billionaire if you help me get El Chapo." Tony walked over to José and put the gun to his head. Then he shouted, "You destroyed my family!"

José responded, "Your father destroyed himself. I didn't mean to hurt you, Tony."

Tony interrupted, "You think you can buy me? You think I'm the type of person that doesn't have morals and values? Well, you need to think again."

"Everyone has a price Tony."

"Not me. Now I'm going to kill you for murdering my father!"

The door on the opposite side of the room popped open as Tony pushed the gun against José's head. José raised his hands in a protesting manner. He knew Tony would kill him if he made the wrong move. Valentina entered the room with an AK-47 in her hands and she pointed the weapon at Tony and said, "Put the gun down, Tony!"

Tony shouted, "No!"

Valentina shouted, "Don't make me do this Tony!"

"Get out of here Valentina and leave the weapon!"

"No! I can't let you kill my grandfather. I am my grandfather's keeper!"

"He murdered my father!"

"I know and I'm sorry, but we can't change the past!"

"I have to avenge my father's death!"

"Don't do this, Tony."

"I have to."

"I'm pregnant, Tony. The baby is yours."

"Stop lying."

"I'm not lying. That's why I've been sick."

"Stop lying, Valentina."

"I can show you, Tony."

Tony watched as Valentina pulled up her shirt. He noticed the baby bump after Valentina put down her gun. He wanted to smile, but the moment was too intense. He was still upset with José for killing his father. All the emotions that he had been holding were released from his body. He didn't even know he had tears in his eyes until Valentina said, "There is no need to cry, Tony. Everything is going to be okay. We're going to be a family." As Valentina let her shirt fall back in place, the lights blinked off and back on. A smoke bomb hit the glass window in the center of the room. Then the smoke filled the air from the bomb. Tony looked over at Valentina one last time as he pulled the trigger. As his gun went off so did Valentina's weapon.

Agent Tadeo and his team entered the room after the smoke was cleared. They couldn't believe that Valentina hadn't been killed by all of the shots that had rung out. As they made their way over to her, they realized that Tony was dead. He had been shot in the heart by Valentina's weapon. Her weapon was lying two feet away from her. The Source was lying a few feet from Tony. Valentina was crying. Agent Tadeo spoke, "I guess it's all over. The Source is dead too."

Dean asked, "What about the girl?"

Agent Tadeo responded, "Lock her up. She's going back to the States with us."

THE SAGA WILL CONTINUE!